"Impressive . . . beautifully drawn . . . The relationships Akhtiorskaya mines are fascinating and tender, her writing crisp and gorgeous in its ability to capture gnawing attempts to piece together an immigrant identity." —*The New York Times Book Review*

"With Nabokovian humor and wit . . . [Akhtiorskaya] gets at capital-T Truth without a hint of sentimentality . . . showing our oft-banal world in a familiar yet astonishing light." —*Elle*

"A riotous, satirical take on the aspirational escape-to-a-better-life saga." —*Los Angeles Times*

"A significant achievement." —*Chicago Tribune*

"[A] spirited first novel . . . Akhtiorskaya approaches the fundamental experience of exile with tenderness and satiric wit."
—*The San Francisco Chronicle*

"Very nearly Nabokovian." —*New York Magazine*

"As Russian immigrant fiction evolves from novelty niche to full-on genre, every new effort faces a higher bar for originality. Akhtiorskaya vaults that bar with ease." —*Vulture*

"Makes something unexpectedly refreshing out of the overcooked tropes of the immigrant household struggling in its new environs . . . One can easily believe that [Akhtiorskaya] may well write a true masterpiece and soon." —*The Jewish Daily Forward*

"Utterly original . . . the reader happily follows [Akhtiorskaya] wherever her kaleidoscopic vocabulary and unpredictable turns of phrase may lead . . . Like everyone else who rightly decides to pick up this book, I will await Akhtiorskaya's next novel with rabid anticipation."
                                                                    —*Artvoice*

"Peopled with smartly drawn, humorously caricatured characters and packed with clever, evocative description . . . a charming, chaotic read."
                                                        —*The Huffington Post*

"For all of the glorious eccentricities of [Akhtiorskaya's] characters, the enduring message of this book is both deeply universal and faithful to the idiosyncrasies on display . . . [and has] humor and catharsis in abundance."
                                                  —*Christian Science Monitor*

"Lyrical, funny . . . deftly crafted . . . Ms. Akhtiorskaya . . . writes like an old soul . . . and . . . Akhtiorskaya's unique linguistic gifts reflect and even illuminate her rough-textured worlds."
                                                     —*Pittsburgh Post-Gazette*

"An impressive tragicomedy about culture shock, integration, and the tangle of family bonds . . . redolent of early Nabokov . . . [Akhtiorskaya's] rich language and ideas sublimate the mundane—'the katastrofa that is everyday life'—into something very special indeed."
                                                  —*Minneapolis Star Tribune*

"Akhtiorskaya writes fearlessly, like a dancer who's never been injured pushing every move to the max . . . reading this giddily inventive prose is like touring a city where you've lived all your life and discovering entire districts you didn't know existed . . . A thrilling debut by a writer with a generous soul."
                                                     —*San Diego Jewish World*

"[Akhtiorskaya] drags the churning hopes, terrors, delusions, and disillusions of emigration in late-capitalist America to the surface . . . crystallizing the experience of three generations, two countries, and an overlooked immigrant community in 300 pages of muscular, unpredictable prose."   —*The Millions*

"Homeruns on every page . . . [an] immensely gifted novelist with a sharp eye for the ridiculous and a bright literary future."
                                                                                      —*Pop Matters*

"An amusingly off-kilter glimpse of a family lost in transition, with jokes aplenty tinged with an authentic Russian Borscht Belt attitude."
                                                                                      —*The Jewish Week*

"[*Panic in a Suitcase*]'s prose truly sets it apart, bursting with such striking imagery, syntactic complexity, and poeticism that it would do its own protagonist proud."   —*Nylon*

"A hilarious debut . . . Akhtiorskaya excels at humorous, slightly overstated character sketches, making each person uniquely absurd."
                                                                                      —*Publishers Weekly*

"Marvelous . . . With beautiful prose that often feels like poetry, Akhtiorskaya portrays America from an outsider's perspective while revealing the collective truths about families no matter where they live . . . A touching and darkly funny first novel that is sure to be adored by readers everywhere. Very highly recommended."
                                                                      —*Library Journal* (starred review)

Panic

in a

Suitcase

YELENA

AKHTIORSKAYA

RIVERHEAD BOOKS
New York

RIVERHEAD BOOKS
An imprint of Penguin Random House LLC
375 Hudson Street
New York, New York 10014

The Library of Congress has catalogued the Riverhead hardcover edition as follows:

Akhtiorskaya, Yelena.
Panic in a suitcase: a novel / Yelena Akhtiorskaya.
p.   cm.
ISBN 978-1-59463-214-3
1. Russian Americans—Fiction.   2. Immigrant families—United States—
Fiction.   3. American Dream—Fiction.   4. Intergenerational relations—
Fiction.   5. Brighton Beach (New York, N.Y.)—Fiction.   6. Brooklyn
(New York, N.Y.)—Fiction.   7. Domestic fiction.   I. Title.
PS3601.K54P36   2014   2013038939
813'.6—dc23

First Riverhead hardcover edition: August 2014
First Riverhead trade paperback edition: August 2015
Riverhead trade paperback ISBN: 978-1-59463-382-9

Printed in the United States of America
1   3   5   7   9   10   8   6   4   2

BOOK DESIGN BY AMANDA DEWEY

For my family

Panic *in a* Suitcase

PART ONE

1993

ONE

THE MORNING WAS IDEAL, a crime to waste it cooped up. They were off to the shore. That means you, too, Pasha—you need some color, a dunk would do you good, so would a stroll. Aren't you curious to see Coney Island? Freud had been. Don't deliberate till it's too late. Strokes are known to make surprise appearances in the family. Who knows how long . . . ? Now, get up off that couch!

Pasha had just flown in last night and didn't feel well—achy joints, profuse sweating, a bout of tachycardia. It was as if his family could hear the roar of blood in his ears and tried to shout over it. A sum total of fourteen hours strapped into an aisle seat near the gurgling lavatory of a dented, gasoline-reeking airplane, two layovers, and a night spent in the stiff embrace of a plastic bench in the Kiev airport would've been tough on any constitution, and Pasha didn't have just any constitution but that of a poet—sickly from the outset, the dysfunction lying in the vital organs (heart, lungs), nose and ears disproportionately large for the head, head abnormally large for the body, premature stains under the eyes, spooky immobility of gaze, vermicelli limbs, metabolic peculiarities. If he'd been smart, he would've been born at least half a century earlier into a noble family and spent his adult life hopping between tiny Swiss Alp towns and lakeside sanatoria, soaking in bathhouses and natural springs, rubbing thighs with steamy neurotics, taking aimless strolls with the assistance of a branch, corrupting tubercular maidens, composing spirited if long-winded letters to those with this-world cares, letters that would seem to emerge from a time vacuum, with epigrammatic morsels of wisdom and nature descriptions of the breathtaking but exasperating sort.

Instead Pasha was born in 1956 to a family whose nobility was strictly of spirit. A dusty courtyard was the extent of his interactions with nature, a branch of assistance only in fending off feral dogs. He rode trams, avoided doctors. Correspondences, if initiated, fell by the wayside before long. He grew to be unreasonably tall (a result of too many parsnips—that must've been it, since he never touched a carrot or a potato), though it would've been better were he small and compact, considering the quality of motor control he exercised. His figure moved precariously along the street. There were hovels, abandoned or rustling with elderly squatters, that proceeded to stand while promising to collapse with the next gust. They were plenty on the outskirts of Odessa, but even in the city center there was one on most blocks. They no longer struck the eye as a single entity—a house—but as a pile of boards, bent, twisted, leaning; a heap, rubble, cats. Pasha's skeletal structure was a bit like that. Prophets are not meant to be healthy, wrote Brodsky, who suffered his first myocardial infarction at the age of thirty-six. At least he'd had broad shoulders. A poet must be feeble, ugly, somehow at a physical disadvantage; if not born that way, he'd promptly get to work on his disintegration by way of alcohol, cigarettes, insomnia, depression. Pasha didn't have to put in the effort. His time could be spent on other endeavors.

Pasha's physique resembled Odessa's habitations but not its inhabitants, who were built well (no complaints there). They were tall but not beyond their means, spry and sinewy, with tans so deep they must've had extra layers of skin, crude jawlines, and coarse yellow hair. They ate fried dough, fried cabbage, dog meat, and exuded an obstinate vitality. Yet it seemed as if nature had taken less time with them, not more, as if the craft were in the defects. Their superior biological constitutions were perhaps correlated to the dilapidation of their dwelling spaces; there's an inverse relationship to be found here.

Other relationships, however, required tending. Pasha was in Brooklyn, where both the buildings and the people were in need of fortifying, and he'd be honoring the borough with his presence for all of July—the entire month! There would be no shortage of first-rate mornings, he pointed out to his restless kin, who mistook the manipulations of neuroses for liveliness, enthusiasm. Look out the window! they shouted. Just look out the window!

Tomorrow will be even better, said Pasha. Not as humid.

How presumptuous. What did he know about Julys in New York? As a matter of fact, they were wet, dreary, unpredictable. All of this, however, was beside the point. Having just arrived, he should *want* to spend time with his family. They'd have plenty of opportunities to tire of one another.

If there was tension, it was partly attributable to the way Pasha had dealt with his impending visit, which was the way he dealt with all practical matters—avoid until they could be avoided no more, a point decided not by him but by external forces (however hard he tried to ignore these forces, they wouldn't ignore him). His sister, Marina, had done everything within her power to simplify the process short of chartering a private jet. She'd decided on the dates and sent him the fare for his ticket. They had no money, but Pasha had even less. When he received the envelope with the cash and felt its weight in his palm, it was somehow even less tangible than when he'd been informed it was coming. He put the envelope in the center of the kitchen table and for the next month endured a dread of mealtimes, indulging the preference to eat at his desk. Nothing happened, yet the days passed. He grew pale and perplexed. There wasn't a more horrifying, cold sweat–inducing suspicion than that those external forces had finally decided to give up on him. He spoke regularly with his father, Robert, who wouldn't dare strain relations by mentioning such banalities as a plane ticket. Marina juggled an increasing number of jobs and was always running in and out of the background, passing on hellos. But one day she grabbed the phone. Evidently she'd lost her sense for small talk and banter, the very traits her new land was known to cultivate. What time do we pick you up? she asked. A silence. I'll tell you tomorrow, replied Pasha. The travel agency ridiculed him. Tickets now cost twice the amount he'd been sent, money he didn't have. Marina flew into a howling rage that Pasha couldn't comprehend—really, it was a simple mistake. Then, just as suddenly, the tempest turned off. The abruptness of the switch from stormy to calm only demonstrated how often such a switch had been practiced, how little faith she had in communicating a message to her brother, and how after all these years she'd come to the cynical conclusion, though she wasn't cynical in the least, that to take offense was fruitless, that nothing could be worked out but only buried and masked.

Pasha gave a sigh and rolled to a sitting position. Agreement scattered everybody—they rushed into and out of rooms, to the bathroom, for a drink of water, to pack the cherries, gather the towels, where are Robert's swimming trunks, and what about the beach blanket? Watching Pasha get ready was worse than watching a pot boil. It wasn't that he had a leisurely disposition but that his brain and body had long ago, perhaps at birth, suffered a breach, leaving his body on autopilot. His mind was neglectful, self-involved, preoccupied; its moods didn't reflect on the body, which applied a mechanical thoroughness to every undertaking, whether tying his shoelaces, blowing his nose, typing, or consuming Hunan shrimp, discovered last night to be more effective than corticosteroids for his sinusitis. By the time his shorts were buttoned—or rather his brother-in-law Levik's shorts, since Pasha had brought with him for a monthlong visit only one pair (also Levik's hand-me-downs), onto which he'd immediately tipped the welcoming glass of young Georgian wine—Esther, Pasha's mother, had packed a suitcase of nourishment (apples, cherries, plums, apricots, or the hard balls of assorted sizes and shades that passed for them in this country), replenishment (bologna sandwiches), stimulant (black tea), reward (poppy-seed rolls), punishment (carrots), and something to pass the time with (sunflower seeds, clothes that needed mending). Habits shouldn't be allowed to cement—they must be extracted early on, like wisdom teeth. In Odessa, Esther and Robert's dacha had been a ten-minute walk from the sea, which for reasons that don't translate was considered a long, arduous journey. If a crucial beach accoutrement was forgotten at home, no one would've thought to go back to get it. Decades of this kind of training had instilled a dogged discipline. Now that the ocean was in the front yard of their building, Esther still packed so that nothing would be lacking. The governing rule: There must be surplus, yet nothing should spoil.

At the last moment, Levik decided he'd rather not go—it was Shark Week on Discovery Channel. Tape it, said Marina. But he was developing a migraine. Wear a cap and take two Advil. Where's the sunscreen? There's no sunscreen—what do you think this is, a pharmacy? Well, they wouldn't be long, just an hour, hour and a half, before the sun got strong. But it's already a quarter of eleven! Did they still have that umbrella with the green and beige stripes? Maybe it was in the hall closet with the other junk— Are you out of your mind? It ripped ages ago, not to mention flew off with a not-particularly-hearty gust into the Atlantic. Marina peeked into her daughter's room. Two giant, grimy feet poked out from under a blanket. Frida! she screamed. We're off to the beach without you!

Esther took this moment to corner her son. Her damp face gave off a postmenopausal odor, like overripe apricot flesh. The sweat never had time to dry. And like flypaper it caught everything it came into contact with—hairs, lint, fruit flies. Pasha, she said, can I ask a tiny favor, please don't get angry, just try to hear me out, a bit of patience—

Out with it!

Take that thing off.

Oh, not this again.

Just while you're here—for Frida's sake.

She's nine!

But she's a curious girl. She'll start asking questions, and next thing you know—

She's running off to join a convent?

It's not impossible. She still occasionally makes the sign of the cross over herself.

And that's my fault?

Where else did she get it?

TV. Classmates. She goes to school by now, I hope.

Is it so much to ask, Pasha? Would it be so difficult?

He looked to the side, as if consulting the couch. He'd thought that the combination of circumstances—the separation, his mother's condition, the palliative effect of time—would've finally rendered this a non-issue. Wishful thinking. His conversion was bound to remain an open wound on the family flesh, susceptible to infection. At twenty he'd inflicted the injury. There had been the technicality of the process—an elaborate theater of spite, as Esther called it, convinced that every step of it was being done to undo her. The catechumen period had been auspiciously brief. The priest practically apologized on God's behalf, as if Pasha's soul had ended up in the Yid pile by accident, in a forgetful or clumsy moment. He received the Eucharist like a crying toddler slipped a pacifier. At last spiritually content. He wore a conspicuous though not garish silver crucifix around his neck (later tucked into T-shirts), attended services, believed in creationism, had convincing arguments and logical proofs against Darwin's theory, which had the quality of withering immediately in the convinced person's brain and being impossible to paraphrase, and collected icons. The icons weren't just any old icons, rather they were very old icons, obtained after hours of sifting through junk under the junk owner's suspicious stare and briny breath, plucked from the heaps of vendors who had no clue they possessed anything of worth and wouldn't have believed it if you told them. The Soviet Union's skewed ratio of valuable objects to discerning collectors resulted in Pasha's acquiring a reputation for clutter. Correction: domestic chaos. Someone was usually around to provide the reproaching. One evening he came home holding a tiny wooden panel with chipped, blackened paint in which he claimed to see the Virgin of Kazan. At least two hundred years old, he said, trembling. Ten kopecks! After months of painstaking restoration, the black lady materialized for everyone to see. Not all instances were so exemplary.

To be sure, Pasha was a far cry from a zealot. The conversion was an appropriation of aesthetic symbols and traditions essential to his craft. Did he not consider, however, that he could appropriate them without the theater, as, for example, Brodsky had? Was it really necessary to *believe*? A grand gesture had been in order. Pasha stood too apart, was too achingly himself. Self-consciousness in such extreme potency wouldn't do for a Russian poet. By joining the Orthodox Church with its hundred million adherents (exact figure?), its seventy-five percent of the Russian population, the fledgling Pasha had been fastening a link that would allow him to roam freely without the danger of floating off into the attic of an ivory tower (reverse gravity being the poet's hazard). And through this link he'd stave off tendencies inherited from a line of depressives. Father, grandfather, uncles, great-grandfathers—dysthymic men of Literature and Medicine, oblivious to the political and cultural climate, abiding only mental weather, then wondering how they got caught in this pogrom or that war. Pasha stifled his genetic tendencies before they could stifle him. Tied to a belief system and other souls, he had no choice but to care, to be affected, to be a part.

What an outburst his mother's request would've provoked a few years ago, how indignant he would've gotten, how hot in the face. That he was even considering complying was a sign that he was getting old. But he knew regardless, with or without signs. If it'll make you happy, he said, growing a double chin as he struggled with the clasp.

The beach! Unable to coordinate a mass exodus, they left in spurts, Esther and Robert hauling supplies in the lead, and five minutes later Marina tugged Levik's weight off the couch, instructing Frida to get ready quickly and not leave without her uncle, they'd be waiting in the usual spot, to the left of lifeguard Hercules. The door slammed shut, a reverberating silence spread through the apartment. Frida dashed into the bathroom, tripping over her stocky legs as she slipped into a cobalt bikini, checking in, momentarily, with her recently activated nipples. Esther was convinced the American diet was to blame. What in the diet? No one would've let her administer the experiments she was devising to find out. Frida flew into the living room. Her uncle sat on a footstool, leaning forward to turn the glossy page of a book that lay on the floor. Let's go! she said.

Pasha raised his husklike head. It seemed to breathe from the top.

Look at this, he said, directing her attention to the floor. She fidgeted, her jutting globular knees (like his jutting globular knees) punched the cotton sunflowers of her dress, which even Pasha could tell was all wrong for her. She wasn't an airy little girl. There was something sumoesque in her stance. She was more substantial than many of the full-grown women in Pasha's literary milieu. Her focus was like the seaweed-green vase, Esther's favorite, once transported by way of a dozen anecdotes from Poland, that Pasha had elbowed off the piano when leaning in to hug his father on arrival. It had shattered into more pieces than it had been made of.

They're waiting for us, said Frida.

Don't be egocentric. Nobody's thinking about us. They're probably swimming by now.

I want to swim!

It's good to hold off on pleasures.

Why?

Do you want to get into a lengthy discussion, or do you want to see something and go?

A groan propelled her. She stood over the lower of Pasha's uneven shoulders but kept a distance—it was hard not to consider him a stranger.

Grandpa already showed me, she said triumphantly. It's Japanese.

Grandpa doesn't have this one.

Despair! Once more the exit obscured, Frida dragged to the floor, to a clean white mountain taking up most of the page. Caucasus, she said. But in the lower right corner were little blue squiggles. She knelt, and her head eclipsed the scene. Three little people in blue robes with white plates on their heads. They'd taste sour. But the mountain was of milk. A jagged edge as if the top had been bitten off. On the opposite page was something different—a man with a blue face, black wash of hair, deformed hands. Like Max's father down the hall. His wide mouth filled with ink—or he had no mouth, no teeth or tongue, only spilled ink. I don't like this, she said, and pushed it away. The book jacket snagged on a loose nail to the distinct rip of paper. Something welled up within Frida that made her repeat herself but more venomously and look at Pasha as if he were a monster, and the welling intensified, constricting her throat.

IT WASN'T ANOTHER MIRAGE to which Esther enthusiastically waved but Pasha and Frida in the flesh. The family was barricaded on one side by water and on the other by cherry pits like tiny bullets that had perforated a flock of seagulls. They're organic, said Levik, implying that they weren't litter, though he would never say that as the family had a complicated relationship to litter. But the trouble with cherry pits was their clotted bloodiness and that they carried the ugly secret of mouths.

What took so long? You had to wait until the sun was strongest! Put on a hat. Take a dip. Come here. Don't get sand on that. Want a sandwich, a drink, oh, I know, an apricot? The pinprick sun reigned triumphantly, but the corners of the sky were thick, curdled, darkening. Frida sat between her mother's slack legs, staring up.

Soon there'll be no more sun, she said.

It's out now, isn't it?

But the black clouds—

Go swim with Grandpa.

Frida ran until the water lopped off her knees. Grandpa! she yelled. Twenty men turned around, but Robert kept floating half the ocean away.

Flies attacked Marina's legs. She decided to ignore them.

Not a minute later, bewildered by how painfully they bit, she began to swat. A plastic bag was blown into her hair, sand into her eyelashes. A neighboring family's feral kids were shrieking, Esther chewed a never-ending apple. Helicopters, fading sirens, lifeguard whistles. Marina wiped the perspiration from her hairline, pulled up her straps, raised her head into the breeze. All around, tan, muscular specimens were running, digging, stretching, throwing balls, and then there was Pasha, folded crookedly into a low chair, his face contorted against the sunshine. Since they were no longer around, who fed him, who ironed his pants? Who reminded him to shower, to tuck in that shirt? Certainly not his wife. His visit, they'd decided, would be a chance for rehabilitation. They would pamper him, cram in a year's worth of nutrition, hygiene, care. But then he emerged (last, of course) from the baggage claim, and his belly looked fostered, cheeks buoyant. His clothes were wrinkled, but twenty hours in transit might do that. Esther reassessed with lightning speed. Look at you! she cried. A haircut first thing tomorrow!

Marina peeled her brother off the canvas chair, and they began to tread. This excruciating pace was Pasha's only mode of moving, and to walk alongside you had to adjust yours. Pasha's pace wasn't a deliberate saunter—he had bad lungs and motor difficulties (such was the official statement), an unmanageable thought chorus, and no need to be anywhere, at least not in a timely manner. Not very long ago, Marina herself had been queen of the promenade, most qualified in a city of inveterate lingerers and loiterers to demonstrate how to stretch a quarter mile for hours, how to ping-pong gracefully between the Opera House and the Steps in four-inch heels. She still had trouble disassociating punctuality from the height of desperation.

With her silence she was prompting her brother to say what he intended to say, which was that he'd given the matter due consideration and the answer was yes. Then the real work could begin—compiling a list of people to call, speculating about elements bound to remain uncertain for a while, and the paperwork, my God, the paperwork. She'd actually been expecting the announcement last night, imagining that it might accompany the first toast. A nice thought. Last night Pasha stumbled through the door at ten P.M. (five A.M. in Odessa) and protested, No food, not tonight, a preposterous request that only went to show how long they'd been parted. He began to fade at the dining table while Esther microwaved maniacally, suffusing the air with Chinese take-out smells and plastic. Pasha hated to fly, but more than that he hated interruptions. Packing, relocating, resisting the pull of his daily rituals, all this amounted to a profound psychological stress. So yesterday they'd kept to superficial topics. Today the big issues would be resolved.

She looks good, said Pasha.

She's gotten fat.

She was never a ballerina.

They're operating the day after you leave.

Pasha turned sharply. I specifically asked her to schedule the surgery for while I'm here.

God forbid anything interfere with Pashinka's visit! Marina felt the heat double, the sun's warmth amplified by rising temperatures within. Throttled by her own steps, as if she weren't on her feet but riding in the dim backseat of a Soviet automobile.

I was truly surprised by how vital she looks, Pasha resumed.

It's not the flu.

But if she's strong and in good shape—

Mama, *our* mama, in good shape?

If she's strong, her body will take the chemo well.

No chemo. They said surgery and a bit of radiation should be enough.

Her body can definitely take the radiation.

And I'll have to take care of everything myself! A whimper escaped as a wave rolled over Marina's sturdy ankles.

That's not true. Papa will help, Levik— Oh, my God! cried Pasha.

What! yelled Marina, clutching her chest.

That seagull—it's monstrous!

Pasha paused. He pointed.

Marina appraised the seagull. It's a bit on the large side, she admitted.

A *bit*? That thing's a dinosaur. Pasha took off, as if some amateur had picked up his marionette strings, in the seagull's direction. In no hurry, it began to pump its white-trimmed wings, dragging its body across the sky.

Allowing her brother to catch his breath, Marina asked, What changed?

Nothing changed, he said. I just haven't made up my mind, one way or the other. It's not like deciding what to have for breakfast.

Though you've never had an easy time of that either. Marina wasn't sure for how long she'd been looking straight ahead with painful intensity. She turned and let herself look at her brother. Don't you think we should get the bureaucratic wheels in motion? By the time you're actually called in for an interview—

Better we wait, he said, until I've decided.

And why haven't you?

What could he say? He couldn't admit that though he'd hardly seen a square inch of Brooklyn, it was enough to sour him on it. Anyway, that wasn't the truth—that had nothing to do with his inability to make a decision, it was just what was currently on his mind. Last night, as the car turned onto Brighton Beach Avenue, Marina had exclaimed gleefully, We're here! Eyes glued to the window, Pasha's first impression had been horror. Filth, dreariness, and pigeon shit didn't bother him, but five gastronoms in a row called Odessa did. His fellow countrymen hadn't ventured bravely into a new land, they'd borrowed a tiny nook at the very rear of someone else's crumbling estate to make a tidy replication of the messy, imperfect original they'd gone through so many hurdles to escape, imprisoning themselves in their own lack of imagination, forgetting that the original had come about organically and proceeded to evolve, already markedly different from their poor-quality photocopy. Such a bubble, no matter how enthusiastically blown, would begin to deflate in no time. Hold it, Pasha said to himself. Inner truth police! He had to admit that he'd come ready to discover just such a bubble. And the strong reaction had been at least partly the result of an overtaxed system.

He was losing morale. The wind flung crowds into their path, crying toddlers with bent shovels and tipped buckets, mothers in a tizzy, stately African women with what appeared to be pillowcases on their heads, sand-flinging adolescents, joggers, overdressed ethnic clans. They swarmed in and just as abruptly dispersed, leaving Pasha and Marina gasping for breath. While they were engulfed in one such burst, a hand materialized, a long, wiry hand that clawed the air twice before hooking Pasha's bent shoulder. The hand's owner and Pasha stepped aside to examine each other by the water. The man was the size of a tiny, desiccated tree that had withstood brutal winters. Clumps of coppery hair, a tight, aggravated mouth. Now the other hand stretched for the other shoulder. They embraced. Marina looked away, wary. Was this someone she also knew? Would his wife appear?

That's Bronfman, Pasha whispered as they slipped away. Marina, relieved, only half listened. But Pasha was shaken up. According to Pasha's mental records, Bronfman had been diagnosed with a rare form of leukemia during his last year at the Refrigeration Institute and died at the tragic age of twenty-one. But here was Bronfman, very much alive, working for the city's transit bureau. Health insurance! Decent pay! Job Stability! Pasha, he said, you must work for the city. Except it's impossible to find a job—at least it's very, very difficult. The glitch must have been this: Unable to deal with a dearth of information, Pasha's memory had filled in Bronfman succumbing to the disease, though in actuality his family had found a way to take him for treatment to the States, absconding urgently and covertly. In this miraculous land, he was cured, and here he remained.

That's what he told you? Marina asked.

He said he was living in the yellowish bungalow on Corbin Place behind the poodle groomers and I should drop by Thursday evening for his meditation group. You can't tell a man that you were sure he died fifteen years back.

Discovering Bronfman among the ranks of the living put Pasha in a frisky mood. He shook his beard into Marina's face like a lavish, impulsively assembled bouquet, splashed her shins, and laughed in his deflating way, like the sound made by turning the exhaust valve on a blood-pressure monitor (a favorite evening pastime). They got back to find everyone deep into the stern phase of beach time. Esther sat under a giant hat that seemed to have been punched in on one side and chomped sunflower seeds, the gnawed shells lodging in the crevices around her crotch. While she was discarding, Robert was in the process of acquiring. There were no beautiful seashells on Brighton, but Robert was determined to collect regardless, as this was the endangered activity he was known for. Marina dropped to the blanket and resumed her solar torpor. Levik picked his toes, using his free hand to flip the pages of a year-old *National Geographic*. Pasha tried rousing them with over-the-shoulder taps and affectionate pinches, but they grew progressively grumpier until he gave up and waded into the warm, turbid ocean for the prescribed dunk.

While Marina was away, Frida had made a friend. The girls had dug a pit, fortified it, and adorned the fortress with turrets, parapets, some ornamental dripwork. They added a ditch at the base for water to collect and sat in the pit presiding over their domain. The friend was a fine-boned tyrant, making it apparent to Marina that what had been uncovered in her daughter was a tendency. Your side needs more shells, the friend said. Frida, who'd never notice such a deficit herself, ran over to Robert and asked for some of his. Overjoyed by the request, he distributed the shells one by one, holding them up to the light and rotating and telling a story about each. But the friend didn't approve of this strategy. Those aren't shells but scraps, she said. Frida scoured the shoreline until finally producing an adequate batch. The friend had a high forehead, a taciturn chin, collapsed blond ringlets crusted with sand. She pointed to where Frida must put each shell and once they were perfectly spaced granted Frida entry. With erect spines they sat in their puddle, laughing into the faces of those who made pleas to join them in housekeeping. After being turned away countless times, one persistent boy returned with a pancake. The friend admitted she was ready for a snack. Attempts to divide it into three pieces were unsuccessful—it was one slippery, tough pancake. They would have to go in a circle, taking bites off the edge.

Marina watched as the jellyfish was passed around. She couldn't decide: to intervene or not to intervene? Instinct told her to go, but her body remained grounded. As Frida's turn neared, Marina looked away, aware of an unreachable dread.

LET'S HEAD BACK, said Levik.

Why must you spoil everything? said Marina, herself in the first stages of heatstroke. You think I don't see you checking your watch every second? No one's keeping you here. Only next time we're with *your* family, see how long I last.

Just then, the wind turned up. Esther's hat flew high off her head like a puck in a strength-tester game. The ocean started to bubble, as if a colossal motor had been turned on in the depths. The bottom of the sky overtook the top, plugging any remaining holes, and the celestial concoction began to stew. A lost balloon was like a soccer ball being kicked around by an invisible aerial team. The ground tipped, and a sheet of sand slid eastward, burying blankets, towels, bags, and knocking vertical tanners, proselytizing proponents of upright sunning, off their feet. A protracted moment of stillness was had as the atmosphere held its breath, turning greenish blue from lack of oxygen. A lash in the distance was followed by an audible inhale of determination, a generative buzzing, an interspecies murmur. Airlifted off her throne, Frida's friend thrashed wormlike until a bald, barrel-chested man set her down and landed his ringed hand on the weedy nape of her neck. A minute ago the collective focus was directed outward, to others, to the horizon; now it was sharply rerouted in. The rest of the world disappeared. People gathered, grabbed, collected. The sky, done stewing, began to crumble on raw, sunburned shoulders. Hunks of ice the size of pinecones. The more it came down, the darker the sky turned, like those who grow angrier as they rage.

When the cosmos broke open, Esther was expected to take a miraculous split second to bundle belongings and snap fingers to safety. She was equipped with a top-of-the-line primal-mother tool kit, with which she could produce a week's worth of meals from iron shavings, lint, and maybe a wilted head of cabbage, use a threadbare curtain to dress her family (distant cousins included if need be), cure the common cold and any other malady non-emetic in nature (puking elicited no sympathy), and get her family out of a disaster without a scratch. But they were witness to a terrible malfunction. Esther kept sitting, squinting and blocking the hail with her hand as if the sun were too direct in her eyes. As she finally got to packing, time halted emphatically. She attempted to shake out her towel and seemed to consider the usual ritual of changing from her swimsuit before heading home. They stood frozen, stunned. A green chair was hurled through the air. Boardwalk waiters hadn't managed to collect dinette sets in time, and they flew off, doily tablecloths along with tables. The furniture, sand, even ocean were fleeing. Only buildings stood heedlessly. Awnings suffered most, as they tried desperately but failed to disengage.

The beach almost fully evacuated, the remaining few were the elderly, moving as fast as creaky joints allowed. Lifeguards ran back and forth, tooting whistles. They soon abandoned the task of retrieving every last human scrap from the water and scurried to their stations. The scraps were insane, homeless, or drunk—what happened to them was already technically in the hands of fate. A pillar of dust came into view, tall and swirling, distorting everything in its path.

Run! screamed Marina, and herself did just that. Blazing the trail, undoubtedly. But she didn't turn around once, and unlike Esther she didn't have a second pair of eyes installed in the back of her head. Crossing the boardwalk, they doubled over, struggling to secure each step, gripping their heads lest they, too, should blow away like the countless plastic bags. At a critical moment, Esther outran Marina, swerving into a nearby nursing home. The steamy lobby was packed with drenched, shaken beachgoers seeking refuge. A drowsy security guard made it known that she wasn't pleased. Over her head a banner drooped—FABULOUS AT 90! HAPPY BIRTHDAY ALICE! A paper plate with a picked-at slice of triple-layer cake was being eyed by so many that she slid it into a drawer and turned the key.

Just in time, said Marina, taking a deep breath and checking to see what was clutched in her hands: a pair of giant denim shorts and an unfamiliar towel.

Have you seen Frida? asked Esther.

Marina gasped. People turned to look. My daughter, said

Marina. She began inspecting small faces in the vicinity—they were strangers' children, almost hers. They shrank away from her fierce stare, not wanting to be recognized. Marina ran through the lobby, taking a harder look at anything with the potential to transform into Frida.

Boo! cried Frida, crawling out from under a marble table. Catching sight of her mother's face, she began crawling in reverse, seeking the shelter of the stone. But she couldn't move fast enough. Grabbed by the ear, she was dragged to join the rest of the family.

Remember you have just one mother, said Marina. Better not rush her to the grave! Though Marina had grown up with such reminders from her own mother, she could never get the tone quite right herself.

They finally settled in to watch. The gods were redecorating.

Two years ago in Denver, Oregon, was a terrible hailstorm, said Levik. This storm caused almost seven hundred million dollars' damage. People think storms aren't dangerous, but even small storms are very dangerous. He swallowed. Did Pasha go to the restroom? I wouldn't mind myself.

Pasha! They hadn't seen him since . . . Esther bolted outside, immediately thrust flat against the door. A young man with quick reflexes managed to tug her back in. She couldn't steady her breathing—not enough air in that tight space to fill her breast. The security guard unenthusiastically relinquished her swivel chair, and Robert lowered Esther into it. Here they were, sweaty, in T-shirts on top of drenched bathing suits, huddled in the lobby of a nursing home. The storm pressed right up to the building. Windows trembled in keeping out the weight. It became black as night, the atmosphere thick and interwoven like a muscle. Along the sinews, threads of electricity traveled.

Aside from everything else they were feeling—worry, guilt, clamminess, a spreading itch—they felt betrayed. There was no way to address this feeling, nobody to yell at. It was foolish, senseless. Having been born and raised by the sea, they hoped that an allegiance had been established. They hoped by asserting, by claiming to be a coastal breed. They were people of the margin, of the edge of the land. If destiny wasn't mentioned, it was meant. Inland folk weren't expected to understand the distinction, just respect it. The particular body of water didn't matter—coastal peoples from across the globe knew when they were among their kind. They dealt in axioms. They were spoiled for any other type of existence. The power of the ocean wasn't questioned. Aquatic mystery was steady stock, safe to invest in. Living by the ocean was like going to third grade with someone who went on to become world-famous. The relationship became an integral part of one's identity. That the ocean never entered into the agreement was forgotten until a reminder was issued.

The storm had a Slavic temperament. It arrived with great force, bells and whistles, but burned itself out in less than half an hour—the vending machine didn't run out of Coke, the security guard wasn't used for meat (she had plenty). Upon return the sun shone brighter than before in compensation or apology or in an attempt to lure back the masses. Only degenerates and conspiratorial herds of pimply boys were enticed. Tousled neighbors poured out of building lobbies. What in the world, they said. Never before—a first! A tornado *here*? They hurried home, where, though it was very hot, they made gallons of steaming borscht as if to concoct the atmosphere in their beloved Soviet vats.

Emerging from the nursing home, they observed the river of people drifting away from the beach. Then they inhaled and pushed against the current, shoulders colliding and feet stomping. They managed to squeeze up one bottlenecked ramp, then helped one another climb over the railing to forgo another. They walked slowly, and even though they could see from a distance that no one was there, they didn't stop until reaching the exact spot where they'd been sitting. Marina flagged down a lifeguard resuming his post, but her tongue tangled. Too frantic for sense. Robert went straight with an appeal to the ocean. Did it have his son's body, and if so would it kindly return it in any shape or form?

Luck, usually so elusive, was in their favor. Levik in his search stumbled upon a gold Rolex, the clasp broken, camouflaged, sticking out of the sand, while Frida, sitting in a foul mood on a jagged rock near the jetty, pointed limply to a figure one bay away.

That he was actually there was a shock. What did they expect? Maybe what they were used to—Pasha in Odessa, keeping guard over their memories. Not all six feet, three inches of him staggering disoriented and pigeon-toed in the midst of their sand. They were still yards away when he began to relate that under the boardwalk was an entire city. Tents, upside-down garbage cans, a mattress and a stove, he said, evidently unaware that he'd been separated from his swimming trunks. His figure was as unobstructed as the horizon (though on the Steeplechase pier, the fishermen, as if glued to the railing, were back to sipping from their long straws). His nakedness wasn't startling—Pasha hardly relied on the basic buffering that garments afforded, not at all on the various boosts. Clothes detracted from his quiddity. In the nude he was uncompromised. Esther approached from behind, wrapped a towel around his rubbery hips.

A homeless enclave, he said, intricate, set up just like—

Was there a flash? asked Esther.

A flash, said Pasha.

He was struck!

Don't shout.

He doesn't look struck. We did just get a good look.

Are you hurt, Pasha?

They were very nice, actually, he said.

But maybe, said Esther, pointing to her head.

Robert cleared his throat. Chin raised, eyelids lowered, he dropped his voice an octave to recite, The tempest spreads a mist across the sky / frosty whirlwinds spinning wild.

Like a beast it begins to howl / now it cries like a lost child, said Pasha.

Let's drink, dear friend / to my poor, exhausted youth.

TWO

THEY HAD LANDED IN AMERICA in the middle of a heat wave, temperatures soaring into the hundreds, the streets streaked with fire trucks and ambulances, shabby businessmen, water-selling opportunists. A blackout was wreaking havoc on the outer boroughs to which they didn't yet know they belonged. Greeted at the airport by friends and relatives whose faces were incorrect in the flesh. These people were all arms anyway, gripping, squeezing, strangling, gesturing, and yanking them out of the frenzied arrivals area. It was night. They were distributed into two cars and taken by way of roads so potholed and fractured it was hard to believe they'd gone in the right direction on the three-rung world ladder to a low-ceilinged apartment with vicious air-conditioning. Sweat beads frozen off, sinuses excavated. The food on the table was identical to the food on the table in the kitchen in the apartment in the building in the city in the oblast in the republic in the Union they were prepared to never see again. But the table looked the same, faded oilcloth from the shop off Pushkin Street (they had the same one in their suitcase), as did the buttery pelmeni, vareniki in cherry sauce, brick of black bread, dill potatoes, cream herring—identical if a bit more gray and deflated, as the spread had been left out ceremoniously while the greeters, Levik's father and stepmother, waited for them to clear customs. Everyone was ravenous except them, who claimed to have eaten on the flight. They were pale, emaciated, dazed. Toasts were raised in a perfunctory spirit. Exhaustion and fright appeared to win out over the magnificence of a soul reunion. Marina put her daughter and her brand-new Barbie to bed. A cigarette disappeared in two puffs. She excused herself to use the bathroom. Half an hour later, Levik's stepmother found her in the bathtub sobbing noiselessly. The friends left hours earlier than planned, looking out car windows on their drives back to Long Island, knowing that they'd also been like that not too long ago but finding it impossible to imagine.

That was seven hundred fifteen days ago—they were still counting, though it was getting less clear to what end. At first it made the change manageable, marked progress. It'd seemed that if not counted, the days might either not pass or sneak by in clusters, two or more at a time. One thing a Soviet upbringing taught you was to pay attention. Not like these lax Americans who didn't even monitor their nickel-and-dime transactions at the grocery store. But what about the pennies—should you bother with those?

Since Levik's father had issued the official invitation, Pasha wasn't able to legally tag along. The understanding was that they'd collect twigs for a nest, then send for Pasha and his humble flock. But he put a freeze on the plan. Why? The many reasons he provided never quite added up to an explanation. But then the Soviet Union fell, Esther was diagnosed. . . . Visits hadn't ever been part of the plan at all. It was strange. There had been all this tragedy and finality, and suddenly you just had to have the money for the flight. No matter—soon they'd get Pasha over here for good. Notions were flying about. Considering Pasha's allergy to life-decision discussions, the plan was to trap him into one immediately, get it out of the way. They'd agreed not to relent when the hostage began to squirm. But after what Pasha had been through, the scheme couldn't be put into action. They weren't monsters. Pasha's talent was to shift dynamics until all sympathy was directed toward him. A steady current flowed his way. He aroused feelings without necessarily returning them and was permanently enclosed in an aura of exemption. It was inadvertent, though Pasha himself claimed that nothing was inadvertent, that there were no such things as accidents or coincidences.

They believed in accidents and coincidences, but too many of them happened to Pasha. Whereas they were admirably bronzed, he looked like he'd barely escaped a house fire. Last night they'd bathed him in ice water cooled with rubbing alcohol as he slipped in and out of feverish delusions about an underground washing-machine city and a trash-can blues band; this morning he seemed better, certainly quieter, but the water blisters hadn't improved and the thermometer, slipped out of a mossy armpit, read 38.6 degrees Celsius. And in such a state he was headed to Manhattan, no stopping him—as if anyone were trying, other than Esther with an appeal of, Wait one more day, and Robert's hushed plea, Wait for me! But he was off. Damn him, Esther spit. Where's he going? What does he know about this godforsaken city?

He knew that he couldn't bear another minute in their little kingdom by the sea. Locating a chariot to take him out was no challenge. The entire neighborhood—cardboard castles, sand fortresses, Chinese take-out joints and all—went into Richter-worthy convulsions whenever a train pulled into the above-ground station. Stepping into the subway car, he took a seat with caution, as if someone might intercept and make him stand. His discomfort wasn't physical—the air-conditioned car pro-vided great bodily pleasure—but stemmed from the sense that a secret code was being intentionally withheld. He alternated be-tween peering into faces and focusing on his knees. On Cortel-you Road a spark of panic flashed in his yolky eyes, and he said something incomprehensible to no one in particular. There was no response. He fell back into a glassy stupor. Another spark and he spoke again, louder. The car was packed with Russians who saw that he was in need of help, but some implacable force prevented them from becoming heroes. How bewilderingly Russian he was . . . it was simply indecent. His flailing let them possess their own proficiency, which was nevertheless too tenu-ous to be tested. And they knew the importance of being dis-creet. Someone was always watching. Luckily, there was Joe from Sheepshead Bay to come to the rescue. He screamed, he forced the Russki to repeat himself, making one wrong guess after another. But there would be no giving up. The destina-tion, it was finally determined, was Manhattan Island. Did this trolley take him there? Manhattan's big, said Joe, looking around. Where in Manhattan you wanna go? But Pasha had stopped listening. He was satisfied, requiring no more.

Deciphering maps wasn't one of Pasha's fortes. Languages were. He knew English, but strangers in an existential hurry did not. To be locked into the most desperate exchanges, from which both parties left aggravated, with a residue of elemental human failure, wouldn't do. In the margins of his notebook were the phone numbers of old acquaintances and friends of friends whom he hadn't the least intention of contacting. But there were pay phones on most corners, and a few even produced a dial tone. Hello, Arkadii Gulovich, this is Pavel Robertovich Nasmertov, currently in your monumental city, doing very well, positioned at the intersection of street number fifty-three and Avenue of the America, having just visited the Modern Museum of Art. Can you direct me to Guggenheim?

The individuals he wished to see he'd refrain from calling until getting his bearings in their city. Too many warnings were tacked onto this metropolis. You'll be overwhelmed and disoriented, you'll be yelled at, robbed, cheated. Nothing like it. It may have taken two hours to find his way out of the Met, but he could now be tested on the medieval wing. When with utmost satisfaction he decided to return home, he placed his final call to one Renata Ostraya. This turned out to be a bit of a blunder. The lady introduced herself as the spiritual custodian of the émigré literary scene. She was extremely glad he was touching base. There were a slew of not-to-be-missed events throughout the month, most of them held at a venue for which she could vouch—her place. These were the poets Pasha had to be introduced to, and these were the poets, entre nous, it was better to avoid altogether. Pasha took truncated breaths, repeatedly failing to insert a comment that might extricate him from the litany. He didn't have it in him to stop feeding coins to the machine. He nervously fondled its bendy spine. When Renata ran out of steam, he asked about a direct route from Madison Avenue to Brighton Beach. You're staying *there*? So began another round about the unfortunate Brighton ghetto and the gorgeous Upper West Side. It was very soulful in that part of the city—just like Europe. Then the coins ran out. A robotic female voice warned of impending doom. The pay phone shuddered, Renata dispersed.

The train was waiting for him to saunter inside before it closed its doors. Wedged into the corner, feeling mighty, Pasha went to work sifting the free literature amassed at information desks, making two piles, one to discard and one for further study. He next looked up when the conductor shouted, Last stop, last stop, train going to the yard, everybody off! He grabbed a pile, suddenly unsure whether he'd grabbed the one intended for keeping or for tossing, and scrambled out onto the platform. He'd arrived at Woodlawn, in the Bronx.

IF ESTHER AND ROBERT NASMERTOV were to give an official account of their son's relationships (which, to be sure, they'd be glad to do), the name Misha Nasmarkin would be assigned, with harmonizing confidence, that parentally beloved distinction of *best* friend. In accordance with the rule for household-endorsed friendships, it had its origins in tender youth. From first grade all the way through to tenth (the last year of schooling prior to college), with the exception of that one year Pasha stayed home due to let's not get into it, the two boys had been in the same class. At thirteen they both made the leap to the gifted-and-talented high school (unhindered by the four layers of added hurdles, one for each Jewish grandparent). They'd taken up a common cause—the death of Ms. Pulvitskaya, enemy of literature (a cause of which even the parents approved). And the surnames! It was as if the universe had, in the spirit of economy, created two boys but one desk. Day after day, year after year, it was their four legs, twitching and kicking or lifeless and numb, Misha's on the left, Pasha's on the right, but regardless because all four belonged to the desk. Ten-year-old Pasha had already demonstrated a catastrophic intolerance for the idiocy of others, yet he found a soft spot for Misha, not in response to a quality inherent in Misha but to Misha's struggle with the class, which met his ceaseless attempts at fitting in with merciless contempt that in turn sparked in Misha a still more fervent desire for acceptance. Misha was the pit stuck in the windpipe of a burly beast. Pasha adopted him, allowing him to get away with remarks, tastes, and habits that from anybody else would've been grounds for that person's obliteration from Pasha's psychic radar. In a room of thirty, Pasha might acknowledge the existence of a handful. Many of the obliterated were teachers, their assignments obliterated along with them. Pasha would've been expelled on more than one occasion had his father not been *the* Dr. Nasmertov. For those deranged teachers with no mortal fears (Ms. Pulvitskaya), Robert would bring smoked pork sausage wrapped in yesterday's newspaper. The taste bent her soul in such a way that even outside her stomach nothing could remain as stark and unbending.

No longer bound by the 120-by-70-centimeter wooden board full of obscene and graphic carvings, the boys would've drifted apart in one of a million ways. Instead Misha's father was tipped off to a very likely arrest—he was the director of the vodka plant, a position that rarely ended in leisurely retirement— and they scrammed. The friendship was embalmed. That they lived in different countries and continued to correspond was seen as a testament to their bond; in fact, it was the only reason for its survival. Minimal maintenance required. A seasonal phone call, a rare letter of personal updates peppered with unavoidable literary pretensions, a warm sentiment or two about one day living in the same city or at least on the same continent.

Misha had arrived in America at an odd age, too young for the usual immigrant dance step of struggle and settle, sweat blood for two years, then fall into a respectable career with decent pay and a retirement plan, fueled by the hope that your progeny will have a better go of it but too old to attempt camouflage, hoping only that the seams don't show. His father belonged to the businessman species, one of those hastily assembled men with an electric stride, a plethora of tics, and an inability to sit at dinner tables. They abridged the struggle and settled for nothing short of the full American-dream package, which included a certificate of struggle completion, Park Avenue penthouse, tasteful collection of automobiles, new face for the wife even before the old one went to shit, and a downtown apartment for their artistic son. Artist was preferable to writer— why set limits, and didn't he also have an interest in film? They provided the best platform for success that money could buy, enrolling him in non-degree programs, financing interactive projects, and passing along relevant phone numbers, which he used unabashedly, because timidity was the quickest route to nowhere. With an accent he thought to be his only hindrance but was actually his edge, Misha asked the local literati out to dinner and to drink the fine champagne (cognac) at his loft. In return he expected to be taught the ropes, the implicit request being that a cushy spot in the front row of the American Parnassus be freed, dusted, and prepared for his soft, pasty, not overly demanding tukhes. Meanwhile he'd be following in the steps of Conrad and Nabokov and transmuting his literary output to the only language now acknowledged.

Nobody protested when Misha offered his loft for Saturday soirees, sampling of his liquor cabinet, laughing at sloppily told tales of backward life in the old country—they distill their own moonshine on the job! drink their mother's perfume! pay doctors in sour cream whose quality is tested by sticking in a fork!—but upon being handed a manuscript of his novel-in-progress they became unreachable. Though there were those, too, who prioritized a good time and would wiggle endlessly to get it. I haven't had time yet; first chance I get; my mother's sick; so much potential. As these wigglers assumed, Misha tired of asking or finally noticed the darting gaze of a friend yet again being inconvenienced to lie.

If Misha couldn't be great, he'd be contemporary—he returned to composing in Russian, making "shocking" use of its wealth of profanity and thereby alienating the friends of his parents, a not-insignificant demographic when it came to sales. But Russian friendship, unlike American, was burdened by loyalty—a chapbook came out in Moscow and was translated into Turkish. He tried to live as if his life were a success, which inevitably led to discrepancies and incongruities. Reality was a bad choice of enemy—it had no need for disguise, didn't respect the rules, and hit below the belt. Every new and/or unknown situation (in which reality festered in its most virulent strain) had to be met with all available shields and methods of defense at the ready. A reality-twisting muscle developed, which converted raw contradictory information into what should have been, bridging every inconsistency, manually returning everything to the shelter of sense; with time the muscle's power grew, and by now it worked almost at the speed of reality. The "almost" was tragic. It revealed the muscle's existence to those who were either very intimate with Misha or very perceptive. Pasha, who was both, posed a significant threat.

A reunion on his turf made Misha nervous. He'd been using his letters to Pasha as opportunities to flesh out fantasies. So he forgot about Pasha's visit until one night when he was flossing his teeth after an insipid evening organized by the elusive, mentally disturbed Plinsk and the phone rang. Of all people it was Robert Grigorievich, Pasha's father, inquiring in a voice throaty and hoarse whether Pasha didn't happen to be in Misha's company at the moment.

No, said Misha tentatively.

Did you see him earlier today?

I don't think so, said Misha, leaving room for possibility as he rushed to the calendar where he jotted everything from Mama's Birthday to Buy New Toothbrush so that each month became a solid ink-black block of accomplishment. The date of Pasha's arrival was nowhere to be found. He's not here, said Misha. I'm not sure where he is.

The line went dead.

Misha didn't finish flossing his sculpted popcorn molars, though the upkeep of his teeth was the closest he had to a sacred rite. He dropped into a regal velvet-cushioned chair at the head of his oval endangered-wood dining table, which as a bachelor's dining table was strictly ornamental and somewhat forbidding. It was sterile, strange, a place he never sat. The apartment looked different from here, longer, the ceiling lower.

Why did he feel so unsettled? Pasha was in the city, out wandering the streets, catching up with someone more important. Misha had held back from asking Robert when Pasha had arrived—the question would only prove that he didn't know, implanting doubts in Robert's mind as to their friendship. Misha was proud to be the one called for information on Pasha's whereabouts. He didn't want cracks in Robert's perception of their bond. It was suddenly very important that Robert consider him Pasha's dearest New York friend. But after he dug around in his brain, he seemed to recall that Pasha had been scheduled to arrive on the eighth. Today was July 6, which meant that Pasha had been in the city for a month with no word. A month! Misha sat with perfect posture at the dining table (his mother had picked it out, and it demanded perfect posture), overtaken by a vaporous distress, which was replaced by anger at Pasha, because who did he think he was, a hypocrite surely, but this accusation stuck to Pasha like paper snow, since Pasha was unhypocritical to a fault. The anger petered out, and Misha was returned to nipping sadness, or had he just forgotten to turn on the air conditioner?

MARINA, juggling bags, arms, appointments, swooped into the living room to peck her grounded brother good-bye. Overscheduling led to domino-effect lateness, threadbare excuses that no one demanded or believed. Pasha tugged an appendage, toppling bags, plopping her into his lap. Why has Mama never had any patience with me? he asked.

What are you talking about?

Everything I've ever done has been met with disapproval.

When I stayed in bed, reading, she'd yell that I needed fresh air, but when I took up soccer, she mocked me for days. Who are you fooling? she said. Her reaction was never to the activities but to me, like that time with the stamps.

An undeniable thrill in being confided to. Pasha had never spoken to her this way before, his fingers locked around her wrist, the immediacy of his hushed voice and strained mouth— Marina couldn't help feeling deemed worthy. From the youngest age, Pasha had given the impression that the family was a nuisance, their clannish mentality a constraint; their affairs didn't merit a second thought in his globally scaled brain. Evidently this impression couldn't have been more false. Deep-seated grievances and injustices had been eating away at him all these years. He mentioned minor events from adolescence the way he'd refer to a passage from the Old Testament. He put on the professor face. Switched into lecture mode. Let's look at the incident of May 18, 1972, when Mama took my entire collection of literary journals and. . . . Having exhausted the list, he asked Marina to provide some insight.

Insight? she said. I'm sorry, Pasha, I don't have it.

How about more memories in the same vein? It took hundreds of hours of psychoanalytic toil just to unearth these. There must be more. My tendency is to bury traumatic episodes. Your memory should be terrific for the stuff. That's why I thought you might provide—

Some insight, yes, I get it. But I've got nothing. She kneaded the dough of her knees. It's a hot soup, she said, and time is like cornstarch. Last week I locked my keys in the car, poured milk into the washing machine. Though on second thought, she said, is it possible that the psychic work didn't retrieve memories but invented them? Take your literary-magazine episode. I remember it differently. You found out the KGB was on its way, but it was Rema who called to tell you. And Mama didn't burn your magazines. Mama wasn't even home at the time. You dumped your magazines into the fireplace yourself, forgetting, though you later denied having been told, that all of Mama's valuables—her jewels and heirlooms, gold coins and cash— were hidden in a little sack under the grate.

Pasha's arm slackened, allowing her to disengage. That can't be, he said softly.

Marina gathered her bags. It's incredible that you don't remember. I'd bet all of Odessa remembers Mama's screams.

Robert came to Pasha's rescue. He brewed a pot of Earl Grey, spooned some syrupy quince jam onto a saucer, and snuck into the living room, where the desquamating inmate lay under a massive heap of art books. Flaps of skin hung off his nose and ears, his chin finding a new shape with each scratch. It looked like a root vegetable that had been partially grated, then thrown away because of pervading rottenness.

I don't want, said Pasha.

I come with an offer, Robert said, setting the ruse on the floor. We say we're going for a walk on the boardwalk but really sneak off to Manhattan!

Pasha reached for the jam. No way, he said, licking the tiny spoon.

You mentioned the Frick.

It's two hours just on the subway.

We'll take a cab.

The last thing I need is another scolding.

Pasha's refusal only restored his father's ease. Here's the phone, then. Call Misha.

I'd rather hold off. He doesn't even know I'm here.

Don't be so sure. Robert shuffled out, a sad sight. Though America filled people out (with such tasteless food that you had to keep on the search for flavor), Robert proved the exception: America shrank him. Over the last year, he'd been dragged to doctors, had his organs inspected, put on a strict diet of lard, red caviar, and French fries. Nothing was wrong, and nothing worked. The admirably, reassuringly plump Robert, a stern doctor with a double chin so perfect it served as a guiding credential, whose paunch pulled taut his striped gray vest and made any neurosurgery seem hopeful, was no more. He was gaunt—every surface that had been convex had concaved, as if a vacuum cleaner had turned on at his core. He became wholly implausible as a physician. Luckily, most of his remaining patients lived in other cities, consulting by phone. His clothes hadn't changed, the same two charcoal suits that now looked like bunkers in which Robert was hiding. The curse of shabbiness—when a barber cut Robert's bristle-thick gray hair, the result was that it stuck out more sharply in every direction; shaving with these disposable razors, he bled; his shirttails went untucked; there was always a button to miss, a zipper to overlook. What had Esther done to deserve this? The shabbiness was innate, but how well it had been hidden under layers of respect and busy living. They'd been so involved. A stethoscope and a reflex mallet had done wonders for Robert's image. With the layers peeled away, the shabbiness was profound. In fighting this impossible battle (Pasha had inherited the gene, and Marina and Levik were inveterate slobs), Esther forgot herself. She lived as if the Master Photographer would arrive at any moment to snap the one photograph that counted, to be filed away into the Permanent Records, yet she never took into account that as part of the family she'd also be expected to pose.

Pasha found her duct-taping the split slits of the yellowed blinds clattering with the breeze. Art project? he asked.

It's not even a project. I'm not even here. I'm actually where I need to be, which is in the oven. Come, take this. She handed him the duct tape, clamped his fingers over the cracked slit she'd been holding perfectly aligned.

By the way, Nadia called while you were out. She's not very happy.

Is she ever?

She's particularly unhappy, then.

Her moods aren't my responsibility.

Calling your family is.

I've hardly been here a day!

It's been a few.

Well, you know what they say, time flies . . .

Don't you care how Sanya's doing?

He's grown. Takes care of himself.

He's sixteen! Do you need me to remind you of yourself at his age? Nadia claims you don't make any effort with him.

Since when do you listen to Nadia?

Since she's allowed by law to call me Mama.

Mama, she's unhinged!

That much was clear the moment you brought her through the door.

That happened on the same day she started calling Esther

Mama. In that time, in that place, everyone had been in a rush to the altar. For good reason—a walk down the aisle with nothing but butterflies or buckwheat in the bride's stomach was unheard of. But marriage was by no means a life sentence. The babies matured quickly, becoming adults by their sixth or seventh birthday, and the guys, however decent, often returned to the streets, though never for long. Nets were ubiquitous, vision blurry. All of this was understood, not necessarily openly talked about. Adolescent Pasha had been ahead of his peers in his grasp of certain subjects (those that came with a textbook) and equivalently behind in what Esther called the Life Subject. Of course it was the only subject at which he wished to excel. When at the age of eighteen he introduced his new wife, Nadia, Esther asked with resignation, When's she due? He laughed. We're not expecting! Esther spit on the floor and reddened. You married her just to marry her? What a romantic! You could've at least had the decency to knock her up. Now how am I supposed to explain this to everybody?

By twenty-one Pasha was a father. No longer ahead or behind but, along with the rest, somewhere in the thick of it, he felt sorry for himself—while Esther felt obliged to side with her daughter-in-law, who had the valid complaint that not long after they exchanged gold bands, Pasha stopped paying attention. Esther sided with Nadia, partly for revenge. Much heartache could've been avoided had he taken to Dora: sensible, warm, from a nice Jewish family, a good cook, not too homely (a beauty in comparison to Nadia). She would've treated Pasha like a king. Instead he chose the cold, insane, pasty, pear-shaped, droopy-haired Northern Nadia, who didn't even give off the good-in-bed aura.

Pasha was handed the phone well into the second ring. Sanya picked up. Mama's catatonic, he said. Half an hour later—that's half an hour of international-calling minutes—Sanya managed to coax his mother to the phone.

We miss you, she said in an evaporated residue of a voice. We want you back.

Pull yourself together. I'll be back in no time.

When?

You know when.

But that's so long from now, Pashinka. . . .

During her lethargic slumps, lasting about a week, Nadia became as pitiful as possible. A burst of household activity ensued. Hopping out of bed before dawn, she'd mop floors without sweeping or use a wad of wet toilet paper to smear window grime. The fervor amounting to nothing, she'd yell, This is why we never have company! You should be ashamed! How do you stand to live in such filth? These scenes took place in front of Nadia's toothless mother, who barely reached Pasha's hip bones and wore a kerchief wrapped twice around her shrunken face. She slept in the kitchen. She used to share her thoughts, then began to think better of it, and by now had reached the ideal state of not having a thought to hold back. She didn't speak, so it was hard to tell to what extent dementia had eaten her brain. When there were shouts—and when weren't there?—she sat by the window with eyes shut, smacking her lips. This deactivated mode had its disadvantages: She stopped helping around the house. The apartment suffered, but dust balls and vermin were easier to ignore than Olga Ivanovna's screech. At one time he'd been afraid for her life—the woman's histrionics could've made a strangler even out of her angelic Lenin. And she probably wasn't even that old. At her pace she could easily persist for another half century. But why think of such horrors when they existed in a different time zone?

Esther was rushing out of the kitchen when Pasha said, Wait. I wanted to ask you something.

Quickly!

What do you think of when I say fireplace?

Chimney sweep.

Oof, said Pasha, relieved. So you don't think about—

The time you burned to a crisp everything precious to me in a fit of hysterical paranoia?

THREE

TAKE THE Q TO 14 ST/UNION SQUARE, keep to the back of the train, get out the narrow exit behind a long-haired man tangoing with a life-size doll, cross to Virgin Megastore side of Broadway, go in direction *away* from George Washington on horse (numbers get smaller) until E. 4 Street, cross to corner with Tower Records, summon willpower to resist revolving doors, find door a bit farther down, tell Jamaican doorman with lazy eye you're there for Mikhail Davidovich Nasmarkin, confirm you mean Meesha in the loft, sigh with relief as he directs you to an elevator and illuminates a button, launch up to some preposterous floor, shut eyes to avoid surfaces busy with your decrepitude.

The blob of color at the end of the hall was Misha. Gold sneakers consumed his ankles, denim shorts fell almost to those ankles, and a yellow carnation peeked out of the breast pocket of his camouflage T-shirt. Flattened by their embrace. His corkscrew brown hair could've been apportioned into five poodles. I can't believe you're actually here, he said in a way that made Pasha wonder, Why not? The next half hour was spent getting the atmosphere just right. What was Pasha's beverage of choice? There were cocktail mixes, espresso varieties, iced herbal teas, fresh-squeezed juices, and vintage wines. Bob Dylan was laid on the gramophone but, failing to satisfy, was replaced by Charles Mingus. Misha announced them as if they were coming out onstage to perform. Pasha took a seat on a stiff couch but was moved to a stiffer couch, closer to the skylight.

I see you eyeing that beanbag, said Misha. Don't be shy.

Pasha plopped down—it was harder than he thought.

Tell me everything, man, said Misha, sitting at last. He switched the cross of his legs. Pasha opened his mouth, but Misha stuck up a just-one-moment finger, flew out of his chair, rounded the corner, and was back with crocheted coasters for their sweating drinks. Force of habit, he apologized. But once again he was stooped over the gramophone, fidgeting with the volume knob, because Mingus was getting out of hand. Returned with a bowl of cayenne-smoked pistachios. Don't blame me when you're addicted. Pasha obediently popped one into his mouth. Rotated it around in his cheek. Within several seconds his eyes shrank into slits of water and a trickle could be seen dangerously near set-off in a nostril. Attempts to bite down proved futile. Misha pretended to look out the window. See that hotel across the street? he said. There's a pool on the roof. Models sunbathe topless. He craned his neck. Not right now, though. Pasha reached for a napkin to spit out the unbroken nut. Something in the apartment intensified its whir.

Weren't we going to go somewhere? said Pasha, sinking deeper into the chair's loosely packed, grainy cushion.

Misha turned sharply. My place is stuffy, isn't it?

It's a superb apartment.

It gets OK light. I didn't even pick it out, to be honest.

And location—it's the artistic crux of the island, no?

Don't remind me. The hood's gone to shit. It wasn't like this when I moved—much grittier.

Looked very respectable to me, said Pasha.

Exactly. There used to be bums, whores, syringes. Now it's bearded collies and NYU baseball caps. He sighed. Where I'm taking you is the real artistic crux. It's as avant-garde as it gets. I guess we probably should be going. We don't want to miss the free wine.

They walked under an awry drizzle, getting sprayed in odd spurts. The sky, however, was a flat, far, uniform blue. Air-conditioner piss, Misha explained as Pasha looked up in concern.

Shopping bags knocked against Pasha's knees. He stepped off the curb into the path of a bicycle. Misha pulled him aside. The cyclist, on a food-delivery mission, swerved and yelled, baring teeth, disappearing into traffic. Evidently, visibility was determined not by air quality but by motion. You could see for miles on end in an open field or on a beach because there was little movement to absorb. In Union Square visibility was never more than an arm's reach. Misha indicated a turn. They veered into deeper, darker, more substantial avenues. Men on corners demonstrated the hot dog as a two-bite affair. The top of Pasha's head felt, oddly, lower than his feet.

Misha decided to recruit an artist friend to show them around the galleries, which had only recently colonized the area and weren't so easy to navigate. The friend was advertised as a character, one of those larger-than-life personalities, a bit of a sociopath—but who isn't, really?—and a brilliant conceptualist. He'd be perfect for the task, insisted Misha, as if trying to convince Pasha. They stopped at a pay phone, and Misha pulled from his briefcase the fattest most bursting soggy tattered crumbling spine-disintegrating phone book Pasha'd ever seen. And a zip bag of quarters. The artist friend didn't answer. Misha persisted, trying every pay phone they passed as if the problem were with them. When he finally got through, the conversation lasted ten seconds. The artist was reposing in his country home. Misha walked on, deep in thought. He suddenly had another friend, an art critic, who would do an even better, certainly more thorough job. In this case the conversation lasted past the minute mark, interspersed with several desperate laughs. Alas, it was a no. The art critic was staying true to his title, composing a piece of criticism due last Monday. He's always behind, said Misha. It's a mystery how he still gets work. They kept on. Pasha could tell that Misha's brain kept on, too. The fire escapes, gnarled, rusted, rising, were like the waste of his thoughts. And indeed it wasn't long before another call was placed, this time without the phone book's assistance or any information about the man being dialed. Misha looked over both shoulders before being engulfed by the booth. Pasha stood in the center of the sidewalk until a man snagged his arm and yelled a brief phrase that definitely included *fuck* or *fucker* or *fucking*, a word Pasha realized he'd been waiting for. He squeezed against a building. Misha hung up. He said, I had to call back this guy, Gerbil, and he happened to ask what I was doing, so I told him, and now he wants to meet us there. That won't be a problem, will it?

Pasha shrugged. The next pay phone was his turn.

Esther picked up in her usual way, as if distracted from battling a furious blaze. Pasha asked how she was feeling.

I feel fine, she said, then got angry. How could I possibly feel?

Maybe you need help around the house?

Are you trying to make an old woman laugh? What's going on? Where's Misha?

Right here.

So what are you calling for? Enjoy yourself! Have fun! Don't come back till next week. Give Misha a big hello. Better yet, pass on a kiss.

My mom wants to adopt you, Pasha said as they resumed their trek.

Perfect timing—mine's just about ready to disown me.

Your mom worships you.

First of all, said Misha, you don't know. You haven't seen the woman in ages. She's down to ninety pounds and comes with a crew of surgeons. She looks like a tiny greased manne-quin. But somewhere inside there's a pea-size gland where all the remaining humanness is concentrated, and this gland wants one thing. A grandchild. That's all. No substitutions. A god-damn grandchild. She says to me whenever we talk—which, yes, is still daily—that it doesn't even matter what kind, a girl, a boy, sick, healthy, even a mulatto, anything with a heartbeat and tiny feet at this point.

And is that such a hard thing to provide?

Misha scratched the back of his head. There was this one girl, Lisa, a Spanish translator, not drop-dead, but sexy. Big tits. And smart as shit. Spoke like fifteen languages. We dated. After several months, several outta-this-world months, I must admit, she made the inexplicable move of leaving her husband. Scared the crap out of me. I was young. Zero regard for the average human's timeline. Later I discovered that a brilliant, sexy, down-to-earth girl in this city—not as common as one might think.

And what about her now, this Eliza?

Lisa—remarried, two kids, lives in a wealthy suburb outside Paris. But maybe it's for the best. She liked Tolstoy over Dostoevsky and had teeth so large her lips didn't meet.

They paused on a scorching corner alongside a construction fence and a stretch of road being drilled into. They had arrived. Yes, really. Misha explained that as of recently this was home to all things visually groundbreaking. He pushed his shades up his slippery nose. Now they would make the rounds. Five, or was it fifteen, blocks of galleries, many of which were sure of little but their names.

It was necessary to see only a fraction of Chelsea in order to stop wanting to master it. What had Pasha imagined? That was unclear. In fact, in his disappointment he forgot that he'd imagined nothing, having come with no expectations. What he found were industrial spaces, blinding neon lights, maniacal wall scrawlings preserved with such care it was as if they were from the dawn of time, flashing signs, buttons to press, levers to manipulate, a heap of recyclables, something vaguely totemic, prim girls paired with oversize desks, an upside-down dining table, footstep echoes, a defeated feeling, white, an elephant made from ostrich feathers—but no wine. Misha charged at the desk with hair to ascertain the situation.

Only at the openings, he reported back with a shrug. In the background, a recording of a woman's staccato shriek played on a loop, as if she were being torn to shreds and eaten alive, which had about as unnerving an effect on them as a pestering fly. Meanwhile no sign of Gerbil. Misha acquired a stricken look.

They stepped outside, letting the sky drop over them like an old quilt. Headaches were like electronics-store flyers—you had one before you realized you had one. Both of them privately wondered whether they could just abort and go home. On such hot days in the city, people were known to walk out on their families, even their jobs, so what was a friend who lived on the other side of the globe?

Misha went around the corner to check for Gerbil, returning solo but with a brilliant idea: the flea market. He'd remembered Pasha's dedication to the one in Moldavanka, that gathering of useless objects laid out on bedbug-ridden blankets or wobbly tables by Ukrainians who sat on rickety stools, a bottle tucked behind their feet, soggy bread in their fists. Misha had never understood why objects with no inherent value should suddenly acquire it when lumped together, but for Pasha the market had been a passion.

Pasha's gloom lifted. For two hours he was transfixed by junk, of which he acquired a fair amount. His bags were so heavy that dinner had to be at the diner one block away. Collapsed into a booth, Misha sighed with exhaustion, Pasha with contentment. A miserably thin waitress appeared overhead, prompting menu misunderstandings, what was what, so many pages, each item trailing a baffling list of ingredients, all overlapping. Pasha made a joke that it was like the poems of someone Misha didn't know, and the waitress disappeared. Hamburgers arrived, deconstructed, plastic-looking tomato and onion slices fanned out on giant plates.

Misha had kept his accomplishments to himself long enough.

He began to spew. There was a residency in Montana for which he was a semifinalist, a book of stories coming out in Germany next spring, a reading he was asked to do with a très famous Russo-Francophone novelist whose name he couldn't reveal. I'd tell you, but I'm under contract to keep the matter private. Pasha didn't press. Misha had more breath stored up but had run out of things to say. He raised his fork, perplexed.

Pasha wasn't coordinated enough to tackle his burger. After he'd tried various strategies, the patty was chopped up into tiny pieces, which were chewed only on the left side of his mouth. Whenever the meat snuck over to the right, Pasha winced in pain.

The teeth were tea-stained, wobbly; there were gaps, silver crowns, recessed gums swollen with blood. Misha ran his tongue over his own set, where order reigned, but was only partially reassured. A clammy streak formed at his taut hairline. Any doubts as to the benefit of immigration could be assuaged by one glance into Pasha's mouth. Pasha didn't notice the horror with which he was being analyzed. The bags applied a pleasant pressure to his feet, the way a securely potted plant must feel.

How's Marina doing? Misha managed to ask, though not without his ears turning the shade of Pasha's grape juice. The infatuation had begun early on. Marina wasn't yet twelve when Misha began eyeing her nervously. The frequency of his visits intensified. Often he'd drop by when he knew that Pasha was at chess club or in detention or under the guise of chess club or detention attending samizdat activities that Misha was too cowardly to join. When Marina bloomed officially, Misha lost his capacity for speech and practically moved into the Nasmertov household. He once obtained permission to play with Marina's beheaded dolls (proof of Pasha's capacity for violence), but no further progress was made. Though at first his presence served to highlight Pasha's absence, eventually he was accepted as a surrogate. After years of inept wooing, Misha's only success was with Esther. His emigrating was detrimental to Pasha in that once again son services were in demand.

She's fine, said Pasha. He'd give no more. First of all, she wasn't a woman but his sister. Second of all, she was hardly a critical subject.

What *were* the critical subjects? And why did it feel as if they were forbidden to broach? Had the weighty material been sectioned off? They had to make do with surrounding nonsense, barred from drawing closer to anything of substance. Maybe it was just too obvious to ask the obvious questions. Or maybe they feared that if those subjects were too quickly exhausted, nothing would be left and the hollowness of their friendship would be exposed. They clung to the general stuff, steered clear of secret vulnerable wealth.

A lady named Ostraya, said Pasha. Do you know her?

Try not knowing her! She's a character, a larger-than-life personality, said Misha, instantly reminded by the phrase's taste of having used it not long ago. Embarrassment invigorated his chewing.

She talked my ear off the other night, said Pasha.

That means she likes you. With me she's an ice queen—I think because I never dug her, physically.

She can't like me—we haven't met.

She's heard good things, then.

A gaping void opened up, about the size of Pasha's book. Or not so gaping—a hundred and twelve pages, to be exact. Pasha's first collection, *Ancestral Belt*, had been published last year. Not only did Misha know about it, he had a copy. After finding it in his mailbox, he'd called Pasha. Congratulations. The thing's a beauty. Can't wait to read it. And then—nothing. But there was an unexpected breadth of response from strangers with no reason to read poems about Pasha's dead family members. The book was receiving a cadenced, still-unfolding, thoughtful and respectful reception; it was following an aberrant trajectory, gathering momentum in erratic increments, by elusive means.

I'll see her this Friday, said Misha. There's this event, it's basically a who's who of the literary scene, a talk-of-the-town kind of thing. It's a secret ball in the style of a Masonic meeting, but women are allowed, and it's technically a fund-raiser, happens once a year but never on the same date or in the same place, and this year I finally got an invite. I've been looking forward for months.

Pasha took a long pull from his straw. So you're saying that thing on Friday is worth going to?

If you were invited, said Misha. It's guest-list only.

OK, said Pasha.

You mean you'll be there?

I don't see why not.

WE LEAVE FRIDAY AT FIVE SHARP, said Marina. She stood in front of the TV, demanding attention. Images flickered behind her, commercials, which constituted their first major disenchantment with the States. How did people cope with these constant interruptions? This was no way to watch a program.

They'd asked around, friends and neighbors, to see if it was possible to rewire the TV or pay somebody off so these commercials would stop. If a democracy made everyone sit through these idiotic advertisements, it wasn't for them. You don't have to sit through them, said friends and neighbors. You could get a sandwich or take a piss. The country's bladder condition was clearly contagious.

Esther asked a question to which the reply was bathing suit. The commercial over, Levik yelled, with an intensity that shocked even him, for Marina to get out of the way. She disappeared. Pasha stopped leafing through Levik's *National Geographic* and went to track down his sister.

Why not go on Saturday instead? he said.

And kill the entire day? Out of the question.

There may be less traffic, he offered.

Crouched over her suitcase, Marina froze, an alerted bear. *You're* worried about the traffic?

It was just a thought.

You do enough thinking—leave traffic to me.

Pasha's weight shifted. He looked at the suitcase with concern. Will we be back late? I promised I'd go to a poetry thing with Misha on Friday night. If we're back around nine, I can still make it.

We're going to Lake George! Yes we'll be back late—on Monday! Do you have any idea how many times I've said this?

A lake? said Pasha. But, Marina, you know how I feel about nature.

Mama's birthday is on Sunday!

Since when does she like lakes?

What's all this about canceling your plans for me! yelled Esther, floorboards creaking as she bolted into the room. Don't listen to her! Go with Misha!

A cigarette appeared between Marina's lips, crackling, a second later eaten down to its filter. The lake is not optional, she said. Everybody goes.

If they didn't feel festive yet, they would once they got there. It was Esther's sixty-fifth birthday. If not for her, they'd be scavenging garbage dumps for carrot shavings. Prisoners in labor camps hadn't exerted themselves at an equivalent level of intensity for such hopeless durations. No one knew when Esther awoke, because whenever they rolled out of bed, she was already at it. Shortcuts and better strategies had to exist, but this was an inkling that no one dared mention. Running an investigation into the matter would be highly dangerous for the investigators. They weren't foolish enough to think they could stick their noses into the shit without getting mired themselves. If she wanted to pickle her own vegetables or spend an extra hour or two on homemade soap and glue in order to save pennies to be used for her exercise regimen of dropping pennies on the floor, then stooping down to pick them up one by one, what was the harm? When she complained, it was only of what she wasn't doing: working and traveling. She wanted to make money, take trips. But the only phrases she'd been taught at the complimentary-with-immigration language lessons held at the local junior high school were *Excuse me, how much does the menorah cost?* and *Shana Tova to you and yours* and *This challah tastes delicious.* Until two years ago, the future of Odessa had been in her hands—all the children were under her care. Mothers had no regard for nighttime. The phone was constantly ringing in their communal apartment. For nine families there was one phone, and it had to ring loud enough to wake all nine families up. Though everyone knew that the call was for Esther (even Robert's terminally ill patients had more restraint), they still went to the door to demonstrate that they'd been dragged out of bed. If they weren't satisfied with how disheveled they looked, they'd mess up their hair, roughen nightgowns, moan, growl. Now the phone calls weren't for Esther, but she answered anyway and attended to household duties as if they were children with fevers and murky urine, hoping to show how irreplaceable she was. In such a situation she'd done the worst thing imaginable—found a lump in her breast.

FOUR

THEY MADE IT OUT TO LAKE GEORGE still on speaking terms, a not-inconsiderable feat for which the reward was being presented with a vast array of separate directions to go off into, the newfound spaciousness startling less in comparison to the car, dubbed Green Cow for a reason, than to their apartment and to the whole city they'd been so inexplicably hesitant to leave behind. Esther headed straight for the kitchen, attacking drawers and cupboards, sniffing wherever something may have been left behind claimable as theirs. There's olive oil! she yelled. And coffee grounds! Two squares of paper towel! Not bad at all. They'd brought their own provisions, of course, and she began sorting through plastic bags, operating on a damaged eggplant, installing the meat grinder, but suddenly stopped, went to the window, ran her finger along the sill. She stared at her furry fingertip. Took a breath. The dank air was satisfying. One gulp and the entire summer lodged in your guts. She took in more and looked at the untended garden, almost crying out, We forgot the television!

Gaze refocused, there was no garden to speak of. An open

field of matted grass, weeds like gray hairs, a patch of turned-up soil, two stolid motels undulating across an overheated road. She turned and was slapped by an unfamiliar kitchen.

Old habits had conjured up their dacha.

Oh, their dacha. But there was no garden, and she was in a cabin with fake wood paneling, Formica countertops, a neutral blur of smothered smells, deflated polyester comforters whose floral pattern mirrored the sensibly sized nature paintings. Esther's hands itched to plant tomatoes and hang up the hammock; she half expected to see Robert crawling on all fours with his tool kit and overhear Levik's under-the-breath cursing as he battled the metal shutters, then his full-fledged fit as he changed the propane tank so she could begin to cook. Two trips were necessary to haul everything from their apartment in the city to their dacha on Tenth Fountain, of utmost importance, for everyone's sake, the television.

Pretending to be consumed by tasks, they were really just observing their arms in motion. Murky sensations nagged. After the initial ecstasy of freedom, time stalled. The vacation seemed to hover over its beginning, unable to attain liftoff. Doubts arose. They became aware of what could go wrong and how far they were from home and pleaded to be quietly (without fuss) returned to their bedrooms, where time resided effortlessly, like a mouse whose peep was heard only occasionally in the depth of night. Pasha's CD player had a tiny knob for adjusting volume and muting murky sensations; he used it freely.

Don't you think it's time to wake Frida? said Esther, standing in the doorway under a stuffed moose head wearing a far pleasanter expression.

Marina, engulfed in an easy chair, looked up from the

"Visiting Lake George" brochure. But she was carsick the whole way up, she said.

Just don't complain to me when she keeps you up all night.

A quarrel ensued, alleviating the existential disquiet. Esther won. They approached the king-size bed on the far end of which Frida was balanced like a glass half over a table's edge. They stood above her, engulfed in a warm cloud of sleep. Go on, said Esther's elbow. On being awoken, Frida gasped for air, convulsively catching her breath. Her gaze scaled the walls. No lilac wallpaper soup-streaked and lumpy from air bubbles, no drab macramé curtains, no glistening Russian tram slipping into the painting of a glistening Russian street. Frida's long in-breath was interpreted, by both mother and grandmother, as a cue to exhale, but then she was seized by violent sobs. Marina barged into the hall. Esther smothered Frida's tears with a breast and began to sing her favorite song—no, not the one about the orphan boy on the street after the war selling papirosi and not the one about the obese beauty with an elephant step, the other one about the swaying rowan tree and the tall oak that stand on opposite sides of the road never to meet.

THE FOLLOWING MORNING marked a momentous occasion: the Nasmertovs' first encounter with freshwater. All their lives steeped in salt. It was nothing short of a rite of passage. First, however, they learned the meaning of the phrase *in the vicinity* and got to the bottom of the reasonable rate for the cabin: When Marina asked the elderly man at the reception desk how to walk to the lake, she got deadpan instructions for a four-hour trek along the highway.

Out of the car, the cash unloading commenced—they paid for parking, for day passes, for plastic chaise longues on the carpet of pebbly beach. At last they were paddling their arms and legs inside the square allotted for bathers. There would've been no harm were the square a bit bigger, the swimmers fewer. How much progeny did a single family require? They'd always considered one the ideal and two the limit. But here five, six, even seven children all addressed the same elderly lady as Mommy. At first the Nasmertovs thought they were observing an aberration, but after further observation they were able to recognize that the aberration was them. All those children! An ocean was a dominant force. Whoever partook of it was subservient, abiding an implicit understanding that it was letting you in and could just as easily rescind the invitation. But a lake was the bathtub of these snot-faced kids. After flopping around for two minutes, Marina remarked how difficult it was to stay afloat, and returned to her chaise.

Esther distributed bulki, stale white buns with an inedible crust that was softened by the damp heat from palms. Growing garrulous, she let slip that what she'd actually wanted to do for her birthday was see the Russian Marionette Theater. Obraztsov was performing in Millennium this week. It would probably be the last time he went on tour, considering he's a thousand years old. Why hadn't she said anything before? Well, she hadn't wanted to stand in the way of their plans. But she did understand, didn't she, that this was all being done for her? Maybe they could still get tickets, suggested Robert. If the vacation had to be cut short a day, so be it. Tonight's the final performance, said Esther. The clouds went like this and like that, the bread got soggy in their fists.

Cotton balls had been stuffed into Marina's cheeks. The corners of her lips pulled taut, the dark side of her eyeballs throbbed. Was it Esther's remark about the marionettes? Was it that no one had thanked her for putting all this together? That no one even acknowledged the effort involved? Maybe it was that her thighs were now large enough to rub together when she walked and a few layers of skin had scraped off. She sat with her legs on either side of the chaise, letting the wounds breathe. It was probably general exhaustion—she hadn't been sleeping much lately. Things called out to her in the night. *Things?* There were no distinctions such as animate/inanimate, living/ dead, past/present—it had all gotten hopelessly jumbled into one mass, and at night this tumor of concerns called out to her in its indistinct voice. During the day you had appointments, papers to fill out, people to speak to. At night there was no one to address. Marina was being bothered, but there was no one to bother back. Everything ended with her, prone, unmoving. And she burped up the strangest, most disconcerting concoctions. She was ashamed and frightened of her dreams. And she certainly wasn't sleeping the nine hours she used to claim that her body needed in order to function, as if she were a car that only took premium. If I get even an hour less, stay away, she'd warned. All exaggeration, it turned out. Now she regularly did with half that and was fine. Only hurt, terribly, overwhelm- ingly wounded and hurt, in giant wraparound sunglasses and a new one-piece that concealed her new flab. Her stomach wasn't so bad, not yet, but all she had to do was look slightly to the left to see what it would look like in maturity. Esther's belly stretched her swimsuit until the individual fibers were visible, the parts that hadn't been dyed. Her black swimsuit petered to

gray over the mound of stomach—the stomach that had wanted
to tremble with laughter at the marionette theater in Millennium Hall.

ROBERT AND PASHA were getting the hang of it, their oars
moving swiftly, in unison. Objects on the shore dwindled to
insignificance as they leaned forward, leaned back, pumping
their arms. Yes, they had arms! Those arms had biceps and tri-
ceps and all that stringy stuff. This had been Robert's half-
hearted suggestion, an idea nixed before uttered, and Esther,
overhearing, experienced head-to-toe convulsions of mirth that
didn't stop until fat tears launched down her cheeks, and even
then, wiping them away with her handkerchief, squealing in
pain, she continued trembling with joy. Her allegiance was foremost to humor. Blunders, missteps, and odors were her comic
fodder. People's sensitivities, like their food allergies, were tiring. But by the time she was done appreciating the mental image
of her husband and son manning a canoe, there was no chance
they weren't going to do it. Without a word Pasha followed his
father's lead to the rental station, claiming they weren't in a position to turn down anything gratis.

Gliding farther out into the boundless lake, they were
noticing superbly, noticing splotches of light dancing on the water's metallic surface and how the clouds receded from their
advance—OK, so there wasn't much to notice, until the houses
dotting the shoreline metamorphosed into mansions, each
guarded by an obedient yacht. Such commodity fetishism
wouldn't have impressed them, but arduous teamwork and ex-
posure to direct sunlight operated in conjunction to make a man

inclined to be impressed. Look over there, said Robert, nodding toward four stories of architectural sleekness, glass walls, extraterrestrial sensibilities. And this one, said Pasha in reference to an ocher villa of palatial proportions. Pasha used his oar to push aside a turgid log. Robert steered them clear of rocky terrain. The sun drilled into their curly backs, extracting sweat. Shirts off, legs spread, breath labored. Conversations were initiated, but none stuck. Grunts and groans would have to suffice. Talk was superfluous. Sweat, toil, brotherhood.

The necessity of a major life change became glaring. Robert had always enjoyed working with his hands, pruning the garden, cracking walnuts, repairing the fence that one time. A primordial feature was activated. He became more spacious. The fog lifted from imaginary distances, extending the inner horizon. And he had an advantage. Levik may have been more naturally gifted in the handiwork department, but Robert didn't have a tizzy the moment a switch failed to turn something on, no tantrum when a few bolts didn't fit into place. He had no temper to lose. But everybody (Esther) ridiculed him whenever he set to tinkering with a broken contraption or went to do his sport (a set of torso twists and toe reaches performed on the boardwalk). A muffled clap of thunder in a distant valley set off the tremendous nature poetry of Tyutchev. The lake itself began a plangent recitation of Bunin's "Returning from Nazareth" and "Summer Evening."

The water level in the boat was rising, and Pasha ingeniously thought to put his new baseball cap (Levik's old baseball cap) to use. The damp cap would then be refreshing on his scalp. As he ladled capfuls and flung with gusto, his oar came loose, plopped into the water, and sank to the bottom. It happened so fast it might not have happened at all. Pasha squatted to peer into the lake, but the boat's sway forced him back into his seat.

A glance of uncertainty passed between father and son. Flanked by dense rows of huddled, inscrutable trees, the lake was congealed sky, the sky an emptied lake. Absorbent and reflective properties made it a challenge to panic properly. They were nowhere, nobody around to incite distress. And they wouldn't incite each other's. In predicaments Robert and Pasha served the same extinguishing function. They were the turgid logs that killed the flame, and if they happened to ignite, it turned into one massive blaze—a purely speculative metaphor, as in their many encounters with disaster they'd managed to steer clear of that one element, having never tempted fate with grills or space heaters.

So I guess, began Robert, but he aborted. A moment later he tried again. What probably happened, he said, but decided not to. Hmm, he said, hmm. See this metal ring that's holding my oar in place? It was probably already damaged on yours, and when you let the oar go, the weight finished off the job.

Oars aren't supposed to sink.

Damaged! Nothing's really free in this world!

It's our luck that's the problem, said Pasha.

Will we be charged? How much does an oar cost?

A million dollars. Are you about to go down there?

Robert seemed to consider it, peering into the clogged drain of the devil's bathtub. Price doesn't matter, he affirmed. Let's head back.

But the second oar wasn't decoration. Circling in one spot as if caught in a slow-motion tornado, they succeeded only in getting disoriented. You have to alternate sides, said Pasha, and grabbed his father's oar, which also came out of its lock with ease, making Pasha feel strong and mighty. In trying to alternate sides, he flooded the boat more. Their shoulders ached. Blisters stiffened their palms. They decided to wait for a boat to pass, meanwhile drifting into a dark, narrowing nook of the lake shaded by grotesque trees that obviously had to find circuitous ways of meeting their nutritional needs. There was a smell of damp, verdurous pulp, as if at the end of the lake a giant grinder were mashing the lake, trees, shrubs, and sky.

A few minutes passed in silence before Robert recognized his fortune. What more could he want? Locked with his son in a capsule, stranded in the American wilderness with nothing to occupy Pasha's interest, no one to divert his attention, no disciplinary interjections from Esther, no impossible-to-keep-up-with ideas from Marina, no CDs, books or art catalogs, no phones, friends, subways, no Chelsea or Guggenheim, just trees and a few clouds, which they admired, appreciated, perhaps willfully sustained around themselves, but without true investment. Trees and clouds were the natural world's equivalent of TV, which someone always kept turned on. Robert and Pasha were at most peripherally tuned in.

This reminds me of our plane rides, said Robert.

Are you afraid of falling to your death?

I'm enjoying your company.

Pasha shoved his arm under Robert's nose, pointing to a crescent-shaped scar on the inner wrist. That's Yerevan.

Robert laughed. And I've always considered myself a non-violent man, he said.

Arm flipped—bite marks. Tomsk.

I took you to Tomsk?

Where didn't you take me?

Arkhangelsk?

You mean Talagi Airport? Twice.

As the city's leading specialist in clinical neurology, Robert had been ordered by the Ministry of Health to constantly engage his phobia, which, considering Soviet aviation statistics, one would be hard-pressed to call irrational. He gave consultations and seminars in small towns, but he also paid visits to the central hubs, where innovations in the field were taking place. Best of all, he attended to emergency patients in remote villages, flying in dilapidated toy planes equipped with thoughtful holes in the floor—rides were so bumpy the doctors usually vomited. An initial romantic plan to forgo flight and ride the rails proved unreasonable; Robert only had to look at a train in order to be robbed blind. He began pulling Pasha out of class, bringing him along on the flights. Clutching his son's hand, he could overcome the fear just long enough to enter into the vehicle of fiery torture and death. Stuck in these capsules above the marching clouds, Robert shed poisonous sweat, convulsed, clawed the armrest and the pale forearm of his son. In his university days, Pasha became more reluctant to put his life on pause, and in the fall of 1982, the phobia abandoned Robert, like a neighbor that moved out of the building—the claustrophobic atmosphere dispersed, everyone rejoiced, and a replacement neighbor moved in.

Are you homesick? asked Robert.

Pasha was stripping bark off a wet branch like string cheese. He shrugged. I don't consider Brighton home.

I didn't mean Brighton.

Can't say I've thought about it.

Means no.

Probably. I'm a little tired of it all.

Robert hiccupped. It all?

Nothing, I shouldn't complain.

But you did say you were tired.

Nadia.

Oh.

Having never stooped to the subject of women, they weren't about to begin now. They had an understanding. Robert didn't need to know about his son's emotional or sexual entanglements. He had no advice to give. That part of Pasha's life could be as fraught as necessary and belonged to Pasha's future biographer, who'd surely take an avid interest in such matters, probably even amplify, adding her own artistic touches. It was preferable that Pasha maintain a high level of activity and complexity in his personal life. It would be suspicious if a poet didn't do so. Still, Robert couldn't help but find it distasteful. Get a wife and stick to her. Robert was starving for news of Pasha's career, foremost his current literary projects but also about the other poets in Odessa, what they were up to, suspecting that it was delightfully mediocre yet needing the facts in order to condescend responsibly. Pasha was cautious with this information, distributing it in meager doses. At times Robert had to wonder whether withholding didn't provide his son sadistic pleasure. But occasions when Pasha disclosed generously didn't go smoothly. When he touched on the Odessa poets and their versified propaganda, Robert was all frothy spittle and dilated pupils. Enthusiastic agreement irritated Pasha. In response to an outpouring of convictions, he demanded thoughtful contradiction or silence. And when he detailed a current project, Robert's follow-up questions were inevitably concerned with how the undertaking might further Pasha's standing, because, my dear, one collection of poetry does not an established poet make.

And otherwise, said Robert. How's the institute?

It looks like I'll finally be getting that assistant.

You need an assistant? I never had an assistant.

It should've happened ages ago, said Pasha, who'd been working at the Filatov Institute of Eye Diseases for a decade, because the rule in Russia, perhaps not exclusively, was the greater the writer, the shittier the day job. The job was just one more thing for which Pasha could thank his father, who for years had treated the epileptic daughter of Amalga Svinovna Allergiskaya, head of the institute ("one of the leading ophthalmology centers of Europe") and creator of "the first in the country Center of Treatment for Severe Eye Burns."

Why's that? It's busy over there?

I'm busy over there! On top of everything, I've been put in charge of a weekly newsletter. Don't laugh. It's not funny. I'm the one writing everything—reports of ongoing construction projects, future construction projects, profiles of new equipment, personal accounts—

Personal accounts?

Like success stories, very gruesome, with the same ending tacked on—Thank you, Filatov Eye Institute, for giving me back the ability to see my glorious country in all its fine detail. Something like that anyway, patriotic, good for business. The patients are encouraged to write these. Being illiterate and legally blind doesn't stop them. Nurses deposit giant stacks on my desk daily. I used to go through them, salvaging anything I could, but now I write them myself, though the guilt of throwing them out makes me read them first.

Let me guess—Amalga Svinovna's brilliant idea.

She retired. Actually, I believe she moved to Brooklyn. Now the head is Ivan Kopeyk. You may remember him, that small fascistic burn specialist with the cleft lip. He's singled me out, in a good way. The man has literary pretensions. I'm not complaining, but an hour in his office can be draining. Aside from the assistant, he keeps promising to get me a raise.

Then I take it you're not even considering . . .

Considering what? said Pasha.

You know what!

Pasha sighed. Just because I didn't come the moment you guys beckoned, that doesn't mean I'm not considering.

I know, said Robert. And it's not my place. Either way I'll understand. Whatever you decide.

But *they* won't, said Pasha, thumb pointing backward. Even in the middle of a lake, they were over his shoulder.

They will, too, in time, said Robert, pleased. *They* were the bad guys, he the understanding papa. (Ashamed.)

Pasha leaned over the boat's edge, wanting a gulp. His mouth was dry, forehead burning. Somewhere along the way, he got distracted—fingers dipped in water, none on his tongue. Am I considering moving here? Either they tiptoe around the subject or they ram right into it, as if their approach could steer my decision, their choice of words or the tone in which they're said influence the outcome. But this need for techniques only reveals an inherent fallacy, thought Pasha, whose aversion to life-decision discussions arose foremost from his skepticism of the very concept. If decisions existed (he'd never seen one for himself), they certainly weren't born on the same plane as conversation. Decisions ripened in the moldy darkness of the cellar, whereas articulation needed windows. There's a lag, thought Pasha, a distinct lag, between the inchoate stirring forces and the perceivable world. But what was he getting at?

Pasha's lower lip jutted. His eyelids sank. The strength required to keep them lifted was now aiding the mental process. When Pasha thought, bodily functions dimmed significantly. He was the biological antithesis to the concept of multitasking. Robert panicked. He feared that Pasha's wilting meant that his son had grown desperate for a return to land. Robert began twisting his torso this way and that, hoping to indicate through fruitless motion that he was addressing the issue. Meanwhile the sun spilled like syrup over treetops and it got colder. Wind gathered over the lake, abiding clearly demarcated roadways and traffic regulations as it traveled.

It's too late, thought Pasha. These conversations are like seeing the light from a star that hasn't existed for a century (because that's how poets think). Two years ago it was too late, and now the matter's dead. There's no tiptoeing around a corpse, and neither would bulldozing be of much use. His decision to stay in Odessa had been made long ago, only why hadn't he realized until now? The lag!

His son losing patience, Robert needed to forge ahead, no more beating around the bush. What about the book? he practically screamed. Any news?

What news?

Reviews, remarks . . . My God, Pasha, absolutely anything! Here and there. Nothing substantial.

What's here, what's there?

I got a letter.

From?

Massachusetts.

Who?

Some academic.

Why?

Wants to translate my poems.

Robert tried to fight off the glow. You must write back, Pasha! Don't miss out on such an opportunity. Maybe you can arrange to meet while you're here? Did he say where exactly?

Cambridge.

But Pasha, Cambridge, that's where—

Shhh! Did you hear that? said Pasha.

What?

Suddenly, in an amplified yet familiar voice distorted by distance, their names were called. Caught! It was as if they'd committed some petty crime and were about to be uncovered. The terror pulsed through their thighs. The voice was shrill, blaring. Was it too late to disassociate from their names and hide behind the mirror of the lake? A boat soon came into view. Levik sat in back with widespread arms. Marina perched in front. A lightning-shaped vein throbbed down the length of her forehead, and her neck was double its usual size, engorged with blood. An outstanding feature was her stillness. She seemed to have been frozen as she raged. A large, open sky was the background to this disquieted woman, who appeared manipulated by a force of which she wasn't aware (like the mute button on TV). Levik's discarded *National Geographic* had contained a photo spread of tornadoes, or killer wind tunnels as the magazine referred to them, in the act of destruction. One of the images particularly confused the senses. The left half of the photo was an intact shed and an automobile whose rear end was beginning to lift, and the right half was exploded debris, pixels in chaos. The image was highly polished, colors vibrant and provocative. Now Pasha's senses were similarly confused. An implicit contradictory quality detached the moment from the present, exposing time's scaffolding.

Marina's stillness was concentration. She'd been putting off a visit to the ophthalmologist and was having difficulty ascertaining whether the objects in her purview were father blob and brother blob. Once this was confirmed, her spine turned to string.

Marina! yelled Robert. Are you OK?

OK, OK, OK, echoed the lake.

We lost our oar, Pasha said as Levik drew level.

Levik's cough sounded a lot like idiots, but this wasn't the time to interpret the coughs of heroes. Levik was prepared to give up an oar. He began by inspecting the oarlocks, ended by attempting to rip the oars out of them. Neither stick came loose. How'd you—cough—manage? He regrouped. In three spasmodic strokes, he docked the boat. With a grunt he dove into the lake and bored a trail of froth up to Robert and Pasha's feet. He thrust his weight upward like a flying whale (propelled by sheer mania), grabbed the oar from Robert's hands, and docked their boat alongside. A finger pointed. Robert and Pasha, unsteady on their feet, got out of their boat and into the one where Marina lay with wide, unblinking eyes, looking rather peaceful. Levik got in and pushed off. The boat wasn't meant to hold this much weight. They were sitting below water level, in a ditch. Pasha resumed his project of ladling out the water with his cap. Robert assisted with his hands.

But they made it back and weren't even charged—a measly victory, insignificant when faced with Esther, who blamed them for the fact that she'd originally found humor in their enterprise. Laughter had been the wrong response. None of this was funny, because they *were* idiots. Nothing was wrong with Esther's throat. They were also to blame for the worrying she'd been obliged to do, when the doctor had specifically ordered her to manage the stress, and for the fuss she and Marina had been obliged to make. They'd bothered the lifeguards, harassed two suntanned and dazed park rangers, thrown a fit at the rental station, threatened the adolescent staff, requested to speak to managers, who turned out to be the ultimate in suntanned and dazed. No one was inclined to go on a search for two grown men in a rowboat after an hour and a half. That's because no one could imagine what sort of grown men these were! But Esther could. Image retrieved, she began to quiver.

A CEREMONIOUS BIRTHDAY BREAKFAST had been mentioned, not a ceremonious time. Quarter to seven probably wasn't what had been meant. It could still be hours before the others awoke, but stomachs were antisocial and had no regard for ceremony. The fridge's purr drew the early birds near. Pasha and the birthday girl eyed the steely beast with desperation, avoiding coming irrevocably close but not letting it out of sight. Did Marina's enforced fantasy of a lazy Sunday start, a phrase she'd been repeating these past few days like a mantra, mean a breakfast time of nine, which was a reasonable duration to make their grumbling stomachs wait, or some preposterous hour like noon?

To hell with it, said Esther, and charged. Pasha disengaged her from the cold cuts. They set out on a nice morning stroll to break the fridge's spell.

Directly behind their cabin was a road, more of a highway, and in front was a scorched field, twigs scattered in loose clusters and patterns, as if a giant bird's nest had exploded. Just past the field, a few interspersed willows seemed promising; they had no choice but to. Amazing that a human could cover distances. Tread in place long enough and the earth turned underneath. A time curtain fell over the field. Hopscotching from willow to willow, they kept hoping they were not only getting farther but deeper, about to hit wild country at any moment, but the density of flora refused to increase. They thought they'd at least find a creek. Instead they found that the highway curved. They saw no option but to hike along the shoulder. Cars were few and far between. When they did fly by, it was rather thrilling. And hilarious—every blur of solid color that shot past, honking at their pedestrian recklessness, made them wheeze with delight. The tension in Pasha's shoulders released as he realized that Esther didn't intend to torture him with questions. He'd braced for another interrogation, but her mind was elsewhere. Too much so. Pasha almost wished she'd intrude. He was ready. Defenses, disclaimers, diversions, open-ended promises, even jokes—by now he'd worked out a repertoire. Instead they focused on breath, following the highway's turns, its snaking white line, until coming to a broken stoplight. All three colors flashed in confusion. The earth grew sidewalk. A defaced street sign cast a cactus's fat shadow. Sluggish humanity had entered the atmosphere. In the distance Pasha spotted a steeple. He gently guided them toward it.

Trying to kill your mother on her birthday, said Esther, catching wind.

Ten minutes, no more, said Pasha.

A Jew has no business in there. Not even a second's worth.

Think of it as sightseeing.

Esther's ears perked. She looked up, considering the architecture.

No, she said. It's only sightseeing when there are stained-glass windows.

Often they hide in the back, over the altar. Sightseeing involves going inside.

Esther's veiny hand was resting on the railing. A swollen foot had been raised onto a step for elevation. Sounds issued from the depths, and she was once again alarmed. It's alive, she said. It's not sightseeing when the sight's alive. It's attending.

The pope uses the Sistine Chapel—would you not visit that?

Don't pull your tricks with me, she said, taking hold of the railing. She yanked herself up step by step until eventually reaching the top, where Pasha already held open the door.

SHE ACTUALLY GOT UP THERE and danced, said Pasha, arms shooting into the air, hands twirling in demonstration. Levik steadied the wine bottle caught by Pasha's elbow. She fit right in. The black ladies took her for one of their own. And not only was she prancing around up there, her mouth was moving, which means she was either singing along to the gospels or speaking in tongues.

I wasn't about to sulk in the pews like somebody here, said Esther.

And wasn't there stained glass as promised?

The church equivalent of a bathroom window, said Esther as she tried to curl spaghetti onto her fork the proper way, which looked deceptively simple.

They were at what was supposed to be the ceremonious breakfast but, considering the birthday girl's disappearance and return in such a state that several valerian pills and a nap were required, had been revised to a late lunch in a seafood restaurant that Kelly, the landlord of the string of cottages to which theirs belonged, vouched was the fanciest in the area. For the paper tablecloth, Frida was given a plastic cup of gnawed crayons but took little interest. They all intentionally pointed to different items on the menu but got identical creamy shellfish dishes on giant plates too heavy to take part in their habitual plate-swapping ritual, so they just threw white globs of mysterious seafood at each other, finding that their dishes didn't only look the same but tasted the same, too. Feeling cautious and uncertain, they offered toasts that grossly overcompensated: May Esther make a quick and easy recovery and have perfect health for a hundred years to come and continue to take trips to places like Venice and Vermont. Pasha added how happy he was to be able to be there for her birthday, to which she replied that if he wanted to give her a real gift, it would be permanently relocating to Brooklyn by the time she turned sixty-six. After thinking about it for a moment, she said, Queens would also work, but that's the limit. Pasha was oddly relieved to see the subject revived. That night Robert and Pasha convened at the chipped toilet bowl, which looked as if a bear had taken a bite out of it. No, a woolly mammoth. Their unsettled stomachs gave them plenty of time to study the tooth marks and argue. Frida got a plastic tub so she wouldn't have to get out of bed.

They left satisfied, enriched. There had been a moment of calm, hadn't there? They'd forgotten that such a moment was possible—everyone together and at peace. Such a moment was created in retrospect. Treading quietly side by side along a dusty trail of allergies, trudging up a comely hill, tugging at their insolent shadows, panting ecstatically, pointing out fungal colonies and rattlesnake-like twigs. Esther hadn't even complained about the cardboard-stiff comforters, stained sheets, mildew splotches on the ceiling, the death rattle of the ventilation system, the bizarre centipede population in the bedrooms. A vacation was a vacation out of their awful personalities; it was permission to not be themselves, and everybody would get angry whenever those selves showed up in an unsuppressed comment, an impromptu two cents.

On the six-hour drive home, the improved personalities were shed. Traffic. Frida had slept sweetly over the numb laps of Robert, Esther, and Pasha while their car made a valiant attempt at speed limit, but the instant it came to a stagnant, sweaty stop, she swallowed awkwardly, bumped her head on the rolldown window handle, and awoke for good. She didn't feel well.

Nobody feels well, honey, said Marina from the airy front seat.

She might have a fever, offered Esther.

I'm sure she doesn't. Everybody's hot and uncomfortable.

But she's particularly hot.

I don't feel well, whined Frida.

They took turns feeling her forehead with the backs of their fingers. The count was three to one, no fever (Levik refused to participate, as he was driving). Fury made Esther lose her voice. She stopped responding to her name. Frida found a dog in the window of the car to the right and switched complaints. Why couldn't *they* get a dog? They'd been promising her a dog for years. The drain unclogged, movement reentered the universe. Soon they were lost, driving circles in a town with boarded-up windows and no one to ask for help. How about that man? said Marina, but Levik sped past all human beings until, almost two hours later, after he'd taken every possible wrong turn twice, somebody took pity and inserted the needed highway underneath their wheels.

Their first American vacation, and its chief discovery wasn't where they went but where they returned. Brooklyn took them back. They hadn't the strength to wish for anything else.

FIVE

SPUTTERING DOWN BEDFORD AVENUE was a giant rusty green automobile. Marina clutched the steering wheel, the tip of her nose almost grazing the windshield. She was of the belief that one must change lanes—if one didn't, one wasn't really driving. Her tendency was to choose an inauspicious moment. She chose not entirely at random—a lane change went into effect once every fifteen minutes or on an in-breath, whichever came first. Before attempting the maneuver, an inner voice started up: Just do it, show those other cars, Go Go Go, you're the big Green Cow, why not now, the big Green Cow, OK now, Yes now, Go Go Go!

Marina tended to get things she didn't deserve, a driver's license being no exception. The midnight before her exam, their friend Yuri, a doctor who lived with his perfect family in a three-story house on lordly Manhattan Beach, administered Marina's first driving lesson, which had to be cut short because of uncontrollable laughter (his). During parking practice he said, No more, you'll kill me, I'm going to have a heart attack. He shared a parallel-parking technique for idiots who knew how to waltz, and said, Good luck, you need it. Six hours later Marina was in the driver's seat a second time. Initially she suspected that her DMV examiner was drunk. But no, she was just hysterical—her mother had taken a turn for the worse in Coney Island Hospital, where the examiner was going right after Marina did her thing. Mothers and hospitals happened to be two topics in which Marina was a genius conversationalist. She forgot the turn signal and straddled the curb while waltzing, but the license was hers, like a key into a house of horrors. (Just learn to drive before you hit the highway, her examiner advised.)

When honks or ugly gestures were insufficient, people lowered their windows to better transmit obscenities. Marina lowered hers to better receive them. A car that would've drawn a groan of longing from Levik went out of its way to draw level, and behind the triptych of glass was a man possessed. She slammed down the brakes—and with what mad speed the chiding party scrammed. After outwitting her attacker, she was blasted by a fury of honks. But by then she was impervious. Cars quickly sensed when their aggression would go unappreciated.

Marina, admittedly, had her own aggression to release. Not only did she have to go to work on this gorgeous Saturday afternoon while the rest of humanity enjoyed its slice of paradise on earth, and not only was this the absolute worst of her countless jobs (as it was the one she was going to at the moment), but afterward she had to drive to the Upper West Side to fetch Pasha from his party. His party! Those were Esther's last-minute orders: Deliver our precious boy home safely. If fully sober, he went to the edge of the Bronx; after a few drinks, he'd end up in a dumpster on Staten Island. Of course, Marina had replied, I'll pick up my dear brother. But that dear brother hadn't even told her that his plans included a party, not to mention invited her. She wouldn't have gone, but did it hurt to ask?

Merging into the right lane before her exit, all she got was a measly middle finger, which had about as much effect as a blown kiss or a catcall—the juvenile methods of American men. The frequency with which these methods were applied to her was an absurdity of daily life. Though it wasn't really an absurdity if you looked around. Women left home in unfitted pants, wrinkled jackets, and the ultimate ignominy: sneakers. It didn't have to be a stiletto, but anything less than two inches was indecent! Of course she'd been prepared for the sorry state of the American female; the stereotype had spread across the globe. The surprise was that her friends—Lyuba, Vera, Irina—hadn't wasted any time. Their physical assimilation had been total. In the few years Marina hadn't seen them, they'd lost their waistlines, cropped their hair to ear length, and fully converted to the religion of comfort, wearing trousers that could fit a diaper inside and the modern equivalent of bast shoes. They'd all been equally brusque with themselves, as if one day they all shook hands on their resignation and since then held monthly evaluations. Marina made a promise not to succumb. She smoked twice as hard and pretended to dislike the taste of French fries. A passion for Coca-Cola was impossible to conceal.

She pulled into the cobblestone driveway of a house at which it was best not to look directly so as to avoid being overwhelmed by its dimensions. It was two houses, really, conjoined. Better to take it room by room, which she did every Saturday, though a once-a-week scrub-down hardly kept the place out of the grip of chaos. A concatenation of bolts was unlocked, and the fancy door from the Russian-owned door store swung open.

Oh, said Marina.

It's me, said Shmulka. Charna fled today.

Shmulka was younger than Marina but had six kids under the age of ten, all boys, all running around the house in formal attire. Isolated locks of hair hung like the strings you pulled in the old country to flush the toilet. Charna, who usually opened the door, was Marina's age and had her own flock. The patriarchs were brothers. They wouldn't have hired Marina were she not Jewish, but neither did they consider her Jewish. She considered them the filthiest people she'd ever met in her life. They paid by the hour. Maximal accumulation didn't take much ingenuity.

Charna's out? said Marina, eyeing the carpets.

She had to go by the hospital, said Shmulka, relocking bolt twelve.

Everything OK, I hope?

Another tsibele in the bake, it looks like.

Enough! At this point the functionality of Charna's oven was suspect. The tsibelach she baked in there were deteriorating in quality. The last one looked plain inedible. But what would Charna do without recourse to being out of commission? As a girl she had laughed. She had that look, as if her mind had been blasted by laughter. Her eyes were like neglected goldfish bowls, the water unchanged for months. Surrounding wrinkles were many and deep. The laughter had leaked out for the most part, but occasionally it still shook her. It hadn't evolved—little girl's laughter. She was squat, haggard, prematurely aged, and she was always home, whereas her sister-in-law, Shmulka, the size of a pinkie finger, was hot with ideas, always hatching up plans about opera drapes or flowerpots or skirt-length alterations and out attending to them. But here was Shmulka with her round brown eyes gleaming under a heavy, dead wig. Her entire life force battled that wig, which nevertheless remained fastened to her scalp, though not securely; she clawed at it so hard it slid onto her forehead or down one side. Although a shaved head was supposed to be underneath, Shmulka had a full head of thick chestnut curls. The layering probably caused discomfort, but Shmulka wasn't one for shortcuts.

Though Marina arrived early and left late, the husband-brothers rarely made an appearance. Being tall, broad-shouldered, handsome, they confounded preconceptions. They were like actors playing Hasidic brothers in a Hollywood movie. Marina dreaded their entrance. Only when they were around did she suddenly transform into a cleaning lady. They could step over her abandoned ankle without a glance in the direction of her head. It was hard to maintain illusions around them, though objectively it would seem they were the ones to have strayed from reality.

You need what? said Shmulka.

Marina looked at her, not comprehending.

To go by the closet . . .

Don't—I know where is all what I need.

She began with the basement—a windowless space filled with every gadget and contraption ever created and put on this planet. She intended to compile a list of these devices—or rather their descriptions, since aside from the few she recognized from late-night infomercials, the majority of their names and functions eluded her—and submit this list to a committee that kept track of . . . Jewish history? Hoarder mentality? Basements of the twentieth century? The problem would be figuring out which committee most deserved the list, and if no one knew what to make of it, at least they'd put it on file. The fact that she might be the only person to set eyes on this basement was disconcerting. Of course other cleaning ladies had seen it, but they didn't count, because they were cleaning ladies. Marina was cleaning only because life reserved its most pungent humor for those special enough to get the joke.

Though the bathroom was often cited as the horrible representative of cleaning-lady duties, Marina enjoyed her time there. It was dense and fertile ground, offering plenty of opportunities to linger. The shower curtains were where the cash was. Marina took her time with every fiber and slit. Then she moved on, with less enthusiasm, to floors. Wall-to-wall carpeting was a chief discovery in terms of pure shock value. Marina had just one question: Why? The carpets were like a bib for the house, soaking up everything that never made it to the mouth. As Marina was brushing the crud out of the carpet, Shmulka burst into the room. An emergency had come up, and she needed to go out, but would be back to the house in twenty minutes max. The only emergency was that if Shmulka stayed inside five more minutes, she would spontaneously combust and pieces of her flesh, which Marina suspected would be very tough and rubbery, would have to be brushed out of the carpet fibers. In Shmulka's eyes: guilt, apology, a plea for understanding. She and Charna obviously had an agreement that the cleaning lady should never be left unsupervised. When Charna was around, this wasn't a problem, as she would've gladly spent the rest of her days without another gulp of fresh air, but Shmulka had ideas. She was addicted to the world's possibilities.

I'm fast, said Shmulka with her emaciated neck. Watch the kiddies. Make sure they don't . . . you know.

How many kiddies were currently in the house and to whom they belonged was irrelevant. They were runty, underdeveloped, somersaulting. Once in a while, they flew down the stairs, let out a shriek, carried on. In their crooked mouths, the true shapes of which couldn't be determined as they were never closed for long enough, was a sprinkling of tiny teeth. Teeth everywhere. A few half-submerged molars inside their large ears would've been no surprise. The older kids knew who was one of them and who wasn't better than anybody, and to them Marina was a large cockroach methodically covering their house. They couldn't kill her (she was too large), so they ignored her. But Shmulka's three-year-old, whom Marina called Krolik because his real name was unpronounceable, followed her around as she cleaned, rarely deviating from her path. She would've chosen him anyway. He was more aristocratic in the cheek. And Marina's principle with babies was the fatter the better. She encouraged largeness, equating size with importance: A big baby mattered more than a small one. Krolik could beat up his older siblings, which was admirable. Not to mention he liked Marina and wanted to hold discussions with her. Marina's English was roughly on a par with Krolik's—both could use the practice.

But today he wasn't in his usual good spirits. Still trailing

Marina, but sulkily, he ignored questions and commands, resisting the minor tasks she tried to assign. A grumpy little man with descended brows, he threw her sponge back at her. Almost toppled her pail. Laughed only after she'd tripped over the vacuum cleaner's cord. An extra burden was something she didn't need. Her probes into his psyche were unsuccessful until turning to a subject that quickened the pulse of even the most hopeless candidates. Krolik didn't have to think long before proclaiming his absolute favorite: kugel.

OK, said Marina, a bit mystified. But what does Krolik feel for pizza?

Pizza! cried Krolik. Pizza's existence had slipped his mind.

Does Krolik want surprise?

Surprise! he screamed.

Her finger instructed patience. Her purse was upstairs. She managed a puff of a cigarette—from Shmulka's secret stash—before returning with a triangle of tinfoil.

Getting wind of what was about to happen, Krolik hiccupped from joy, a sudden shift of fate. His gaze was superglued to Marina's chafed hand as it peeled back the petals of tinfoil with agonizing slowness. The boy stopped breathing. He stopped blinking. He stopped—

But when Marina finally presented the slice, Krolik's excitement transformed. He gawked. He seemed befuddled, stumped.

My daughter's favorite, said Marina. You don't like?

Krolik's head shook, though without conviction. His jaw had fallen open. He continued to stare at the cold slice, tomato sauce on the surface like burst capillaries, neat circles of pepperoni with curled edges, little red bowls.

Try, said Marina, her own mouth filling rapidly like the bathtub on the edge of which she sat.

Krolik took a few greedy bites and ran off with the rest of the slice. Marina set off after him, but it was as if he'd vanished. She moved on from the basement to the first floor, and upward. It was slow going, rough. She was unable to summon the Cinderella sensation, the famous-actress delusions, the good-for-my-biopic mood. Her arms and legs were heavy. The house leaned on her. Neither could she work up momentum or recall why she'd thought this was funny. Where was that pungent humor? I'm an actress, she said to herself, an undercover agent, a spy, as she scrubbed around the house's hundredth toilet bowl. I'm a Russian lady embarking on middle age. That term— middle age—never failed to lower the sluice gate of self-pity.

YOU'RE *the* PAVEL NASMERTOV, said a woman with eyes taking up half her face, further enhanced by dramatic, expertly drawn shadows. Perching on the sofa, she gave Pasha a moment to acquire that face, which she'd borrowed from one of the nocturnal animals kept in special enclosures at the zoo. Renata Ostraya, she said, as if this were the elusive title of a painting, meant to illuminate something while giving nothing away. Otherwise she was a regular plump lady, apologizing for not being there to greet him when he'd arrived, which she hoped wasn't too long ago. Pasha confirmed that he'd walked through the door no more than ten minutes ago, fifteen at most, but Renata wasn't paying attention and he also wasn't sure why he was going into detail.

In any case, she said, at last we meet.

The introduction took place only on the surface level of consciousness and was performed to appease that level, so its security guard wouldn't get suspicious. Ancestral intermingling in more formative times was possibly at the root of this feeling.

I've deemed you guest of honor, she said. I hope you don't mind if we ask you to recite a few poems.

What poet would mind?

A modest one. But that's pure speculation.

You could smell the stories. If men hadn't spilled blood over her, they'd surely threatened to. She found in all of it a good laugh. She was an actress, her flesh involved but spirit unconvinced. As a lady poet, she fought frivolity with exaggerated expressions of seriousness—frowns, gathered brows, pursed lips. Now her face leaked into these masks and had to jostle out of them. She grew increasingly substantial, a matronly effect conjured up by a lack of shuffling. Her body was an extra fixture of the sofa, hips as sturdy and impersonal as armrests. She counterbalanced the anchoring tug of her body with an overly expressive top eighth, though her proportions in this sense, too, weren't the Vitruvian ideal; her small head must've been rather a ninth of her height. Women like her seemed to always be squatting. They were reminiscent of drawers that, pulled open, released a woody, smoky, dusty odor. Not Pasha's type, and surely Renata could tell. She knew she'd been made for particular tastes.

Though the evening's caliber was excessive, shades of sloppiness were ubiquitous. All the elements of a superb party were there—beluga caviar, Krug champagne, a microphone. Maybe this was the problem. A checklist was in the air. People wore their best attempts, no one capable of trying harder. But the plates didn't match, and there were volume-control issues with the speakers, which to some extent had to be the case at every party that tried for matching anything. Usually only the hostess noticed flaws, her guests remaining oblivious, but now no one was oblivious except the hostess. Were these evenings played out, or was Renata exhausted? Prior to settling beside Pasha, she'd picked up a glass of cognac someone had left behind. A hostess's reflex: clear abandoned drinks. But after five minutes of rotating the glass in her fingers, she took it down.

A proper hostess never stayed in one spot for long, even if that spot was beside the guest of honor. A goosey girl with hypersensitivities and self-abnegating tendencies took Renata's place, balancing a large plate on her bony knees. The food was artistically arranged. The colors, the proportions—marvelous. The creative act was still in progress as she commenced moving the food around with delicate but assured strokes of the fork. That she was coming to public events was a miracle—or a modern psychiatric marvel. Pasha found a window. A joint was being passed around. It didn't evoke the appropriate Russian-intelligentsia-dabbling-in-dope feel but a cows-out-to-pasture one. Admittedly, he was afraid of it and looked in the other direction while remaining acutely aware of the joint's location, particularly as it neared him. The roach was tiny and wet when he lent it his own dab of saliva. The smoke scratched an itch in his left lung, an itch he didn't know he had. Renata Ostraya began to seem like a tragic figure. Misha circulated throughout the room, manic, a brochure of twitches. It was as if time were manipulating him more savagely. He shot glances at Pasha. His eyes were like photographed cat eyes, not glowing neon but glowing paranoid. Who was Pasha talking to? And did Pasha notice who Misha was talking to? Because Misha talked to a bouquet of interesting, accomplished people—poets, critics, the painter Dolbintsov, prose writer Bliznyats, Misha knew them all, and the young woman by the glass menagerie collection, too, the one in the black dress, a turtle in her palm.

Pasha, evidently, had been staring. Her composure captivated—amid a murmur of still-crinkly conversation, the handling of drinks and utensils, crowd maneuverings, female and male laughter (starkly different), the young lady gave the impression of perfect stillness. Which was advantageous, as it afforded an opportunity to admire her plump white arms and champagne-glass waist.

That's Lilya, said Misha. Her father's an experimental filmmaker, mother a Bulgarian puppeteer. She drinks coffee, translates ancient Bulgarian philosophers. I tried, most do. Her younger sister, Elza, is even more beautiful, but haunting. She lacks something human.

In another corner, an hour or so later, Ostraya's crystalline voice: Not enough affection from your mother. A distant relation put a curse on you as a child. It hasn't been lifted. You trust people too much. Don't eat mushrooms. Incorporate more alkalizing fruits and vegetables. Relationships don't grow on a foundation of humor. You need to be tickled occasionally. Watch out for unusual headpieces. Loyalty is respectable until one day you find yourself the patron saint of a Potemkin village. Look around, be tempted. She leaned in. Dewdrops stood out along her hairline. This is the center—it's thriving.

I've never felt a strong pull toward the center myself, replied

Pasha. Maybe I'm a provincial at heart, rather like Gorky with his Nizhniy Novgorod than Chekhov, who thrust Moscow down throats. The center is dangerous. You can visit—in fact, you must—but it's not wise to roost. Furthermore, are such matters so easily delineated? Is Brooklyn still the center? Different languages must have different centers. How do you repudiate Moscow's claim? We are Russian speakers after all. Not to mention that the center shifts as one gets older. Bach, Shakespeare, Pushkin. Listening to the cantatas, am I not in the center?

How much of this had Pasha said? Aloud he'd probably no more than shrugged. When he looked up, Renata was nowhere in the vicinity—or there she was, across the room, petting a young woman's braid. Maternal, vicious. But Pasha continued responding to her . . . question? accusation? Since when was simply remaining in the city of one's birth an act of loyalty, as if a person without will would just float off across the Atlantic?

Though Odessa wasn't the city of his birth. Of this he often had to be reminded himself. Pasha was considered an Odessite of the first order, nobody aware that a technicality eliminated him from the running. Somehow an aura of secrecy, a stigma, had been generated around such a trivial circumstance, that Pasha's birth certificate said Chernivtsi. This, too, the fault of his mother. Esther had chosen to wait out the last months of her pregnancy not in Odessa, where she'd been living with Robert's parents (meaning, for the record, that's where he was conceived), but with her own, in a house of wooden boards on a dirt road. There had been valid reasons for doing this, and she'd had to enumerate them so many times that she ended up questioning their validity herself, wondering if maybe there hadn't been a bit of transgression to the decision after all, perhaps a response to the Nasmertovs' city-folk pride. Her plan had been to return to Odessa a month or two after giving birth, but with the birth of a poet there were bound to be complications. Pasha first entered city limits at a shameful eighteen months. Arguably the most critical year of his life, depending which Freudian you asked, had been spent struggling for survival in Chernivtsi, a fact he could wield in response to the numerous accusations that his poetry didn't comply in this or that way with the spirit of Odessa. The Odessa poets felt that he was making use of the city without paying the obligatory dues. He could've renounced his claim on the city; instead he felt the opposite pull, to out-Odessa them all.

Why don't you sit down, said Misha. That was strong stuff.

What did you tell Ostraya about me?

Not a thing. If she knew anything, it was intuition.

They stood by the table picking at olive puffs and soggy crostini. Misha pounced on the trail of a pleated skirt. Others swarmed around the guest of honor. They asked questions, requested opinions, and, having tasted of the evening's exotic fruit, went on their way. A few poets remained. Pasha was enjoying their company. They were ensconced in a fog of their own making. In reaching for a pig in a blanket, a pale lady elbowed Nurzhan Bozhko, whose poetry was passable and nose exquisite in its resemblance to Pushkin's—long and straight, keeping neatly to the face, with an extended tip like a dagger. Startled, he picked up the entire serving plate and handed it over. She, in turn, was equally baffled and stared imploringly at

Pasha, who burst into preposterous laughter, since it seemed as if this young lady were delivering the massive platter personally to him. He relieved her of the burden, finding it far heavier than expected; if not for Bozhko's quick reflexes, there would've been quite a mishap, but as it was, only a few piggies tumbled to the floor.

An inexplicable charge passed through the group at the appearance of a physically unremarkable man with a pink face and small gleaming eyes. Andrei Fishman, the man said, and zapped Pasha with a handshake. Andrei clearly had many abilities, but standing in place wasn't among them. He led the group up the building's stairs until they arrived at a steel door that yielded when pushed hard (at least it appeared to take considerable effort) and emerged on a roof. The bottoms of their shoes scraped against a sandpapery surface as they stepped into and out of overlapping shadows, navigating incremental darkness. Finally they came to the edge and overlooked a black crater that slowly began to inflate. It grew upward at them. Central Park. The night was starless, but the stacked and staggered lights of distant skyscrapers served just as well. Pasha, a nonsmoker, partook in the collective cigarette breath and was just about to hear a thought for the first time in hours when snatched up by Andrei, whose outsize libido powered myriad undertakings that were quickly interwoven into conversation. Editor of two journals; head of an émigré reading series; poet and prose writer and Pulitzer Prize–winning journalist (for his series on the mentally ill in adult homes); presided over this and that board; psychiatrist; second residence in Moscow, third in Tuscany; about to get married to his fifth wife in Montreal;

accompanied to the party by one of his ex-wives and her elderly father, who'd once spent a weekend at Pasternak's dacha and could tell Pasha all about it. Pasha observed without attempting to keep up. To watch one of Andrei's pale, freckled arms slice the night air was enough. He had a giant watch and healthy fingernails. Probably in response to a question, Andrei said, At night I sleep very well. None of my previous wives could sleep, and maybe that's why they're not my wives anymore. I can't be kept up. Their anxieties inexorably came to a head after midnight. They preyed on my rest. So this time I chose differently—Martha's a superior sleeper, the best I've met. Nothing can prevent her from it. Whenever there's a break in stimulation, she dozes off, no matter where she is. No available seats on the subway, she naps standing up. She's very resourceful. I think she would've done very well in the gulag. It's refreshing to be with such a fine woman, especially as I embark on my hydro years.

Andrei spared Pasha having to formulate the question and elucidated the concept of hydro years, relying heavily on the fundamental let-lie principle, which required its own brief overview. Hearing himself say worms, dirt, eye sockets, Andrei got intense jolts of pleasure. He closed with a quaint theory of calves. A woman listening in began performing a roof dance, which came with an accompanying chant. That Pasha found this long-haired swaying charming meant he was no longer in his right mind.

The stairs were steeper on the way down, the lights dimmer. Fortunately there was someone leading the way and, if need be, a cushion. But had they gone up this many flights? Peeling gaze from shoes, Pasha found himself alone in the middle of a landing. The other set of footsteps had just been an echo of his own. The building, called Eldorado, really was a vertical city. He was stranded somewhere within it. Misha had brought him to Renata's door, Bozhko had delivered him to the roof—the apartment number, even the floor, was a mystery. Doors were duplicating, noise tangled and muffled and coming from everywhere at once. What was being played was a programmed memory of building sounds. A flare of panic unsteadied Pasha's footing. He gripped the railing, lowered himself onto a step.

There was a desire to get back, an urgent need for reintegration. He felt a danger to himself. If left to his thoughts, he would have to think. Much had been riding on his having a mediocre time tonight; instead he was being a fool and enjoying himself. Excitement spoiled solitude. He'd grown accustomed to stimulation coming strictly from within. The dose could be regulated, specific flavor chosen. Sometimes satisfaction was two scoops of vanilla, other times Milton, Brodsky, a Gregorian chant or two. Laughing at a joke wasn't without risk for someone like Pasha, who was often described as absorbed in his own thoughts. This wasn't, as people supposed, because they weren't interesting enough to engage him but for his own protection, the irony being that had they been interesting he would've been helpless against them. An inherent flaw in the heavy-duty defenses Pasha set up against humanity was that regardless of heavy-dutiness they could be demolished in an instant by exceptional people—such rarities in certain parts of the world that defenses were erected without them in mind, just as you wouldn't install floodgates in the Sahara.

No napping in the stairwell, said Fishman.

Pasha was returned to civilization, but it wasn't the same. Something had changed, though he couldn't put his finger on it. Perhaps it was the odd configuration of chairs. Stumpy-legged Renata swooped in, and before realizing for what, he was making excuses. We went up to the roof, he said. Some people wanted to smoke.

People are smoking in here! Don't cover for that prick. Andrei knows the roof is off-limits. Last time the alarm went off, neighbors called the cops. They dial 911 if the wind blows too hard. And they want me out of this building. They're praying for something like this. The sad part is that I never learn. I just figured he'd left, but he'd never leave before every last drop of life had been squeezed. And you wouldn't go without a good-bye, would you?

They'd missed the reading, during which Renata had called on the guest of honor, a tremendous poet and our new friend, Pavel Robertovich Nasmertov, to share a few of his poems. Pegging him for a low tolerance, she'd prepared a copy of his book and used colorful Post-it notes to mark poems she deemed it best to read (not the wordy ones or those mentioning the camps). A simple mistake had set her on this path. She was confusing Pasha with men who resembled him in superficial ways. These men, like Pasha, lacked spatial awareness, peripheral vision, guile, and garrulity; their height was excessive, only accentuating their infirmity; structural idiosyncrasies were respected with a limited, very particular range of motion that made them identifiable from miles away; their plates remained white until you put something on them; they were known to wander off without warning; in the act they groped blindly, pawing like cubs. Such men wouldn't know what world Post-it notes came from but would appreciate their not-so-subtle assistance. Equipped with a nonverbal breed of gratitude, they rarely acknowledged the deeds on which their existences relied. It remained unclear whether they even realized that effort and care were taken on the part of another, and in this helpless opacity there was something deeply perpetuating.

But these men were undeviating versions of themselves—and they certainly weren't performers. When giving a reading, Pasha underwent a transformation. Before an audience Pasha embodied, occupied, seized. The capacities and drives assumed absent or atrophied appeared fully formed. He was forceful and aggressive. He was loud. Renata would've whispered her instructions into plugged ears, catching Pasha devoid of a shred of receptivity. After reciting a few poems, he'd notice that he had something clutched in his bloodless fingers. By this time he would've forgotten who introduced him or where he was. A sealed realm of acute nowness could get direly claustrophobic. To fend off this threat, any available vents were used, including objects that had accidentally slipped into this realm but still smelled of the outside world (think of prisoners who emerge with the collected Voltaire memorized). Discovering that he was holding his own book and that it was filled with flapping sticky neon squares, Pasha would've made a stab at the gesture. Renata would've been wounded for years. Any chances of hurt feelings had been averted. Renata could continue to brim with maternal sentiment. Equally fortuitous was that he'd missed the other poets. In the meantime Misha's powers of rationalization had been called in. It was all very plain and understandable: The reason Bozhko, Fishman, and that whole gang didn't take an interest in him was that he wasn't a poet but a prose writer, and too Americanized at that. The only prose writer in their circle was Rosa Salem, and she didn't count for two reasons: She was an attractive woman (despite the nose), and her prose was as incomprehensible as contemporary poetry. But it was only natural that Pasha should fall in with them.

Lilya, of a dark magnetic beauty freshly extinct in Odessa, whose ghost still haunted the streets, was gone. She wasn't using the facilities or tucked into a bookcase shadow. As long as she'd been pinpointable, Pasha could happily keep talking to somebody else. The reconstituted atmosphere brought a whiff of party death. What had been ambience was noise, uneven and jarring. The number of people had been cut in half, and the remaining half had to laugh harder, take up more space. The room had been plucked clean of beautiful women. The remaining ones looked as if their feet were killing them. They wore overcompensating blouses, hoping to draw attention to breasts with which they'd struck a deal that was now dusty. Like broken contraptions about to be pawned, their faces had been tinkered with at the last minute, using makeshift tools and a bit of improvisation to attain a precarious guise of serviceability that with some luck would hold for several hours. Smiles like grease smudges hastily wiped. It was impossible to imagine his wife among them. With brazen makeup and a blouse, she'd look absurd and savage. Not in a million years could she manage a grin like that. Pasha was filled with pride. No, his wife never smiled.

As a matter of fact, I often forget the good-bye part, he said. But I'll try to remember you're particular about that. Here goes: Good-bye.

You can't leave yet. Look how much watermelon's left.

There's an entire train journey ahead of me, said Pasha, though he did love watermelon.

Oh, of course, Brighton Beach! I won't hear of this train ride. There are extra beds, couches, closets, whatever you prefer. . . . Sleep here, and tomorrow we'll go for brunch. I'll show you around a real neighborhood. Do you know what bagels are?

Very kind, said Pasha, but my family—

Call them. Say you'll be back tomorrow afternoon, Renata will make sure of it. Nothing will happen to their little boy. I'll get you the phone. As she was turning, a young lady, freckled and flushed all over, took her by the elbow and leaned in, conveying pure flustered youth. Renata's eyes widened, and with a pregnant look she put the girl on pause. Seems like an urgent matter has come up, she said to Pasha with a discreet wink. Shouldn't take more than a minute. You wait here—I'll be back with the phone. Renata's experienced arm slid around the young lady's emotional shoulder.

Pasha was deliberating on Renata's proposal when a harried and winded Misha sidled up to him. It was Pasha's turn to see if Misha was OK. Misha replied with one of his jarring laughs. It poured out, a cascade of giggles as effervescent as his hair. They'd called him Masha because of those curls. Pasha felt a hand on the small of his back, surprised to find Misha in such a demonstrative mood. Perhaps that's just what they needed—a little old-fashioned affection. They were childhood friends after all.

Hello, boys, said a familiar voice. I've come to break up the party.

The party's just beginning, said Misha. Now, let's get you a drink.

Designated driver here, said Marina. Actually, personal chauffeur.

What in the world are you doing here? said Pasha.

On second thought, said Marina, I'll take that drink.

Misha tenderly disengaged from Marina's arm and trotted across the room to the refreshments.

Unbelievable! Mama didn't tell you I was coming?

It's nice that you're here, said Pasha with zero conviction, but, frankly, entirely unnecessary.

Misha trotted back with an urgent delivery.

Marina laughed. Who do you think I am, Semyon the second-floor neighbor?

A little classier than that! Semyon cooked up the moonshine. You always went for the Stolichnaya.

I was fourteen. Now I'm a lady. Our species drinks wine.

Misha's quick fingers were ready to take away the shot glass and, once it was drained, they did. She hadn't lost the macho habit of pulling her lips back, exposing teeth, after taking down the strong stuff. And her throat made the hiss of a freshly opened can of Coke. Misha placed a more species-appropriate beverage into her swollen hand, which took the glass's stem as if it were a grip test.

Your timing's auspicious, said Pasha. A minute later and you would've missed me.

Maybe you got Mama's telepathic message after all.

Esther Borisovna does have supernatural powers, said Misha. Remember when she predicted that blaze in the Preobrazhensky Cathedral?

The courtyard lady, Vedama, always did call Mama a witch, said Marina.

What I meant, said Pasha, was that I'm ready to make my exit.

You'll just have to wait a bit, said Marina, lifting her glass. She had an adamant stance on waste, at least when it came to alcohol. A ruddy flush crept up her cheekbones, bulges that had always perplexed Pasha. Marina the Tatar, he'd teased, but she actually got upset, wanting only to be Marina just like everybody else in the family. She brought the glass to her mouth so often it would've been easier to keep it there. Her eyes were already losing their wideness, her forehead smoothing, focus melting. Her fanned teeth tended to turn blue instantly. Looking around, she nodded in approval. Not too shabby, she said. Though I wouldn't want to be the one to clean it.

I have a lady, she's superb, said Renata. Gets the place spick-and-span in a few hours, charges practically nothing. An illegal, from Kharkov, where she taught literature. I can give you her number, though she's overbooked as is. Renata turned to Pasha and held out the phone. Here, dial your family. Tell them you'll be back tomorrow afternoon. If you prefer, I'll do it.

You just did! Marina began to roar. The laughter pumped in waves, jostling her organs, rising upward from her core.

Your older sister, Renata said to Pasha, or a Brighton aunt?

Marina continued, helpless. The production was turning hysterical. Tears blurred her vision.

And she didn't even smoke anything, said Misha.

They stayed the night. They had to. Marina, at last managing to regain composure, realized she wasn't drunk as much as cosmically exhausted. If they drove back, she'd be asleep by the

Columbus Circle roundabout. Renata put them in the office where she took her patients. I'm a psychoanalyst, accredited, been practicing for ten years, she said, her stare directed at Marina. This got Marina started up again, to everyone's dismay but Misha's. He was prepared to trail-laugh up the steepest slopes, to absurd summits. This time Marina's laughter quickly transitioned into a painful case of hiccups. Misha called a car service home.

The futon's seen better days, said Renata. Patients developed attachments to their psychoanalytic cocoons. It would be a betrayal to change it. Marina was left to do battle alone. Pasha knew better than try to solve a mise-en-scène riddle. Technically, somehow, the chrysalis had to unravel into what in this case would undoubtedly be a very crippled butterfly. But you couldn't just jostle your way to a metamorphosis. The key, it turned out, was simply to lift the front leg while holding down the stretcher rails and punching in the back cushion as the hidden deck was tugged out from underneath and the wooden frame kicked, but gently, as it already had a crack. Then the thing opened up like new.

NOT THAT MARINA HAD MANAGED to sleep, but she awoke to a barrage of numbers. This occasionally happened—nightmares lingered in code. Digits swirled down the consciousness drain. They banded into sequences that senselessly harassed. If the numbers were vivid enough, she took it as a sign to buy a lotto ticket. Clearly misinterpreting the message. But this unassuming morning, after a hasty raffle, a number stood out in pure gold on a backdrop of red velvet—seven hundred and thirty. Two years! It was the anniversary of their arrival, the realization a shock, as if she hadn't been obsessively counting. It was an occasion, not an accumulation. The others had been unusually tight-lipped about it. Was it possible they'd forgotten? Perhaps after the previous year's hullabaloo, they felt the need for understatement with this one, a measure of nonchalance. Pasha was loaded into the car and made to wait as Marina picked up some understated pastries and nonchalant champagne. They got back to an empty apartment. While arranging the fruit bowl, which took some mastery, she noticed the phone light blinking red.

A man's gruff voice, heavy accent. Her heart thumped throatward. It was one of the Hasidic brothers—addressing her! Too overwhelmed to listen, she played the message back, and again. It was brief.

Fired! said Marina. Sitting around the table, they'd lifted glasses, hadn't yet clinked.

Esther grew indignant—who'd ever heard of one of their own getting fired? But she dropped the act and put on the kettle when Marina began to rant. The families were slobs, treated her like shit, were practically abusive, never offered anything to eat but forbade her from bringing her own food into the house because of their wacko laws! Kosher shmosher! Food was food, something they would know if they had ever suffered from a lack of it! They hadn't liked her from the beginning, something about her specifically, say, her long hair or the way she dressed, and yet she'd done the best she could with their pigsty. A handkerchief, warm from Esther's breast, wiped Marina's eyes. The tea made her chapped lips tingle and swell, and she slurped loudly, trying not to recall Krolik's perplexed expression at the sight of pepperoni, his tense forehead too new to wrinkle. How quickly he'd swallowed those few bites, hardly chewing, before taking off with the evidence.

SIX

ROBERT WAS FIXATED ON THE MAN from Cambridge, the fact of whose existence Pasha had let slip and then promptly forgotten. This man accompanied Robert throughout the day but became central at night. He started to say things, such as, Get Pasha to contact me, this is very important.

Who are you? Robert asked, but the man would say no more. Robert's questioning persisted, and a few hours later the man introduced himself formally as professor emeritus at Harvard and foremost translator of Russian poetry into English. I've worked with Brodsky and, briefly, Nabokov. I'll translate Pasha's tome and, once it's published, secure him a position as lecturer. He'll be in Massachusetts, more convenient than Russia. It's quite close, just consult a map—anyway, it wouldn't hurt to brush up on your American geography. There are trains, expensive but the height of luxury. And when the time comes, Frida has an easy in.

Here Robert felt obliged to kindly object. Don't you think you're getting ahead of yourself? How old is Frida? Ten at most. And at what age do they finish school in this country, twenty?

So you see it's still a while before she applies to university, and besides, an easy in will not be necessary. But I do think you're onto something with translating the book, hardly a tome, and getting Pasha a position. He'd be very good with the students. He's always exhibited a pedantic sensibility.

Then he must respond, said the man from Cambridge. I've read his book and sent him a long letter introducing myself and extolling the virtues of his poetry, going through a few of the poems in significant detail. It's not every day that a collection by an unknown Russian poet moves me to propose a translation. There's no money in it for me, you understand that, I hope. And I'm not dying for an additional project—as is, I'm drowned in deadlines. The point being I've done all that I can.

Robert thought long and hard. Being forthright would be foolish. Pasha wouldn't respond positively to news that his father had been conspiring with the man from Cambridge. But if Pasha complied, he was essentially a step away from fame in America and a respectable position that would leave him time to write. This was a matter of objective significance. Much was at stake, and Robert couldn't afford a careless approach. He needed to be strategic. But Robert had no sense of strategy. Shameful as it may be to admit, he avoided chess. And he invested too much trust in a higher system, underestimating contingency. He believed that if you put everything down at once, the veracity magnets of the universe would sort through the mess, set it in its right order, and see through to the correct outcome—hence Robert's characteristic sloppiness. Suddenly he heard the lock turn and footsteps. Esther let out a groan, rolled onto her side, and began to snore.

Robert sat up, electrified. An epiphany: Pasha had the letter. He may have been obstinate, but he was also a Nasmertov, which meant that he came equipped with a reserve of relentless, pestering doubt. If he didn't leave a bit of space for a change of opinion, he'd get claustrophobic. Robert imagined Pasha opening the mystery letter from Cambridge and devouring it in a gulp, then deciding for whatever insane reason that it must be ignored. Pasha would've put it away and spent the following days trying to forget its existence, until realizing that he was only driving himself to the point of having to reply. He needed the space to rethink his decision in order to not have to rethink it. So he retrieved the letter and took it to New York, figuring that if he did decide to call or write, he'd want to reread the thing first. Robert clutched the blanket, breathing hard. He looked over at Esther to see if she was hearing his thoughts, but she was asleep, head cocked back and mouth agape, screaming breath. He looked at the clock—quarter to three. He lay down, now convinced that Pasha had the man's full contact information with him. But Pasha was going back to Odessa tomorrow evening, and if he hadn't contacted the man yet, he wasn't about to. Robert had the sensation of flight. He was weightless, the wind under him pumped in powerful rhythmic bursts. He was exhilarated—these were real developments, though confined to his throbbing brain. But no more new developments were coming. A small rock rolled onto Robert's chest, and its weight pinned him to the mattress. So Pasha had the letter with him. What exactly was Robert supposed to do with this knowledge? He remembered the semi-lucid dream that had led to the breakthrough: He was in a canoe with no oars. He began to search for something to paddle with, up to this point a recurring dream, but this time he found under his seat a suitcase that crumbled to dust the moment he touched it.

IN ACCORDANCE WITH THEIR WISHES, Pasha had filled out over the course of the visit (he'd developed an addiction to Ritz crackers, keeping an amber stack torn at the seam in his pocket at all times—so everybody's happy, said Esther, the roaches and the mice). His grooming had improved, he'd acquired a healthy dose of color, and the result was that he no longer looked like a poet but a computer programmer, which possibly had something to do with his wearing Levik's clothes, sitting on Levik's couch, getting tended to by Levik's barber, using Levik's toiletries and, unintentionally, Levik's toothbrush (neither used it very regularly). Pasha was a stable poet of even temperament, Levik a tortured coder. Pasha slept soundly, had a calm demeanor and steady output not widely ranging in quality (on his off days he was great, on his good days he was excellent, and his genius needed no equivalent). Levik was volatile and moody and regularly stayed up into the wee hours, staring into the screen. He muttered, gnawed his fingernails, tugged out fistfuls of hair that needed no help in disappearing, shut himself in the bedroom for hours; cursed when he was failing, cried if he ever broke through to a solution; hid jars of unidentifiable liquid around the house; bought vast quantities of Febreze products in compulsive splurges. Passing him in the corridor, you never knew whether he'd ignore you or try to dance with you, as he was the type of man occasionally so stirred he could express himself only through dance, though an impartial observer would hardly know to call it that. This reaction to his work was odd, since the only scripting language he knew was Visual Basic. Don't let the name fool you, said Levik. What about the fact that it had been created for beginner programmers? Levik held an entry-level position he'd secured because he'd lied on his CV and had twenty friends vouch for his credentials and because Americans refused to believe that a Russian might not be proficient in technology. A nerdy eighth-grader with too much time on his hands could've done Levik's job, but looking at Levik at four in the morning in front of a massive black screen with an arrangement of code on it and a cursor blinking in the same spot for hours, you'd think he was making an effort to decipher the secrets of the universe.

Pasha poring over a lined page was a far cry from Levik's impassioned computer sessions. Face expressionless, equanimity unruffled. Marina composing a shopping list seemed more inspired. And he worked so early in the morning he was essentially still asleep. The only other person awake at the time was Esther, which had been a source of much bristling. Dawn was a very particular time, unlike dusk, when a million things could be happening. At dawn there were silent missions, at dusk predinner drinks. Esther and Pasha didn't like to share their precious matutinal commodity. But Esther set up base in the kitchen and bathroom, two places difficult to avoid for long. She'd fix Pasha with a piercing gaze, judging every food and drink decision he made. Why take three spoonfuls of instant coffee when one sufficed? The wafer should go on a plate, but why should he care about that if Mama's there to wipe away the crumbs? Today wasn't just any morning, however, but Pasha's last. She'd made a fresh batch of cottage cheese for the occasion, and he wasn't being shy with helpings. She felt an urge to hug a little boy to her breast. Instead, finding herself behind her pasty giant, she pinched his back fat (the drawstring of Levik's pajama pants cut into Pasha's skin, creating convenient bulges).

How's the writing going? she asked, eyes ablaze.

Fine, said Pasha, on guard. The question came out of the blue; it was, in fact, the first time his mother had mentioned his writing. She'd never been the most supportive of the poetic endeavor. But maybe, Pasha thought, she's come around. Perhaps the question constituted a gesture; she was reaching out. Actually, he said, it's been a little rough—they say the second book is where it gets difficult. Why do you ask?

You've been eating a lot.

Not any more than usual.

More frequently than usual.

What's that got to do with my writing?

Maybe you're compensating.

Do you think it's been easy to get anything done in this house?

We manage.

You make soup.

And you eat plenty of it!

Pasha repackaged the wafers, spooned cottage cheese back into the pot, poured his coffee down the drain. I'm going for a walk, he said, and, not entirely sure why, as he wasn't actually angry, headed for the door and executed a dramatic slamming.

Robert dragged himself into the kitchen, grumbling for having overslept. The concept, however, was no longer relevant. There were no consequences to snoozing past the alarm, which made him all the more disgruntled for doing so. Being ten minutes late to work was something a person could grasp. It focused and sublimated the intangible unhappy feeling and even made it fun—occasional tardiness was a transgression, a small, harmless one. Now there was only the intangible unhappy feeling.

You didn't wake me, he said.

You were sleeping so sweetly, said Esther.

She gets a boost from seeing me at my worst, thought Robert—perhaps the third mean-spirited thought he'd had since the Second World War. He fell into a dejected slump by the window. A cup of coffee appeared under his nose.

You know I've been trying to cut down.

Nonsense, said Esther. The stuff gives you a pulse. After he'd taken a few sips, she added, Pasha went off somewhere.

I wasn't looking for him.

I thought maybe you had an idea where.

You mean, did I get a dream communication from him? No, I did not. He didn't say a word. But you could've asked.

I didn't want to intrude.

Robert shot her a who-are-you-kidding look.

For a walk was what he said. But Pasha doesn't walk. Now I'm worried.

How long has he been gone?

Half an hour.

Relax for now. I'll tell you when to worry. Is there any cottage cheese left?

The news of a fresh supply lifted the gloom—what a difference between the stiff brittle pellets of a week-old batch and the airy clumps of a new one. Along with a teaspoon of raspberry jam—a heavenly marriage. That they'd been having it for breakfast for the past thirty-five years never diminished the gustatory surprise. Robert had been walking around with white crud in the corners of his mouth for decades.

Satisfied, he was ejected from the kitchen.

And now? Esther called to him. Should I worry now?

How long's it been?

Forty-five minutes!

Not yet! Robert yelled as he lathered the unkempt shaving brush and puffed out a cheek. But he didn't finish because he was standing over Pasha's suitcase. Though it wasn't really Pasha's suitcase. It was Robert's—a patient had once given it to him as a present. The patient was a luggage merchandiser with arteriovenous malformation and early-onset Parkinson's. His name was Volodya Laramshtik and genetic misfortune had tailored his life so that the Nasmertovs never suffered from a dearth of luggage. Robert's slipper nudged the flap. What an unhappy sight: clothes and papers swirling together in a panic. He got to his knees and set to work. Give Robert a chisel, curettes, even scissors, and the procedure was sure to go smoothly. But digging with bare hands wasn't his forte. He was inexperienced in this line, and it wasn't as mindless as he assumed. After an arduous spurt, he noticed that he wasn't breathing. And he was sifting blindly, not registering what he was putting aside. He began again, this time trying to integrate three operations: breathing, digging, and discerning. It was a while before he asked himself, Why am I diligently inspecting every article of clothing when right here is a massive pile of papers? The weight of the papers shocked him. Just lifting them out of the suitcase drained his strength. He divided the papers into several stacks and picked up the first: disconnected stanzas, notes, illegible scribbles. The moment the word *papa* jumped out at him, a creak resounded. Robert turned. The door swung open, and in the doorway appeared Esther's rear end, often of assistance around the house, since her hands were generally occupied. Robert was relieved, not only to see that it was Esther but by the very sight of that rear end. She couldn't really be sick with a rear end of such grand proportions. Cancer ate at people. Left them brittle and emaciated, wasted away. That rear end was absorbing all its nutrients. But now she about-faced, gasped. She stood frozen, wide-eyed—she was bringing in Pasha's laundry.

You scared me, she said, and proceeded to waddle into the room, setting the neat stack on the edge of the couch. Then her legs buckled under her like felled trees. Robert thought she was collapsing and jumped to attention, but she was just sitting onto the floor beside him. What are we searching for? she asked.

I'm not sure, said Robert. To avoid eye contact, he looked down, spotting a letter on top of the second pile, written on Harvard University letterhead. He began to read it and laughed aloud, so stilted and stuffy was the Russian in which it had been composed. The man was John Lamborg, chair of the Slavic languages and literatures department at Harvard University, specializing in the linguistics and semiotics of medieval Rus. He also taught a class that reflected a more heartfelt interest: stylistics of twentieth-century Russian poetry. Robert copied out the address and returned the letter.

I'm done here, an exultant Robert said, and stood.

Well, I'm just getting started, replied Esther.

· · ·

PASHA SURFACED ON THE STREET. An unfortunate turn of events, really. Unlike Tolstoy, Pasha wasn't one for long, aimless walks. But a destination eluded him. Why not look at it as a last chance to explore? Weren't there hole-in-the-wall trinket shops that had tempted in passing, alleyways with a Venetian allure? But the neighborhood had ossified, no longer explorable, just usable. Did he need anything? Perhaps some tomatoes?

In fact he needed to pack, but returning to the apartment wasn't an option. He let himself be carried downstream by a pour of sunlight. Summer had officially overstayed its welcome. Despite a wildly enthusiastic reception, those who'd eagerly awaited its arrival now wanted to be granted relief. Dumb heat was being pumped into a hothouse atmosphere. The inability to sustain a thought made surroundings materialize. What was that? A shrub. And beside it? An old lady scavenging through the trash bin. Across the street scurried Rurik Schvarts. Esther's dearest friend had been Rurik's mother, Raya, a hardened lady prone to fits of maniacal laughter, who died at forty-seven from a lightning strike during a rendezvous with a lover. Rurik was a failed violinist. Fortunately, failed violinists were too resentful to look around when returning home with groceries. He disappeared with two limp bags into a building.

An odor of derangement hung about Brighton, wafting extra from under the train tracks. There were too many instances of household appliances used as hats, baby carriages with things other than babies in them, heated conversations with a sole visible party. The condolences distributed by the émigré poets upon learning where Pasha was holed up for the duration of his visit were understandable, though he couldn't help being suspicious of a response so quickly issued and unvarying across the board. Only his family had a different idea. They said regularly, Isn't it wonderful here? Look how nice it is! They seemed to be neither lying nor telling the truth. Pasha couldn't say he'd come around to their point of view, but he'd softened to the place. No longer did it strike him as a nostalgic bubble beyond hope. Rather, despite its being just that, there were undeniable charms, for example the little grandmas selling prescription pills and old furs on the corner, the physics professor with his pile of used watches, the open-air concerts by ardent if not expert musicians. And if nothing else, there was something to be said for the fact that there were more bookshops in Brighton than in the entire country to which Pasha was shortly to return.

Seeking refuge from the heat in one of the larger bookstores on Ocean Parkway, he was reminded that if Russians put in a decent effort, they could mimic German sterility. The effort was misdirected. The immaculateness of a bookstore or a couture tie shop or a faux-Italian lingerie boutique didn't compensate for the raging chaos in other arenas of Russian life: politics, family, drink. Nevertheless, it was a comforting lie, like the kitchen of a grandmother. Though Pasha himself wasn't neat, sterile, or orderly, and his life wasn't cataloged or alphabetized—not even the genres were distinct—he wasn't impervious to the effect of these qualities in a bookstore. That odor of derangement stopped right at the door. The air inside had been imported from the atmosphere over an Alaskan lake. Outside, the concrete was melting. Here, Pasha's teeth clamored. Thoughts were like warts blasted with liquid nitrogen. The poised saleswomen, the straight-backed stacks. Just as there was a superior class of humans who didn't perspire, there were books that didn't accumulate dust. There was no way to tell which books the public neglected. They were all equally pristine, waiting not too eagerly to be chosen. They seemed to boast of a system of self-grooming, like cats.

As his sister had predicted, Pasha had come to fear his own name. There were creatures that resided eternally in the underworld but were able to rise to street level on the condition that they identify some poor individual by his or her full name: first, last, and patronymic. Using all possible tactics, they tried to prolong the conversation that ensued, because the moment it was over, back to the underworld they went. Pavel Robertovich Nasmertov, the voice said, and instantly grew flesh. Pasha turned to find an interesting creature indeed.

I thought it was you, she said. And where else?

Pasha looked at her quizzically. She pointed to a sign, so large and perfectly positioned that it was invisible.

I'm afraid this is misrepresentative, he said. The majority of my life is spent outside the poetry aisle.

Yet you look quite at home.

On the contrary, I'm finding it stifling. They must've just washed the floors.

And of course you object?

Not on principle. I like clean floors as much as anybody. But the chemicals make me light-headed.

Then you need some fresh air.

Pasha looked abstractly to the stacks. Anyway, there's no room in my suitcase for more books, he conceded.

They nodded politely to the well-built boy guarding the

door from scores of invading armies and emerged into the tightly packed heat. A train pulled into their skulls.

Are you leaving soon? she asked abruptly as passengers overhead were advised to stand away from the platform while the train was entering and leaving the station.

Tonight, said Pasha. I'm sorry, but do I know you?

She turned away in the odd chance that her pale cheeks were capable of mustering color, and said that they'd met, just briefly, at Miss Ostraya's.

Right, said Pasha, though he thought he would've remembered had he met this young woman, if only because of her ear. The right one was unremarkable, but the left was tiny, shriveled, mangled; it looked like a stick of gum that had been chewed not too long, then stuck clumsily on the side of her head as if under a desk. Her copper-in-the-sunlight hair was worn shoulder length and shaggy to best shroud the deformity. A tricky operation. Though small, the ear was jagged—it had a way of poking through. And New York was a blustery city, particularly Brighton. From the direction of the Verrazano, they were being blasted night and day. Each gust defied her efforts. Under the sway of the elements, she couldn't be sure when the ear was hidden, when on display. To check would only draw attention. The technique she'd developed was to check in with her toes, letting the choppy strands brush over her cheeks.

Her name was Sveta, and she offered to escort him home. She was a bit overgrown. She must've been cripplingly shy as a girl, because now that she was in what Pasha pegged to be the twilight of her twenties, she was developing a hunchback. The timidity had matured into wry coyness (or coy wryness). She was a bit spacey, which Pasha took to be an affectation, adopted in order to deflate a constitutional intensity. A very American impulse to dilute—she'd probably grown up here. Thoroughly Russian women exploited to the maximum their God-given powers of intimidation. She was trying to hide that she was fully awake and at the controls. The steering took place far behind her eyes. She spoke quietly and very quickly, as if to compensate for not being able to walk as fast as she would've liked (her step was light and bouncy, like those slender dogs whose paws hover over the ground). She mentioned school repeatedly and the horrid F train. Which school, the nature of her studies, her connection to Miss Ostraya, or where in this capacious borough she lived, Pasha didn't catch. Hearing *Transnistria*, he asked her to repeat.

Where my family is.

There went the theory of an American upbringing—though now he realized he'd never believed that theory anyway, and this only confirmed what he had truly assumed, which was that her relatives couldn't be here, she was too pale. A family wouldn't stand for it. At the height of summer, in a beachside community, to be this devoid of color could only mean she was alone, no one nagging her into outdoor activity, making incessant remarks about her corpselike pallor. And how skinny she was—bones and more bones. Neglected enough to remain uncompromised. Without opposition, her disgust, or perhaps fear, of sunlight, athletics, and nutrition could grow to monstrous proportions. And how terribly lonely it must've been with no one to force you into doing something you refused to do—hence the talking to strangers. She'd plucked Pasha from the poetry aisle. It would be unwise to think himself the first or the last.

He asked questions to keep her voice around. Nearing his

door, her enunciation improved. Pasha learned that her youngest brother had died last year in the War of Independence and she was going back to Tiraspol at the end of something to visit her ailing grand-something.

At the end of the week?

The year, she clarified.

Pasha was so lost in thought he didn't notice that the door into the building was being held for him by his mother.

Pretty, she said, but worth missing a flight for?

THE BAGS WERE PACKED in no time, then unpacked and searched for the house keys, repacked much more sensibly by Esther, partially unpacked again in hopes of finding Pasha's passport, because without it he was going nowhere, he'd just have to settle down for good. Pasha's cot was stripped of bedding and folded up, ready to be returned to the downstairs neighbors. All the mugs and spoons that were missing, for which Esther had searched everywhere and gone so far as to accuse their neighbor of stealing, were found. Pasha's precious junk was consolidated, the plastic bags crumpled together and stuffed into a drawer for future use. A living room appeared, in which the entire family sat down together for the last time. They were quiet and composed. Somber? No, serious. Perhaps solemn? No, no—serious, and a bit tired. Their collective sleep debt could've belonged to a class of medical students.

Robert coughed suggestively.

Davai, said Esther.

We meant to bring this up sooner, said Marina.

But then the whole incident, with the twister . . .

We really should've taken you for a checkup.

But it went so fast! You just got here!

It sure didn't feel like a month. Though it also felt like a year.

But we did have a good full month. And as long as we have your attention.

Try not to scare him, said Robert.

He's not a child, said Marina.

All this is unpleasant to hear.

And it's hard. Life . . . It's all sort of dreadful.

But just deciding is half the—

More than half. Once you decide, it's smooth sailing.

Let's not go that far. It's easy. It can be easy.

Basic steps.

We'll help through them all.

Better not think about it. Worst thing you can do is think about it.

We did it. And you know us. We're not the most organized or intrepid or courageous—

Adaptable.

Comfortable with change.

Practical, financially speaking.

Good with languages.

But you have an ear for languages. That's a problem that can be crossed off the list.

Robert, why must you say there are problems?

Face it, Pasha, there's nothing for you there.

Is it fear that's keeping you?

You don't even have friends!

Here you have Misha. *He's* a true friend.

That's more rare than you may think.

At that party you enjoyed yourself, didn't you?

That you want to deny the fact that you're capable of having a good time at a gathering of like-minded people means there's something wrong with you.

Nothing's wrong with him—Marina, stop being nasty.

He's not denying anything! He knows he enjoyed himself. He never denied it!

Think of Sanya—he's taken a bad turn.

What she means is, he can get a good education, opportunities.

The boy has an entrepreneurial bent. That thing he did with the batteries.

You said yourself he's fallen in with the wrong crowd.

And he's only seventeen. Imagine in a few years.

Here there are special programs.

Here there are no bad crowds.

And maybe you can get in touch with John Lamborg.

Who?

Oops.

Frida can have her uncle around, and her only cousin. He was practically a brother to her.

Not my brother.

She could use the relationship.

I know there's like a silent law that this can't be mentioned, but screw it. Mama's sick. We're going to need an extra hand.

Nonsense! I'll be fine. You can sit on the sofa in the corner. No one will bother you. We just want to look at you.

Pasha, the world is much smaller these days. Trust me as

your father. And I happen to know the brother of the husband of the lady who's the secretary to the senior editor at *Novy Mir.*

I'll bake you honey cakes every day! cried Esther.

It was hot. They hadn't yet come around to the concept of air-conditioning. If it was summer, you had to sweat. And the sweat had to smell. But something about the location of their building, the positioning of the windows, the roof materials— they hadn't suffered through a sufficient number of summers to develop a dependable theory—made for especially stifling conditions. The windows were gasping, yet the curtains didn't stir for days. Even the furniture seemed to languish. This was an unfortunate distraction, which had the potential to obscure what was important. People who focused on their physical discomfort seldom got to the point.

I'm glad you brought this up, said Pasha. A bead of sweat originating in his hair somewhere split in half over his lumpy forehead, and the beads diverged, rolling down opposite sides of his long face. I've given this a fair amount of thought, as you can imagine. My tendency, with poems at least, is not to show them to anybody until they're done. I've never found it worthwhile to hand somebody a mess and ask them to clean it up for me. Mama, don't give me that look. I know I've kept you in the dark. He looked around the room. He inhaled. He picked a crumb off his stomach. I want to come, he said. Let's begin the process.

Pasha seemed on the whole sincere and alert. Pasha was never alert. Except here he was—alert and speaking to matters of true consequence. They were swept up by the momentousness. Of course, Pasha was susceptible to the pressure of endings.

They were sad, but they needed to be successful. That Sunday afternoon, as Pasha sat in a room with sweating wallpaper, surrounded by his family (a tough audience), his last line was so sonorous it made the future palpable in their throats.

Robert and Esther said their good-byes, staying behind while Levik and Marina chauffeured Pasha to JFK Airport. The torture of the drive—the perfectly stagnant traffic on the BQE, then the Van Wyck, the mysterious sounds and smells given off by their automobile—made them sick to their stomachs. They unlocked the doors should they need to open fast and vomit. Pasha regularly vomited in bearable conditions, so it was a surprise that he managed to swallow at all in this hellish toaster of a car. No one spoke, as there was nothing to say. Pasha had the last word. Who was Levik or Marina to meddle with such an ending? Marina rested her head on her hand and looked out the window. In this city you had to become a professional at looking out the window straight into your own thoughts. What was actually outside was of no concern; it might as well have been a mirage. Those weren't cars or people—who knows what they were? It didn't much matter—the chance that she'd see them again was practically nonexistent. My God, Marina suddenly thought. Do we even want him here? Despite the heat she was trembling.

SEVEN

A YEAR LATER PASHA WAS BACK, once again flying into JFK's third terminal, thinned, disheveled, pale. Marina was now enrolled in nursing school, Levik still staring into the void. Frida had been cruelly committed to day camp at the Y, turned over to the American swim director with the toupee, luckily with a taste only for the boys. Robert and Esther were decorating lampshades with beads, claiming they did it for the minuscule fee, though it was obvious that stringing tiny colorful beads was soothing to their nerves. Levik drove the decorated lampshades over to the American lady, Kathleen, who lived on Madison Avenue with two blue cockatoos and in her ample spare time was starting a lamp business. She didn't need the money but got it regardless. Her business was skyrocketing. People just adored those simple but lovely lamps.

Esther had been opposed to Pasha's visit, as it rendered void his application for an exit visa, a stipulation being that during the months, years, occasionally decades that it took for such an application to be processed, the Russian citizen was not allowed to leave the country. Pasha had finally applied for the visa, and why should news of Esther's recurring cancer make him throw that out the window? She preferred to delay seeing him until he could come for good instead of once again flying in for an over-laden visit at the end of which they'd be back to square one. Pasha reassured her that he would reapply for the visa the moment he got home, words that had been put into his mouth by Marina.

In such instances Pasha got confused.

He knew he was confused when he stopped being able to predict what would be wanted of him. For example, he was as-tonished to learn that his sister's demands didn't coincide with his mother's. One afternoon Marina called Pasha and hissed that if he didn't buy a ticket right then, it would prove once and for all that he was as selfish as everybody claimed. Pasha ex-plained that it was a misunderstanding—he very much wanted to come but had been putting off buying a ticket because he'd gotten the impression that nobody wanted him.

A misunderstanding was the natural state of affairs. Pasha made no effort to clear up his end, choosing to ignore, or simply remaining unaware, that motives were being assigned, inten-tions misconstrued, until the moment of eruption—shouts, name-calling, frequent phone calls and hang-ups, the stupefied dial tone. The accusations shocked Pasha. It was one thing when they came from acquaintances and critics, another when from the mouths of the dear. Unless instructed otherwise, the dear assumed the worst, having very little faith in humanity, or perhaps just in him.

You all expect me to die, said Esther when she heard that he was coming. If you think you're visiting a woman on her death-bed, you're quite mistaken.

But at his arrival she was overjoyed. Marina had been right—Esther's wishes shouldn't have been heeded, as they were not what Esther wished. The anti-Esther had been using Esther's voice—Pasha had failed to be on the lookout for such a possibility.

Even Esther found the idea of Pasha's permanent arrival a source of ambivalence. As long as he remained in Odessa, finality was evaded. They'd studied the cases around them—when an entire family was uprooted and replanted in another country—whether it be America, Germany, Israel—and all ties to the motherland severed, the psychological burden was often managed to the detriment of mental integrity. Thus far they'd avoided this burden—by way of a loophole. No strangers were living in their old digs, doing unimaginable violence to their walls, peering out their windows, distorting their left-behind thoughts. If they went back for a visit, they wouldn't have to loiter at a closed door or a locked gate, gathering the courage to knock and ask for permission to peek inside, or debate whether a hurried scanning of their former premises would be worthwhile at all, especially under the mistrustful, inconvenienced scrutiny of the current residents. Their old apartment belonged to Pasha. Pasha belonged to them.

And it wasn't just a regular kommunalka—it was only one room (partitioned off with curtains), and most of the space it offered was vertical, not doing them much good except offering the opportunity to complain about the lowness of ceilings in ninety-eight percent of places (the Opera House, Carnegie Hall, Lincoln Center were exempt), but it was situated in the epicenter of Odessa, perched in the most prime spot by Primorskiy Boulevard, overlooking Potemkin Square, a minute from the Steps and Vorontsov's Palace, two from Deribasovskaya and City Garden. Summers, Pasha relocated to their dacha. This knowledge brought great solace. It was permission to stay sane. Ties hadn't been severed; Odessa remained theirs. This sense of retention, of not having exchanged or betrayed but simply enlarged in scope, kept virulent immigrant manias at bay. They didn't need to compensate for what had been irrevocably lost by polarizing into the hyper-Americanized or feverishly nostalgic, to vanity-publish photo-essays or entire book-length declarations of love to their former city, compose odes to Odessa and perform them on Saturday evenings at Restaurant Odessa, form International Odessite clubs or join said clubs, have strokes and sit in wheelchairs outside their building screaming *Odessa, Odessa!* at passersby with rage and passion and utter incomprehension as to what was going on both around and within.

The chemo was under way by the time Pasha arrived, Esther's wan curls detaching by the fistful. Daylight infiltrated through to her scalp. She'd bought one of those housedresses that came in countless dizzying print variations and hung on the outdoor racks of discount shops along Brighton Beach Avenue, a purchase that infuriated Marina. Esther was throwing up her hands. First it's a housedress, then no desire to live. Marina bought a wig for Esther and a geometric summer dress from Bloomingdale's.

They expected to have to keep her from the housework. They'd permit a little dusting or watering, so she wouldn't feel useless, but forbid the more physically straining activities. When Esther went for the pail, Marina's bold voice resounded, We can do that, you must save your energy. Esther didn't have to be told twice. She returned to bed with a book, leaving the pail out for Marina, as the floors weren't about to wash themselves.

Pasha's help would've been enlisted, but the reward for reaching his ripe age never having peeled a potato or folded a pair of pants was never having to. No one would make the mistake of even turning on the vacuum cleaner in his presence. He was most useful in distracting Esther, who wasn't of the if-left-uninterrupted-will-read-in-bed-for-hours temperament. If left uninterrupted, she'd interrupt. Pasha was deployed. Lying side by side, they engaged in a conspiratorial whisper. Occasionally she laughed. A large ship passed over the open waters that were Esther, leaving the surface unsettled long after the ship had gone. And her face, thought Pasha, had the bloated, grayish quality of something that had spent untraceable years at sea bottom.

It proved not true that a housedress—which Esther proceeded to wear both around the house and outside despite the presence of the Bloomingdale's dress, which even Marina had to admit looked a lot like the housedress once Esther put it on—led to a diminished will to live. Esther's sole focus became survival. She was so determined that the actual process of living became a distraction from the goal. At mealtimes she reverted to Soviet-style nutrient-density assessment (anything creamy, sugary, buttery of highest value), but instead of giving the choice foods to Marina or Frida kept them for herself. This combination of eating nutritiously and saving her energy made stoic Dr. Muckleberg advise a weight-loss regimen. Esther incorporated grapefruit into her diet.

The family outings were to the hospital, where other people's conversations were marked by a subdued intensity. It's good I made you that sandwich, said the small woman with a drinker's nose as she sat wrapped in a sweater in the air-conditioned cafeteria. The bread isn't very appropriate, said the small man with the drinker's nose before proceeding with a very businesslike chewing. Others were peeling hard-boiled eggs and rattling sugar packets, stirring coffee with great determination; still others were reading brochures, becoming informed, asking a question. Esther sat in a snug-fitting armchair that in retrospect would look beige but probably had a specific color, some insane purple. She sat in these armchairs and at the same time refused to touch them. You'd never catch her elbows on the armrests or her fingertips near the fabric—they were holding a book or a paper cup or resting on her knees. Other people touched these armchairs. The problem was, of course, all those others.

Marina touched everything, and everything she touched became hers. How afraid she'd been—but that fear was like a loose thread snipped by the hospital's sliding doors. As it turned out, she was a valuable sickness companion. For the first time, they were seeing her in her new milieu, and it was enlightening. They had been of the opinion that nursing school was a wrong decision. We just don't see you as a nurse, they said. On the one hand, they thought it would be too much—the high-intensity environment, the long work hours—and on the other they considered it below her—a nurse. They had better suggestions. If she was going this route, she may as well bite the bullet and go to medical school, but she should also take into account that hairdressers made a good living in the States, and she'd always been so creative with her updos. Once they became regulars on the hospital scene, the offering of alternatives subsided.

Marina never rested her legs or plucked a magazine from the pile. There was always a slippery personage to track down, some bit of information to obtain, a minor error to not overlook. Marina's voice, unlike those of the others, was loud but never hysterical. Her assured silence was just as soothing as her assured speech. It was only natural that she assume full responsibility for their interactions with doctors, telling them what Esther felt and where and what Esther wanted and how, then telling Esther what the doctors never quite formulated themselves. The Indian doctor hardly spoke, the Australian doctor rattled off warm but unintelligible volumes, and it would've been better not to understand the German doctor. Having long stopped seeing patients as humans and disease as something unfortunate occurring within a patient who was human, he was interested only in recruiting the diseases, in whichever package they were delivered to him (brown hair, blond hair, fleshy, thin), for his ongoing, alternating, and evolving experimental studies.

If it was being offered, Esther was willing, sign her up. Sickness from treatment was preferable to sickness from disease. There was almost an invigorating aspect to it. The fact that she wasn't well meant that she was getting better—the treatment was working, and she only wanted it to work more, fearing that she wasn't suffering enough. She pressured Marina to pressure the doctors for more chemo, stronger radiation, additional sessions, newer drugs—she was strong, she could take it. Sure enough, in many instances the doctors could be convinced.

When she suffered third-degree burns, they saw no reason to take the blame.

At least the hospital had been fortuitously plopped on the Upper East Side of Manhattan—you must take advantage, said Esther. No need for them all to sit for hours in the soul-crushing, disease-saturated atmosphere just because she had to. What a waste of a wonderful opportunity. Robert would keep her company. The two of them would rattle sugar packets, visit bedecked mansions in the high resolution of real-estate magazines, play card games as treatment was intravenously delivered. Marina had done more than enough; there was simply no one left to bother. Hospital employees shuddered at the drum of her footsteps, secretaries twitched as she advanced to their posts. And it must be remembered that Pasha was in New York for a limited time only. Siblings should spend quality time together.

Illness has made Mama generous, said Pasha, falling behind to let Marina start up the revolving door. She must be in negotiations with the mighty powers.

She wants to be left alone.

Don't we all? Pasha was unable to dislodge a bone. She's always terrorized me, a recent claim. Last summer's conversation proved but a glimpse—Marina had no desire to see more. Where to, she said, Metropolitan or Guggenheim?

Actually, said Pasha, I've been intending to make a purchase.

Canal Street was where the train spit them out. Pasha's request, yet he stood frozen. Struck dumb by tourists in bold T-shirts. The insignia on baseball caps bled together into one strange character of an alien alphabet constituting precisely the terrible nonlanguage of the street. Calamity was the result of such senseless diversity. Each nationality had its own approach to shopping. In some countries if you wanted a plastic turtle, you pushed, in others you formed lines and were mercilessly cut off. Everybody, however, regardless of origin, wanted to be heard. And to be heard it was necessary to shout. Second opinions were in urgent demand. Aggressive shopper personalities were activated for purposes of basic protection. People trying to preemptively avoid a mishap in which they looked foolish or got squeezed out of a few bucks were at their worst. They needed to multitask (not the species' strong suit), evaluate several things at once—an object's value in relation to its price, their personal need for that object, how it looked on their head or wrist or dangling from their tan-lined shoulder, how comfortable they were with the knowledge that the object was a replica, and how to deal with this knowledge, whether to allow others to draw their own conclusions or tell everyone, including those who didn't ask, that only four dollars had been spent.

A mere shpritz of adrenaline cut Pasha's whole system off from power. He proceeded to stand, blink, and stroke his beard. Grabbing hold of Pasha's hand, Marina led the way, exasperated by the situation. She'd been employing all her powers of persuasion to push the department-store experience—they could go to a store like Macy's for good-quality apparel, something practical and useful so that he wouldn't always be walking around in ill-fitting hand-me-downs, where they'd also find something for Sanya—a cool pair of jeans, a denim jacket—not to mention that Nadia couldn't be completely overlooked. But Pasha wanted a watch, and only Canal Street would do. This galled Marina. The entire business was distasteful, like the way her friends bought dresses from Saks only to wear them once, then return for a full refund. Not Marina. Since she didn't have the means for brand names, she'd do without.

If a stigma was involved, Pasha didn't seem concerned. Marina gave other options—Kings Highway was lined with stores that sold elegant, inexpensive watches. Look at Levik's. So it's not Swiss-made. Who can tell the difference? Like talking to a wall.

They exited the purse forest, entered a field of dial faces. Ugly fungal watches sprouted from wooden crates, plastic tables, suitcases propped on fire hydrants. Vendors kept up a steady barrage of hushed solicitation. A few reached out and grabbed. Marina shook off their *Hey, miss!* and *Hey, lady!*, knobby fingers, musky smells. It felt like Turkey, 1983. The fear, the shame, the disgust. She stopped abruptly. Her own fingers, giving Pasha much reassurance, unclamped. Go ahead, she hissed, pick.

Pasha weighed a few options but didn't delay, plucking the most sparkle-studded, yellow-bright Rollex in the batch.

Marina relied on facial contortion to communicate her feelings. Pasha advised she buy a pair of sunglasses; there was no shortage of options. Voice would have to deliver. You want *that*? she said.

You prefer another?

They're all hideous, Pasha, but that's an absolute monstrosity. She glumly lifted the flap of her crappy-but-honest purse, proffering a five-dollar bill like a crumpled sock. I just don't get what this is about, she said.

Pasha's wrist held out, Marina fastened the clasp. Tutoring, he said.

Marina failed to comprehend. Releasing Pasha's arm, she recalled walking out along a narrow pier so high that the water underneath wasn't visible and holding tightly on to the arm of a man who wasn't Levik. She stared at his neck as he stared at a tiny cargo ship wrapped in silky flame. There was a terrible screeching sound as he lifted his other hand, in which he held a dirt-caked shovel. Oh, said Marina. For the mothers?

Mothers weren't the issue. Pasha could get work from them regardless. The watch was for the kids, hardly a fitting term for two hundred fifty pounds of pure muscle—adults with deficiencies, a more apt description. They were practically illiterate, spoiled, hopeless, but what else was new? The problem was a rampant obsession with status. At the whiff of financial desperation (and why else would anyone tutor?), they stopped being bored, became vicious. You didn't have to be a hound to smell it on Pasha. In perhaps their only demonstration of logical reasoning, they figured, if you're poor, I should be learning how to *not* be like you. The watch would take care of that. He'd just have to remember to stash it in his pocket before going to the institute, so as not to upset the doctors.

They walked a few blocks north, tending their thoughts. Where next? asked Marina.

Her brother was a weak old man, almost forty, couldn't take more. But if she was ambitious enough to continue to Macy's, he wouldn't mind waiting. Were they far from the Frick?

Speechlessness launched Marina. There she went . . . fiery, short-fused Marina, zooming up the avenue. Her hair looked angry. Pasha could see it from far away, in a dense mass of bobbing heads, by far the angriest hair. Each strand a heated needle. She stopped on the corner, pressed her back to the traffic. In a state, she forgot herself completely. Her arms, too tense to rest at her sides, froze at odd angles, as if she were beginning to lift off. Her eyes searched frantically for Pasha, finding him only when he'd blocked her sun.

THE SILVERY GLEAM under the couch had been spotted by Frida as she was being ushered off to day camp without a second to spare. Eight agonizing hours of locker-room changing, double-line forming, bologna-sandwich deconstructing, back-flip attempting later, when let into the apartment again by Miss Gala, the severe emerald-eyed lady substituting for Esther in pickup duties on hospital days, Frida made a beeline for that couch. All that anticipation proved not for naught. Silvery gleam had weight.

The necklace's appealing qualities (in order from least to most): It was chunky, it had a clasp, it accentuated her breasts. In the bathroom mirror, she kept track of the day-to-day changes. The areolas were fluffy and light pink like inside a conch shell, but the surrounding whiteness, what Frida understood to be actual breast, refused to un-cling from her rib cage. Pushing them together was no more possible than making a joint eye. The first thing that greeted Frida in the bathroom was disappointment, but by the time she unlocked the door, letting in whichever crazed family member had been trying to knock it down, she felt herself the owner of a real set of boobs. There was nothing passive about these mirror sessions. Work was being done, tissue developed. Yet no one mentioned a training bra. To ask for one was against the rules—the world had to offer. The bra had to be deserved. The necklace fell heavily to her navel, on the way outlining each breast, creating visible mounds. Examining herself from every imaginable angle and in all her tank tops of the thinnest cotton, she decided that this time the evidence was irrefutable.

The corridor came alive not terribly long thereafter, introducing a final unpleasant moment: Miss Gala's dismissal. Whispers characterized this small event, as Frida was made the subject of a report. Miss Gala was troubled by Frida's antisocial behavior. When walking out of the Y, Frida tried to fall into step with a group of girls and grimace as if she were interacting, but this tactic didn't always work, because Miss Gala was no fool. Once the door had slammed behind Miss Gala, Frida could at last make her appearance. It was calculated for effect. The only possible result was the urgent purchase of a training bra. Frida knew the exact one she wanted and where it hung in Berta Department Store.

After the recent string of days (one thousand one hundred and twenty-seven), Marina's powers of observation weren't as sharp as one might hope. Frida, torso puffed, had to go so far as point. Once Marina processed what she was seeing, she leaped in her daughter's direction, meanwhile maintaining perfect silence. This made her daughter squeal all the louder. Realizing that her mother was a lost cause, Frida turned her chest to her grandma, who was straining to remove her shoes on the creaky piano bench. No need to know what Baba Esther's words meant to sense the force of profanity. By now her mother, too, had found her voice. Take that thing off! she yelled. Right this instant!

Mission aborted, Frida ran to the bathroom, turned the lock. How could it be that they'd missed the point entirely? Somehow or other, Baba Esther was to blame—if she wasn't busy, she was furious. Most of the world slipped under her radar. When she looked at Frida, it wasn't as one person looked at another, certainly not as a grandma looked at her granddaughter, but as an inspector checking a garment. She was interested only when something was wrong. If Frida had a fever, an ear infection, splinters in her heel, Baba Esther gave her undivided attention. She was visibly disappointed when Frida's cough wasn't a cough but a badly swallowed grape. And she never lacked for the proper admonition: I've seen many girls just like you asphyxiate because they stuffed their mouths and ran while eating.

Too discouraged to conduct another mirror session, Frida climbed into the bathtub and stretched out her legs. The necklace rose and subsided with her rib cage. Its weight instilled a lesson. It wasn't a good lesson, but at least it wasn't algebra and at least her uncle, to whom she assumed the lesson belonged, as her grandma had yelled his name several times, wasn't trying to instill it himself. The walls of the bathtub were rounded and white like distant mountains. For a moment she felt as if her surroundings were open and vast, in contrast to her days, which were crowded with buildings and shadows.

EIGHT

ROBERT'S YEARLONG SCHEMING had manifested such outward symptoms as an acute mailbox fixation, the revival of dusty desk implementa (magnifying glass, makeshift clipboard, pencil sharpener the size of a pet cat), severe bouts of pharmaceutical-resistant insomnia—all of which Esther and Marina misdiagnosed with dread as stage one in the fulfillment of the mythic memoir project. But they need not have worried about their secrets leaking out through Robert's pencil. Thanks to his furtive efforts, John Lamborg had translated half the poems in Pasha's collection. No publisher had taken it on, no lectureship been offered. Robert miraculously kept up the correspondence in Pasha's name until foolishly mentioning that he would be visiting his family in New York this July. Lamborg read this as an invitation. He'd assumed that they both assumed it was important and inevitable that they meet. Perhaps not entirely unintentionally, Robert had gotten himself into a bind and saw no choice but to disclose to Pasha the details of the entire deception.

He wasn't sure what to expect—an outburst of rage at the

intrinsic breach of privacy or gratitude at the sight of the translated poems, perhaps one followed by the other. But Pasha took
the news as tepidly as he'd taken the letter. He'd never had any
intention of responding to Professor Lamborg, having skimmed
his letter with a bit of amusement but a lack of any other sensation. The amusement was partly in response to the letter and
partly to the attached photograph of the Russian branch of the
Slavic department assembled in two paltry rows on a concrete
staircase. John Lamborg had forgotten to point himself out,
which didn't make much of a difference, since the four men
were identical. Their ruddiness was half fresh air, half rosacea.
They had scrawny men's confined bellies and wore quality
sweaters made of wool, the necklines of which were tight and
pronounced; perhaps it was this constriction that caused the
bloom in their cheeks. If Pasha had been surprised by anything,
it was his own boredom.

Fine! yelled Robert. I'll cancel the goddamn meeting!

There's no need, said Pasha. Calm down, Papa. I'll go meet
the man.

But the calm was precisely the problem.

The department photograph must have been a decade old.
Lamborg was gaunt, aged in the haphazard way rosy people
age. His button-down shirt still had the size sticker on the back
(XS), and his hair looked like freshly mowed grass. It was for
this occasion that the man had cleaned up. Having little to
present to Pasha, Lamborg wanted to be presentable himself.
He must have thought that all these months Pasha had been
awaiting news of an English-language publisher.

They met in Brighton, a neighborhood whose pulse Lamborg made a point to check at least once a year. Pasha professed

ignorance, and it was Lamborg who ended up showing Pasha around, leading the way to a restaurant-café that served the most delicate blintzes. A rheumatic finger pointed out that over there was the most sinus-excavating plov and here the airiest meringue, while two blocks up stood white vats of the crunchiest pickles. The only men Pasha knew with such an investment in the matter were grotesquely obese—they ate all day long, did little else—yet even they were less expert in the field. And here was Lamborg, a chopstick of a man, warning Pasha never to buy Korean carrot salad from Gold Label but only from Taste of Russia, which, on the other hand, used the worst dough for its frozen pelmeni. All in utter earnestness, not a hint of sarcasm, not a measly grin. Lamborg was disappointed at Pasha's inability to supply new tips or fill lacunae like Brighton breakfast fare. The only gastronomic wisdom Pasha could muster was that it was truly uncanny how much the food here was like that in Odessa, the only divergence being in abundance. He kept at it until he'd talked himself into admitting how disturbing and pathetic he found Brighton, though he actually didn't feel one way or another.

They burrowed into a corner table under a tiny but very deep TV soundlessly projecting a football match. Lamborg itched for the chance to halt Pasha's menu inspection if only Pasha showed some sign of noticing the menu or any awareness that such a thing existed. Eventually Lamborg simply caught a moment when Pasha's gaze drifted and said, Don't bother with that, I'll order for us, which he did in proud, overstated Russian that failed to arouse admiration in the waiter with black eyes glued to the TV.

Pasha kept Lamborg from ordering chak-chak, Lamborg's

favorite dessert, and invited him back to the apartment. These were the instructions he'd received. Lamborg didn't protest—he was a collector of Russian household experiences. He entered the building lobby and began to systematically take note, inspecting the floor tiles, plants, odd ceramic bowls, and how they were all used in equal measure as ashtrays.

Pasha was caught off guard by what he discovered at home. The apartment was clean. The dining table had been transplanted to the living room (Pasha's foldout cot had disappeared, as had his suitcase) and covered with a celebratory cloth, on top of which stood a city of saucers filled with jams and tiny treats. This was Esther's fancy china set, only admired from behind the glass door of a cabinet, until now. His family members were scrubbed to a shine and dressed in their finest. Lamborg himself was surprised by the magnitude of the reception. Sweat stains deepened the blue of his shirt, and his lips receded, exposing horsey teeth that didn't suit his face at all.

Hardly more than our usual Sunday lunch, said Esther, waving away the concern.

Pasha took Marina aside. Number one, what is all this? Number two, I told you we were going out to eat. Number three, whose idea was this?

Not an ounce of gratitude! You'd think we were doing something horrible. If you really want to know, Papa ordered this up. And it's for Frida as much as for you.

Frida was by then a big girl three months shy of eleven. She had to be impressive when the man from Cambridge came to lunch. Expectations were low. Impressive applied to Frida meant that she wear a dress and sit at the table. No one expected smiles, precocious conversation, grace. She wouldn't have to use a knife.

Even a fork was optional. The man from Cambridge didn't need to leave with a distinct impression of Frida. Better he did not. When a few years later she would be applying to Harvard, he should be able to remember, upon gentle prodding, that sunny Sunday afternoon, that immaculate lunch, that delightful, generous, expansive family of the poet Pavel Nasmertov, and his niece, who just blended into the background, did nothing jarring or off-putting, was in no way insane, misbehaved, or emotionally corrosive, neither capricious nor foul, and so must have been quiet, reserved, and mature, traits meriting acceptance to America's most prestigious institution of higher learning. It would be the least John Lamborg could do after a block of black caviar.

But along with a dress, a proper young lady must wear stockings. No two ways about that. Frida's lumpy, bruised legs, her knees of picked scabs never allowed to heal, couldn't just stick out of her dress. It was a hot day, and just looking at the shiny, airless material created a frantic itch. Frida whimpered and clawed at her flesh. There was a lot of meat to pack into those sausage casings, and Frida didn't deal well with constriction. She wore shoes two sizes too large for her feet, confounding the salesladies with their measuring devices. For months she hadn't allowed a comb near her hair, which grew increasingly lopsided, tangled, lackluster and shaggy, until a bloated white bug stepped out onto the balcony of her forehead. All of it had to be chopped off. It was growing back frizzy and brownish and currently fell just past her ears, her large ears that also seemed to have fought their way out of confinement, to freedom.

After ten too-good-to-be-true minutes at the table, Frida

began to fidget. This during the routine immigration narrative they were replaying for their guest, who'd certainly heard a thousand such narratives with a peppering of charming details like how Marina had thought that in America she would work as a professional clairvoyant because around that time Barbra Streisand gave an interview in which she said she never went anywhere without her personal fortune-teller, Tatiana, and the hearsay was that after that all the wealthy women in Manhattan wanted their own Eastern European fortune-tellers, so instead of learning English in the time leading up to their departure, Marina learned to read palms and Turkish-coffee grounds and was embarking on tarot cards and astrological charts. She usually told the story better—Frida's writhing and squirming distracted.

Lamborg abruptly turned to Frida. What about you, he said, do you like it here?

It was difficult to fathom a more catastrophically off-the-mark question. Here—as opposed to where? If there had been a somewhere else, Frida was currently engaged in an immense struggle to extract every last trace of it from her DNA. The writhing stopped. She looked at the man dead-on from under hooded eyelids. Without uttering a word, without needing to, she made it all too plain just what she thought of him.

She's timid, said Esther. Needs time to warm to strangers.

Answer the man's question, said Marina.

It's OK, said the man, she doesn't have to.

Actually, she does have to.

Just a very sensitive girl, said Esther. Will become a pediatrician one day, just like Grandma.

Frida rose partially off her chair as if about to charge. But

she didn't—she stayed in what appeared to be a very uncomfortable half-squatting position and lifted her hand, in which
something beige was balled up. She flung this ball, which un-
raveled midflight, at Marina's face. The stockings didn't quite
reach the face, landing weightlessly across Marina's plate. Frida
glanced nervously at Pasha, as if expecting him to appreciate
the act, to laugh perhaps, or also toss some nearby object. When
he did neither, his face remaining impassive, his gaze motionless, she ran out of the living room on lumpy, bruised legs.

Anecdotes are good, was Robert's take. His temperament
was conducive to seeing the big picture. Seven years would be
sufficient for any residual unpleasantness to wear off. Bitter af-
tertastes had relatively short half-lives. In six years' time, when
John Lamborg would be reminded of Frida's stocking fling, you
know what he would do? Laugh! Everything falls into perspective. What appears to be a tragedy now will be repackaged as a
light anecdote, a bit of color—crumpled stockings in Marina's
plate of glistening caviar. Answer me this, if the encounter had
gone smoothly, what reason would there be to remember it?

Of course, there was no guarantee that in six years John
Lamborg would even be alive. The man drank a good deal.

Levik had been ordered to pull out the vintage merlot they'd
gotten as a welcome–to–the–New World gift from their distant
New World relatives (scattered in the mansioned pine forests of
New Jersey) and which served, it seemed, as a sort of bribe—we
will give you an outrageous bottle of wine the likes of which
you've never tasted, even though the odds you're able to discern
the notes of vanilla oak and black truffle and hints of plum cas-
sis on the finish are slim, and in exchange you'll never ask us for
anything or expect any sort of relationship or call on the holi-

days. Levik's hands shook violently as he uncorked. He was going through the actions as told, but it was taking profound control to tune out the internal hiccup—Don't, don't, don't.

Such a deep nuanced red came out of the tender opening as Levik poured.

A coy look came over the guest's face. What's this, he said, a Russian household with no vodka?

God forbid. Levik rummaged around behind the radiator that during the winter gave off, if anything, frost, and introduced a family-size bottle of the clear stuff.

And they'd been under the impression that Americans didn't drink. Lamborg's shot glass existed in a perpetually drained, expectant state. Just refilling it (without drawing too much attention to the refilling) was a full-time job. Lamborg had taken to heart the custom that it was rude to drink when a toast wasn't being offered. The Nasmertovs had proposed one or two at the meal's commencement—concise, practical, for health and wealth. But then Lamborg made a few increasingly far-fetched toasts himself—to enviable households, to new countries and new friends, white nights and black seas—and they realized with horror that they were supposed to keep cranking out the toasts so their guest could keep imbibing. Three-quarters of the bottle (which was the size of a child's leg) disappeared with practically no help from them.

Frida had expected the stranger to leave in an hour, two at most. During her brief stint at the table, she had been too uncomfortable and indignant to eat. Once the adrenaline from the tantrum subsided, she found that she was starving. But you don't throw stockings at your mother's face in front of an important visitor you're supposed to be impressing only to return an hour later for some pelmeni. She remembered all the delicacies on the table. Esther's homemade cherry vareniki in thick crimson sauce had virtually disappeared from their culinary repertoire as of late. They were labor-intensive, and the cherries here were not like the cherries grown back on their dacha. But the vareniki were currently in a bowl on that table in the living room, to which Frida could possibly very quietly return once the visitor was gone. She had pride. She would starve to death before facing that man again. And starve she would, because the hours kept passing with no sign of his departure. If the visitor were making an exit, the entire family would escort him to the end of the corridor, where they'd orchestrate a loud, festive, dramatic, prolonged farewell—to seal in the specialness of the occasion and properly launch it up the memory chute. So Frida was prepared to overhear the finale, which, like any proper climax, would be audible through a closed door, a door to which she pressed her ear every quarter hour. What the hell was going on out there? The silence stretched for so long and the cherry sauce grew so vivid that Frida suddenly thought, Maybe I fell asleep without realizing and in the meantime the visitor left? So she cracked her door a smidgen and peeked—to find the visitor's shoes waiting under the mirror. Murmurings leaked out, there was the scrape of porcelain, a muffled cough. She almost succumbed to the urge to rush into the living room and grab as many vareniki as she could with her hands—but they were slippery, they'd slide out. She shut the door and sank into despair.

The knob turned. Esther stuck in her head.

Are you hungry?

No, said Frida. I hate you.

Not even for some cherry vareniki?

Esther was unexpected in the role of savior. Usually she was the one advocating for harsher measures and stricter policies, being of the opinion that naughty girls who don't respect their elders must be taught a lesson and that once you set out to teach a lesson, Marina, you have to go through with it. Marina had a tendency to cave the instant her initial rage subsided. Then it was all kisses, togetherness, laughs—to absolutely no disciplinary result. Mixed messages only made a more stubborn monster out of Frida. When the door opened and it wasn't Marina, Frida felt a flare of reinvigorated anger, as if her mother had broken a promise to relent. But here was Esther with her gray face and ratty wig, her sticky sweat and palpable not-wellness, offering Frida not just sustenance but assistance in taking the first step toward a return to public life. A shame—Frida preferred to regard her grandma as the enemy.

Where'd he go? asked Frida.

Still here.

He's an idiot, said Frida, intending to anger.

And a drunk, said Esther.

PASHA SAW THE ÉMIGRÉ POETS—Renata Ostraya, Nurzhan Bozhko, Andrei Fishman, Efim and Sofya Milturn—finding them, to his surprise, every bit as lively as he had the summer before. This time they came to Brighton, as Pasha didn't want to leave his mother for the entire evening. He thought his refusal to traverse the Brooklyn Bridge would mean that he wouldn't get to see them, but they scrapped their plans and boarded the train, emerging boisterous and rowdy. Pasha was apparently providing them with an opportunity for adventure. They approached Brighton with the attitude that it was hilarious and exotic. They were strictly explorers, anthropologists in an absurd land. Of course a good anthropologist must participate fully in the local customs, no matter how bizarre. Once they got off the train, they piled into the nearest gastronom and loaded up on cheap liter bottles of Ukrainian beer and kvass, filled containers with pickled cabbage and tomatoes, grabbed packets of dried salted fish, then stopped off at the liquor store for that very thing a Russian household couldn't do without. Provisions in hand, they made straight for the shore, for a picnic in the moonlight.

Pasha followed along, feeling vague stirrings of resentment. This was a real neighborhood where people lived, people with families and tight budgets and, furthermore, people who spoke and read in the language in which they wrote. No reason to feel so high-and-mighty, to act like the nobleman who'd put on a peasant's frock to play the part for a night. And his mother was sick—one block away, she lay in bed, vomiting into a tub. Pasha wasn't in disguise. But then they were creeping along on night-trampled sand about as redolent of nature as a bath mat. After finding a spot to settle, he was able to relax. It was as if he'd been collecting evidence against them into a plastic bag that was punctured by one of the ubiquitous glass shards when he plopped onto the sand. All evidence leaked out into the ocean. It was a nice night. So much so that Pasha, after a long sigh, said, What a nice night. Who was it that said one must make a habit of saying aloud when something is nice?

My uncle Dodya, for one, said Sofya Milturn. She'd grown appealing in the dark. What the moon did to the ocean's surface it also did to her hair, illuming a path through the smoothness and ripples. In the light she was gawky, boyish, angular, but now she was lithe—a clean, elegant silhouette. Ostraya was out of her element, breathing heavily and trying to unstick individual sand grains from her large white calves. The group honored a pensive period. But they drank steadily throughout and were returned to rowdiness.

Fishman drummed on an overturned garbage can, Renata accompanied in song, while Pasha told of the time he got caught in a twister and made the chance discovery of an elaborate under-the-boardwalk world—tunnels, stoves, birdcages.

Care to show us? said Bozhko.

Pasha didn't, really.

Come on.

Pasha leaned back, digging his elbows into the sand.

What, are you afraid? Or have you just been using your creative license?

I'm using my go-fuck-yourself license, Pasha said and laid down his head. The sky pulsed with airplanes, one of which was supposed to have been taking him home. Tonight had been his return flight, before they'd extended his ticket. This was accomplished in a manner of complicit silence, a refusal to allow meaning to enter. The pretense was that he could spend more time with Esther, but time with Esther had become unendurable. Her waking hours were devoted to a frantic demand for additional treatment. As she saw it, the doctors were deliberately depriving her of the one treatment that would overcome her disease. Her family was at best not trying hard enough to get her this elixir; at worst they were in on the plan. There's a conspiracy against me, she claimed. Up until then, she'd been rational to a fault.

A heavy object dropped onto Pasha's shoulder—Renata's

head. It wiggled until his arm unglued from the side of his body, became a cradle. Pasha's armpit announced, The sky is the underside of an old mattress with a monstrously obese owner who never gets out of bed.

Pasha, inexplicably overcome with tenderness, kissed the top of her head.

The sky is a turtle's turd, said Bozhko.

The skinny-dipping was Sofya's idea. It was turning out to be her night. Only her husband, Efim, hesitated. He was useful to the crowd in that he provided the brakes. Fishman, occasionally Ostraya and Sofya, constituted the engine, and everybody else gave color to the ride. If you just looked at Fishman, you'd never suspect the frenzy of sexual energy within him, the need that could never be satisfied for long. He looked extraordinarily plain and middle-aged: beady eyes, a nose like a nose, no lips. The face was very red, overheated, which was the only sign that beneath the surface was a barely contained fire that had settled into the most unlikely candidate. Fishman was engaged in a never-ending battle with his own odd physical manifestation, but he had it in him to fight fifty battles at once and simultaneously charm the ladies, because if he wasn't doing that, what was the point of any of it? Along the way he charmed Pasha, who usually had a hard time tolerating the energetic types. But Fishman was less like an overgrown child, the way the majority of these types came off, more like a man in the thick of existence, encompassing all inlaid hypocrisies, chauvinisms, victories, fetishes, guilt.

After experiencing the ocean's cool, slimy touch on every part of their bodies, they returned to the blanket. Only after falling down upon it and releasing a bit of a middle-aged sigh that betrayed the extent of their previous exertion and their joy at the support of the hard sand allowing their lower backs to release, did they find that their party was greatly diminished. Two were missing. There were whispers. Efim looked around with a dull gaze of incomprehension, then alarm. Where's my wife—she drowned? That would've been nice. Neither was Fishman's labored breathing to be heard among the pack. Two interlocked shadows disturbed the equanimity of the water, luckily out of the moonlight's path. Occasionally Sofya's hair caught it. Everybody on the sand felt insufficient somehow, so they had a conversation about literature, digging small holes with unconscious effort.

None of it affected Pasha too deeply. He was the observer, the anthropologist, not them. They, in fact, had it all wrong. But in this role Pasha missed a few nuances. He left with the impression that the night had been a success, whereas they might've been more reserved in their evaluations.

Regardless, the night served its function, casually reminding Pasha of America's positive attributes. Immigrating wouldn't be so bad, now, would it? He had friends. They were lively and witty. And they were somehow not overly discouraged by the predicament of writing in a different language from the one spoken on the street, perhaps because the language most seldom spoken was English. His family was here. And who knows, maybe Sanya would make a lot of money and support them—he *had* done that thing with the batteries. The situation in Odessa, meanwhile, was only getting worse. A systematic deterioration defined every arena of life: Pasha's beloved bookstore had overnight transformed into a casino whose metallic windows reflected his confounded face; the only other poet he tolerated in the entire city had frozen to death last March in a drunken stupor outside the doors of another casino; those coffee-flavored sucking candies had disappeared from markets, and in a way they had been his sole joy.

Back at the apartment, the stench of vomit clung to the air. Pasha found all the lights turned on, needlessly overlapping, imparting an aggressive sheen, while everyone had fallen asleep strewn about the rooms. Robert sat at the kitchen table clutching the handle of a cup of tepid tea, his large head wedged into the crook of his elbow. Marina was slumped on the toilet seat, an anatomy textbook in her lap, forehead resting on the sink bowl. Frida lay in soapy bathwater, chin hooked on tub's edge. Levik had been tinkering with the TV's wiring when he'd dozed off. Esther still clung to the plastic tub, recently emptied and glistening wetly, which was settled on the summit of her stomach. Pasha set it aside and laid his head there instead. Nothing moved. Everything was perfectly, peacefully still.

The funeral was held in a massive Soviet-immigrant death establishment on Coney Island Avenue, a street where cars had many lanes but still bunched together and tiny people on the tiny strips of sidewalk seemed to be crossing a desert.

PART TWO

2008

NINE

EMBARKING ON the Coney Island–bound Q, Marina spotted an inch of bench and reverse-parked herself into it. Was there a greater victory? Pregnant lady looked sturdy, Park Slopey— she'd be getting off soon anyway. Secured in this cradle of human warmth, rocked back and forth, soothed by a lullaby of rails. Too quick to rejoice—at DeKalb Avenue eyes were locked, pupils zapping. No escape. Marina summoned emergency energy reserves, reserves tapped daily and for the most part depleted. Acquaintance swooped in, hovering, head dangling from armpit. This woman, who, to be honest, Marina couldn't place— which former life should be referenced?—began to rave about some novel she'd just finished reading: epic, absorbing, deeply evocative. Permission to tune out. Marina nodded along, studying the woman's chiseled jaw, single chin, teeth aligned in neat rows, until her neck cramped and she looked down. Snakeskin boots, brass buckle, pointy toe, collided head-on with her own pair of subway-rat-gray Reeboks discounted from Loehmann's, a half size too large, extra wiggle room for her toes, hallelujah! A few stops later, the train-evacuating stampede left Marina alone, holding a book. If she hadn't been at the limits of exhaustion, she never would've accepted something that locked her into future interactions with whoever this acquaintance was, clearly someone liable to get carried away in the after-work delirium and make grand gestures soon to be regretted; just wait and see, in a week or two there'd be a phone call, unknown number, this friend of hers wanting the book back or at least feeling entitled to Marina's thoughts, to a meaningful exchange of ideas and opinions.

She'd put off cracking the spine for a long time. In the first place, she resented the imposition on her life. No one knew what she was going through. No one had been through anything like it. In the second place—the cover! A blurry reproduction of a drawing depicting some dim medieval scene alerted her to the likelihood that the novel was historical fiction, a genre she avoided like the plague. Finally there was the size of the thing. It'll build my biceps, she joked. Precisely how long it was, she still didn't know. In the beginning she'd figured that knowing the exact number of pages would daunt and discourage, and now she feared the arrival of the end. Her mother used to say that after a certain age all a woman needs is a good book, a statement Marina found too preposterous to require rebuttal. But . . . The novel was written in a lucid style (so said a back-flap blurb— she agreed) and thus far had been set in seventeenth-century America (witch trials), at the turn of the twentieth century in northern China (Boxer Rebellion), and in present-day Zurich and Moscow (life). Marina couldn't remember the last time she'd been so drawn in, so quick to lose track of the hours.

Interruptions came regularly. Marina's childhood friend called from Tel Aviv to complain about her situation, which had a habit of hitting rock bottom, then getting drastically worse; it began to pour, and the windowsills had to be lined with towels, a plastic tub put in the corridor under the leak; Levik cut his finger making Biff Stroganoff for the guests about to arrive any minute now; the electricity went out during the October heat wave and waited to return until the last item in their fridge had perished; the cat's vomit had to be cleaned; the cat's diarrhea; Robert lost his hearing and began listening to Shostakovich's string quartets at such a pitch the walls shook and reading became impossible, and Marina could only lie on the bed staring up at the ceiling in urgent need of a paint job until she either fell asleep or surrendered utterly to the fury of Shostakovich, the despair, the doom, the colossal force, which happened once. When she began driving to work instead of taking the subway, having started a new job in the cardiac unit at Methodist Hospital, the change made her put the book down for months, and when she picked it up again one evening (the evening she finally tossed the heap of junk mail and found it hiding underneath), she got a pounding brain-on-the-brink-of-explosion headache, so she took two Advil and half of her father's yellow pill and fell into a dreamless sleep. The same thing happened a few evenings later. Every attempt brought on the same damn headache. A protracted visit to the doctor resulted in eyeglasses. For a while she avoided the book in order to avoid the glasses, or more precisely the feeling that somehow, without realizing quite when, she'd become a middle-aged hag with bad vision and achy joints and a host of other stereotypical-for-her-age issues not necessary to mention (she was still a lady after all). Eventually, however, she grew accustomed to the glasses and even began to enjoy the gesture of slipping them onto her nose, notifying her body that it was about to be returned to the realm where it felt happiest, which, oddly enough, was currently in the nineteenth century, at a monastery on a hillside in France.

But then an entire year elapsed, every minute of every day accounted for. There wasn't a single moment when Marina could shut the door, crawl under the covers, and turn on the reading lamp now colonizing her nightstand. On the lamp she'd decided to splurge. It was nice to treat oneself to a touch of luxury. The lamp gave off a peculiar quality of light, intense and ghostly, but Marina figured she was just too used to crappy fixtures, half-dead bulbs, ancient chandeliers. How could good light not seem peculiar to her? But after a month of being no less shocked each time she flipped the switch, she did a bit of research and realized she'd gotten one of those plant lamps. This was for the best, really, as the plants were dying slow, miserable, inexplicable deaths, and anyway at night she fell asleep, as they say, before she hit the pillow. The plants got a last-wish sort of gift. She stopped attempting to make time in her day to read.

Until a few miraculous occurrences: Robert recovered from his lung surgery and agreed to test-drive a home attendant; Marina's on-again, off-again lover, Serge, moved to Cincinnati to be near his autistic grandchild; and most important, after an interim period of living at home and working part-time in a doctor's office, Frida was accepted to medical school in Pennsylvania. They'd failed to get her out of the house for college, though not for lack of trying (John Lamborg was alive and well, still slaving away in the Slavic department at Harvard—and of course he remembered them! How could he forget their generosity, or those delectable cherry dumplings? He looked back fondly on that afternoon but held no sway with the undergraduate admissions board. And he thanked them for the elephant ears, quite unnecessary, much appreciated). Frida had gone to NYU, commuting to class because there was no way in hell they'd also swallow the cost of housing, an arrangement that must've suited her fine, since she'd hoped to continue in the same vein after graduation. But sitting at home and weighing options for an eternity wasn't an option. She had no luck with medical schools in the city and was forced to pack her bags and get out. It was as if Marina found a secret door in the wall and walked into her life: With a snap of the fingers, Frida's room became hers. This was only fair, as Levik and his flock of laptops inhabited the bedroom, Robert had a claim on both his room and the living room, and the home attendant, a West African lady with whom Robert refused to coexist, camped out in the kitchen, where she kept up constant contact with her alcoholic husband's hundred-and-one-year-old mother in Nigeria.

There was time—not only to read but to tell her friends about the good book she was currently reading while they waited in line for the new Almodóvar film at the Angelika, to go for a swim at the Y and take a morning stroll to Seagate, to learn how to ride a bicycle and get a manicure from a Chinese boy in a face mask.

But school years end. In the damp, double-digit days of May, Frida's summer vacation began.

FRIDA CAME HOME, READY TO TALK—about the weather, the new shampoo by the tub, the downstairs neighbors, everything, in short, with the exception of her studies. As she saw it, she didn't owe them a report. They'd gotten their way—she was already *going* to medical school. Wasn't that enough? Evidently not—she had to be forthcoming and positive about the experience as well. Misery was impermissible. She couldn't not like *all* her classes and not find *any* of the other students worthy of companionship and not see *any* benefit to being situated in such proximity to Lake Erie. She'd always wanted to be more in sync with nature. This was her chance. No, simply becoming a doctor wouldn't cut it; she had to be happy about it, too. This need for a positive outlook was more for their sake than hers. They'd forced her into medical school despite vehement protest. She'd put up admirable resistance, but they'd left no choice, attacking like hyenas at the whiff of her lostness, pouncing on her sense of guilt. Did she not remember that ever since she was eight years old, she'd been saying that she would be a pediatrician? Imagine how disappointed Baba Esther would be. After four scholarship-less years of university, did she really have no idea what she wanted to do with her life? It was a common misconception that time was the answer to anything. Time was *never* the solution. Besides, if another idea should ever present itself, a medical degree wouldn't prevent her from pursuing it. The halo of an M.D. over one's name had never hurt anybody.

The moment Frida gave in, the story was rewritten. They pressured her? Don't make me laugh! Who could force Frida to do anything? She was completely incorrigible and always did just as she pleased. Had anybody ever heard her say she wanted to be anything *but* a doctor? Such a story relied on Frida's doing more than gritting her teeth through the rest of her professional life. At the moment, however, she was prepared to do just that.

Robert was particularly distraught at her merciless restraint. He thought he'd get to polish his rusty jargon, banter in doctorly argot, whip out medical arcana, warn of pesky hospital perils, offer seasoned advice. (Marina was just a nurse after all.) He was riddled by fantasies of a wondrous return to the old days, when Frida sat on Grandpa's lap as they hatched plans for fantastic science-fair projects that even when compromised by a translation to reality never failed to take first prize at ecstatic ceremonies in junior high school gymnasiums. Frida's eschewal of any medicine-related topic in long-distance communications had been explainable as typical to Levik's side of the family's telephobia. There was no meaty discussion to be had with Frida unless an interface-to-face was established (an internet-aided one, notably, didn't make the grade, causing her to be even flimsier and flightier than the phone—the more elaborate the technology, the harder to invest concentration). So when she appeared at their doorstep in pimply, ramen-plumped flesh, Robert attacked. What had she learned? Had a specialty been chosen? Waiting for inspiration was futile! Would she be sticking with the pediatrician-like-Grandma line or switching to neurosurgeon-like-Grandpa (a better ring, perhaps)? What about the instructors—did they know what they were talking about of course not! Frida exploded. Get off my back, Ded! I'm on break!

That one subject excluded, there was nothing she didn't intend to discuss. The latest gossip was particularly welcome—was Brukhmansha's anorexic daughter still seeing the balding poodle groomer? Had the Marazams finalized their divorce? Did Lera's daughter get out of rehab, or at least go back into it? Marina found her daughter's newfound garrulity and excitability disturbing and was adopting shameful habits such as turning the lock quietly when she got home from work, loitering in the locker room of the Y, tiptoeing from bathroom to bedroom, where she exhibited all the signs of someone hiding out, strategies that invariably failed at avoiding an encounter. At least Frida had a particular way of leaning her weight on the door handle, allowing Marina a chance to brace herself.

Frida barged in, forehead glistening, hair rising. She looked as if a cherry pit had gotten lodged in her throat and she was about to commence choking.

The firefighters are here, she said.

Give them my regards, replied Marina, not glancing up from her book (unable to make out a single word).

Frida hurried into the hallway. She was worried about her mother. She suspected that Marina had succumbed to clinical depression. She knew the checklist backward, and the signs were impossible to miss: Marina had virtually stopped cooking (once a fervent pastime), lost her joie de vivre, always claimed to be exhausted yet was never asleep when Frida paid visits (Frida took it as her duty to keep her mother engaged). And now her mother was forgoing a chance to flirt with the firemen— unimaginable that the old Marina would have passed up such an opportunity. Admittedly, the opportunity was lately in abundance. Someone in the building—was it Igor from the fourth floor or crazy Marusya?—had gotten into the habit of reporting fires, and several evenings a week the staircases were scaled by firemen. At the identifiable bustle, doors unlocked, men in slippers and boxer shorts emerged, women in hair rollers and bathrobes, gunky spatulas still in hand. Everyone hoped and prayed for a fire, and it was as if the firefighters themselves were failing to conjure the flame. Interest waned. People gave up going out on the landing.

Frida persisted, and not in order to flirt. One must have a sense of ceremony. The men were responding to a cry for help. They wanted to dazzle with heroism. Frida didn't intend to insult them further by not coming out on the landing. A fire, even just the threat, demanded respect. (There was little excitement in Frida's life recently, or none at all.) She stood by the stairs radiating concern. That's the most delicious fire I ever smelled, said one of the button-nosed firemen, referring to Inga-from-across-the-hall's cooking. Frida wanted to congratulate him on his joke but didn't even manage a grin.

They lumbered down the stairs in a fury of grunts, scrapes, burps, and groans. Having seen them off, Frida returned to the apartment, overstepping a mound of spilled cat food and the colony of roaches partaking, skirting the pile of neglected pianos and bicycles and an ab roller like a cherry on top, into her mother's toasty bedroom.

Still no fire, she reported. But the guys seemed in good spirits.

That's nice, said Marina, tucking a yellow strand into her ponytail and leaning into the mirror. Frida hopped onto the unmade bed—a cherished, elusive moment was upon them. The makeup case had been laid out, unzipped. Marina's manicured fingers reached inside, and the plastic tubes and compacts, the lipsticks, mascaras, eye shadows, and rouges began to stir in the dark, rearranging. Marina knew what she was looking for, oblivious to the hypnotic purr emitted by her search. It was as if she were choosing bones from Frida's body. A pair of rusty tweezers emerged, efficiently attacking a chin hair.

You know how Anna and I take our Friday-night walks? said Frida.

You do?

Well, we've been meaning to make it more of a thing.

That's nice.

But yesterday I stayed in—

I remember.

Do you know why?

Nowhere to go. Lipstick found Marina's taut lips, traveling smoothly back and forth like a swinging car on the Ferris wheel.

Because Anna's cousin is in town from Poland.

She couldn't invite you to hang out with her cousin?

Frida swallowed. That isn't the point.

Anna's cousin might be your soul mate.

He's in high school. And they were doing a family thing, a sit-down dinner. I wouldn't even have wanted to go. But I do want to go to—

I told you, Frida, not another word about the wedding.

Have you even considered—

Does it seem like I've had time to consider something? She smudged eyeliner with a fingertip, dabbed a few powdery finishing touches, assessed herself, and gave a long, defeated sigh.

You're not old, said Frida.

But *you* are. Turned away from her reflection, Marina lost the pout and vacant mirror stare, released her belly, dropped to a slouch. And it's Saturday night.

I have plans, if that's your way of asking.

That involve leaving the house?

Fuck off!

Lighten up a little, said Marina.

I'm leading a pathetic existence!

Follow me. Marina looked both ways before crossing the corridor. Dusk was creeping up the walls (crooked, stained, what can you do?), lending a somber touch to their journey. The destination was the computer chair, into which Marina sort of just fell. One hand felt around for her glasses, the other smacked the mouse several times in her particular way of rousing the machine. She typed with one stiff finger, staring down at the keyboard, then up at the screen, then down at the keyboard. Ten minutes later a message appeared. Photos attached. Somebody's perfect catch of a son had split from his girlfriend and relocated from New Jersey to New York—he was shy, he was vulnerable, he didn't know his way around Greenwich Village (liked sushi).

Frida glanced at the keyboard. A different message overtook the screen: GREETINGS, AMERICANTSI . . .

Marina's eyes bulged. Don't forget I was the one who showed you this, she said, and don't make me regret it.

Sanya had gotten engaged, news he deemed worthy of sharing with his estranged Western aunt, who then made the mistake of sharing with her strange, not-distant-enough daughter. Getting married at last, that sullen, mousy boy. . . . OK, so it was hard to get sentimental. The guy was thirty-two and had two kids from two different women, both older and married. Otherwise his record was clean. Not a single divorce. This was to be his first relationship in the eyes of Ukraine. And he was Frida's only cousin—there were dozens of photos of the two of them in the cardboard box stashed away in some not readily accessible nook of the apartment. Though it was probably more readily accessible than she remembered. In her mind it had to be unearthed, dug up. A major effort had to be involved. All those photographs of them together, or not exactly together but caught in the same frame. A courtyard scene: Frida in ballooning denim overalls, staring into a well (old, dry, someone's rubber ducky at the bottom), next to her a ratty courtyard child of indeterminate sex grimacing into the camera, and in the background Sanya squatting over a neat mound of something (probably dog feces; he went through a prolonged fascination, the only time Pasha displayed a measure of paternal concern). At birthday parties they were seated together but never to be found looking at each other or even in the same direction. But at that age a seven-year difference was very significant (this phrase, repeated over and over). Sanya hadn't been the type to take anybody under his wing; he'd needed someone to do that for him, but there had been no takers.

We should all go, said Frida.

Obligations, work, money, protested her mother.

But you're always going on about how you walked him in the baby carriage and his first time saying Mama was directed at you, how everything would be different if we stayed together as a unit, poor Sanya this, poor Sanya that, practically an orphan.

You've certainly changed your tune, said Marina. What happened to not another wedding ever again? You barely survived the last one. This is vulgar, that trashy, the other pathetic. My friends will never let me live down your lovely toast. Marriage—an obsolete institution, remember?

That's here in America, where people spend a decade orchestrating an apocalyptic celebration with registries and flower arrangements and twenty-piece bands. By no means am I opposed to weddings on principle. In fact, I wouldn't mind one of my own. And to be honest, I like the way this sounds. Engaged in May, married in August. That's a proper duration.

She's obviously knocked up, said Marina.

He didn't marry the other two!

This time the girl is high-maintenance.

If Frida wasn't fighting off the accusation that she was singing the same old tune, it was that her tune had changed, and which was the worse offense not even Marina could say. To top it off, Frida was tone-deaf—the intractable pronouncement of her piano teacher, the wife of Rostislav Dubinsky, first violinist of the Borodin Quartet, made after spending two lessons with Frida in 1994. Heartbroken, Esther had demanded a second opinion. Perfect pitch runs in the family, she'd insisted. For the second opinion, Marina had wanted to know, Should we get Shostakovich's widow or Prokofiev's?

The computer made a sound and went black. Marina swiveled her chair around. Though I'm not saying it wouldn't be nice to go. Who knows what's going on over there? Slumped down, arms hanging lifelessly, Oioioi! she cried. Even if we don't go, we'll have to send at least a thousand dollars. That's what's expected of the Americantsi! And if we go, don't even think about it. It'll be a ten-grand affair. Of course, I *do* want to go, she said. She got up and went to the window. Who says I don't want to? Believe me I do. Only it's absolutely a hundred percent out of the question. Papa would kill me if he found out I even told you about this. Though of course it would be good, even necessary, to go. Not that Pasha said anything the last time we spoke. That he was nominated for another prize, he didn't forget to mention, or that he's being translated into Finnish. But about his son's wedding not a word. Either way, we should've gone back for a visit years ago. It's shameful that we haven't made the time.

Frida's face contorted as she ventured to ask, How come *he* never came *here*?

He did, twice—you know that!

It wasn't easy to stir cement. No, she said, what I mean is— why didn't he come for real?

Oh, *that*. It wasn't even something we considered, not in any serious way.

Now who's changing their tune? Baba Esther didn't want her son nearby?

You can't want something from the grave. Pasha did get his visa once upon a time, but there was no longer anyone to nag and yell. The visa went to waste.

And—that's it? That's all there is to it?

There was this, there was that, and the other.

The other?

Sveta.

Frida blinked. How do you mean?

Marina answered helplessly, He wasn't about to leave without her.

Why couldn't they come together? said Frida, in that exuberant way of people with sudden strokes of genius. Her mother's gaze was withering. Oh, said Frida slowly, he was still with—

Lay off, Frida! How many times?

Frida raised her palms, signaling that she had no difficulty laying off, in fact she didn't much care one way or the other, was just making conversation. In heated moments eyes also needed a breather, and in such cramped surroundings this was accomplished by staring with great longing at the foggy windowpane. On the windowsill, lined in cattle-car fashion, were all of Frida's stuffed toys, eye buttons missing, ears torn, fur flat and faded. Here's an idea, said Frida much to her own surprise, how about *I* just go?

The option struck her mother as highly comical.

Am I missing the joke? said Frida.

Well, it's a little preposterous, you must admit. After all these years, the one to go back is *you*. You barely have any connection to the place.

And here I thought it's where I was from!

Seeing the look of pained defiance on her daughter's face, Marina bit her lip but proved unable to stop herself. Do you even remember anything? she said.

I'll make more memories now, said Frida.

You better get a move on it, then.

Are you trying to scare me?

I don't have energy to do anything of the kind. All I'm saying is, Don't make me regret telling you about this. Your father will say all this foolishness is my fault and he'll be right. Besides, you can't go. You have school.

Classes start the week after.

Marina glanced at her watch. Oh, my God. We had to be there half an hour ago at the latest. Levik, she yelled, up!

They were off to Irina Tabak's fiftieth-birthday extravaganza at the overpriced Mediterranean restaurant on the bay, or was that next week? Tonight was the Brukhmans' anniversary at an opera restaurant in midtown, only first they had to stop by

Lera's to drop off a present for her son whose party they'd missed last week because of Vova's backyard fete. They could forget about that! Mascara crumbs were permanently sprinkled under Marina's large, tired eyes. She woke up with a fancy earring tangled in her spray-hardened hair and the necklace Levik had gotten her turned around, the pendant stuck to her perimenopausally damp back. She had more dresses than T-shirts, more gowns than slacks, more absurd open-toed heels and only one pair of brown loafers, the rubber soles superglued. The funny thing was that Marina was enjoying none of it—backyard fetes were tiring, nightclub parties pathetic, no one dancing or letting loose like in the old days, endless dinners at whole-fish-on-a-plate restaurants were taxing on the digestion, and the conversations didn't help the chunks of eel—always so much eel—go down. Momentum kept the gears spinning. Everything had to be celebrated: their birthdays, their parents' birthdays, their grown-up children's birthdays, and now their grandchildren's birthdays, anniversaries, promotions, departures and arrivals, holidays both Russian and American, both Jewish and American. This took care of most weekends, but if one rolled around occasionless, it would be spared such a dire fate by anyone with an aboveground pool or leftovers.

LEVIK WAS NO LONGER IN ANY MOOD for a party. He stared straight ahead into the infinity of segmented boredom that was Ocean Parkway. When the light turned yellow, he didn't sail past but slammed down on the brakes, solely to spite Marina.

You weren't in the mood long before you overheard a thing, she said, so don't you even try.

Whether he'd been in the mood before was irrelevant. He'd certainly been *more* in the mood, but to address this point would be to fall for an ingeniously, if too commonly, laid trap. His jaw clenched so tight his ear canals ached, as he persistently drove and stopped, drove and stopped, while the cars in the other lanes drove and drove and drove.

Marina felt as if she would catch fire at any second. What was I supposed to do? Not show her the message?

Bingo!

She bit her lip. Having moved two blocks in ten minutes, she was growing attached to the people on the benches, the young couples, the geezers, and if given a sack of pebbles, she knew just which heads to fling them at first.

He's her cousin! Anyway, you're taking it far too seriously.

Tell me one thing, said Levik, just one. What did you think her reaction would be? What did you want to happen? Did you expect her to just let it go? Were you even thinking? And how—

You know how she is. By next week it'll be ancient history.

A Hasidic family crossed the street in front of them, four men in tall white socks and sleek black coats, followed by two women of venerable bosom, then three girls pushing baby carriages, bony legs scissoring, and finally a wild tail of children, which, like all tails, relayed the secret message of the beast. The light turned green.

I am in no mood, said Levik.

Why are we in the car, then? You had to wait until Avenue N to tell me?

Only at Avenue H did Levik deign to speak. With utter serenity he explained that he was dropping her off at the restaurant. She could get a ride back with the Plyazhskys, and if they wanted to leave before she was ready to wrap up, Vitalik surely wouldn't mind giving her a lift. She shouldn't worry; he wouldn't be waiting up.

Once again with the Vitalik! Would it never end? Miron, just for example, was far more touchy-feely, yet never a word about him.

Miron's that way with all the girls. Vitalik just with you.

Oh, please. Are you kidding? What are we talking about here? I'm an old lady! Marina flipped down the mirror and began contorting her neck, able to appraise herself only from the oddest of angles. Look, she said, wrinkles, brown spots, splotches . . . But I do have nice lips.

In no mood, repeated Levik.

Where are we going, then? For a little ride?

I'm dropping you off at the restaurant.

Not a chance. If I were you, I'd turn the car around right this second. Your job here is done, my dear.

Levik appeared to suffer a small seizure, then regained control. They kept driving in the direction of the skyscrapers and lights. The highway opened out underneath them, smoothing away the last hour of staccato torture. Soon they were rubbing shoulders with the Hudson, so behaved and placid on the surface, obviously full of its own thoughts in the depths. The great thing about the skyline was that you could say it was beautiful in ideal visibility, everything so strict, intimidating, and contrasted, and you could say it was just as beautiful in fog, such as lay over the city right then, with the Chrysler Building creating eerie patterns of smudged light. If Marina were for some reason forbidden to comment on the view from that one spot on the highway, below the overpass, about four minutes at sixty-seven miles per hour from the Brooklyn Bridge, she almost certainly would've either had to leave the city or go insane. Even now, when they rode past, Marina muttered in amazement. And Levik, by reflex, glanced to the left at the glowing island of Manhattan.

Breath held at the entrance onto the bridge, which their Honda Accord took swimmingly. Silence was maintained for the rest of the drive. At one point, after making a few unhappy circles, Levik pulled over in front of a garage entrance, was honked at, drove a little ways, and pulled over again. Reaching for the glove compartment, he accidentally brushed Marina's knee and recoiled. A second attempt was maneuvered with caution. The GPS was installed in a few spasmodic motions. Suzanna guided the rest of the way to the opera restaurant. A crowd had already gathered. Levik slumped as if he were sitting in his office chair and said, *Davai*.

Marina didn't respond. She sat in dire fear of being spotted by one of her friends.

Please go, said Levik, receiving no reply, which, after a few seconds, became a reply. An increasingly desperate barrage of appeals followed. Get out of the car, he beseeched. Just go! Marina maintained the silence on her end. Levik's back rounded like a tire. Propping his elbow on his thigh, he gently tipped his cheek into his hand and shut his eyes. Through heavy lids, in a whisper, he said, Marina, are you going in there or not?

Take me home, she said.

Why are you being such a—a stubborn! he screamed. His foot slammed on the gas, and the Honda nearly missed a passing car. An explosion of honks almost kept Marina from noticing that Asya Brukhman, whose anniversary it was, was fast approaching with a giant smile, a hand raised in greeting.

The ride back to Brooklyn was calm. A resigned air set in, Levik's preferred atmosphere. They were going home—was that such a terrible thing? He became so relaxed that after recrossing the Brooklyn Bridge he began to whistle softly, not quite noticing it himself. The truth was that he hadn't wanted to go to the anniversary party, sitting for hours on end in a restaurant, making tired conversation while his wife pranced about, getting progressively drunker and more unruly. Now they could go home, he could go back to part three of the Nostradamus docudrama. He let himself believe that Marina's anger was mild and fleeting, that she, too, was enjoying the languor of the drive.

The situation became delicate as Brighton neared. Levik slowed to a crawl when it came time to contemplate parking. It wasn't in his interest that they vacate the vehicle. Only then would he learn the extent of the damage. A performance, he knew, was unavoidable. What he expected: a quickened pace, more ignoring, perhaps taking different elevators and forgoing inquiries as to tea/coffee preference. What he didn't expect: Marina dashing off in her strappy heels in the direction of the beach, over which an impenetrable fog had settled, the kind of raw, curdled air that made fiery Saturns out of streetlamps, a field day for slugs, a density of atmosphere that in the past few years had become synonymous with late springtime in Brooklyn and which was portrayed far too romantically in Italian cinema classics.

Either Marina was deliberately not responding to frantic shouts of her own name or she was outside hearing range, having dashed farther than Levik could imagine anyone dashing in those shoes on a night like this. Though, knowing his wife, she'd already kicked them off. The ocean became fantastically loud when you were deprived of the sense of sight. Levik heard its roar to every side of him, which meant he was already disoriented. He realized that he wasn't moving but standing in one spot, shouting Marina, Marina! and at the same time holding out his arm, not entirely convinced it was his. There was an echo, *Marina, Marina!* And then he was no longer shouting her name, his throat refusing to project a voice. He pushed, but the voice got snagged on something in his chest. He held out his arm and let it drop and hang limply, hoping his legs didn't cave. It was funny when you thought about it: fog. That's all it was, soft, harmless fog. And yet Levik couldn't force his feet to move or chest to steady or throat to produce a sound. This was what they called terror, and it was seizing him for no identifiable reason within several blocks of his home, where he would've killed to be right then, stirring two spoons of instant coffee into Marina's cat mug and pouring freely the nonfat milk. Reminded of Camus's *The Stranger*, a book he'd read as a foolish young man with lots of brown curls and the inclination to like things he didn't fully understand, and even so he hadn't liked that book. Why, then, was it so often on his mind? The accompanying image was Munch's *The Scream*.

Suddenly his arm came into view, as if someone had blown the dust off. It was thin and smooth, with a cold, even shine. Someone kept blowing, and the arm kept extending, growing longer and thinner while remaining defiantly rooted in murk. Levik shut his eyes and heard the chaotic ocean, opened them and saw a railing, an empty trash can, slanted boards intersecting his feet, a bench, then two, then three. . . . The fourth bench had knees and a messy blond bun. He was able to gradually reduce the distance between himself and that bench.

She just lay there. Her hair had exploded, now taking up ten times the usual space. It reached through the cracks, as if growing in the damp darkness between planks. If she sensed a presence over her, she didn't stir. He came around, pushed her bare feet in to make some space, and sat. She made a few adjustments, found a more comfortable position, and was motionless again. For a moment Levik felt insane, as if something horrible were happening, but if he didn't move everything could seem like the height of normalcy, as if he were a child wandering a department store after getting separated from his mother, attaching himself to any serviceable hem. Then he realized everything *was* fine, no one had died, he was still very close to home, even closer than before by approximately thirteen meters. The night was warm, and he could take this moment to breathe, maybe even contemplate something peaceful while directing his gaze into the distance, though there still wasn't much of it.

He clapped Marina's knee. Time to go, he said.

Don't touch me, she said. Her voice was inviting, supple. Yet again she demonstrated mastery of the contradictory tone/content maneuver, which was spiderlike and had a paralyzing effect on the victim. She inhaled deeply. You know what I'd like to be? she said.

How could he know?

Homeless.

Maybe one day, said Levik. Not tonight.

This is so much better than being inside, so much more serene, don't you think? And such a sense of freedom. I'd do well as a street lady—I think I'd have a knack for it. For one thing,

I've never had trouble obtaining free food. I have enough imagination. You know that I never register temperature change. Hot, cold, it's all the same to me. And it's not like I'm particularly hygienic. In fact, there must be homeless people out there more hygienic than me. Forget the street. I'd stay on this very bench. Lie under the stars. Listen to the ocean. Do you think it's saying something? Do you think it's communicating?

No.

Listen, she said.

The ocean isn't saying anything.

Marina's head popped up, her mouth already twisted by an idea. Here goes, thought Levik, wincing in preparation.

We never decided—Paris or Rome?

Levik shuddered. If the ocean is communicating, he said, it's saying, Go home, drink some tea, lock your doors. It's unhappy with us and making it very clear. As long as we're here, there's no telling what will happen. Maybe that Cumbre volcano in the Canary Islands finally erupted and caused a massive landslide. A tsunami is headed our way as we speak.

What difference does it make where we are, then? said Marina.

Don't you want to see your daughter one last time?

She said she had plans.

FRIDA HADN'T LIED—she had plans. She went to her parents' bedroom and rummaged in her mother's makeup case as if in a decorative bowl of rocks. This failed—her bones didn't tingle. She applied lipstick the color of Chinese eggplant and thought about where she could go, then called Gabe, who did a round of verbal cartwheels before admitting he was scouring the internet for men—tonight potential, not life potential, he said, though either would work and the end result would be a new pair of sneakers. I stayed out late yesterday and feel sick, he said. That's fine, said Frida, who anyway didn't feel up to dealing with the train. She turned on the TV and traveled through channels, not letting her thumb rest even if the colors or poses intrigued. She usually guessed wrong as to what interested her. She made her bed, neatly tucking the corners, then got into it, then left it but didn't bother to make it again, knowing that the urge to get in would only strike once it was made. She wasn't hungry, which was tragic.

Marina's perfume and Levik's cologne lingered in the corridor until the downstairs neighbors began their supper preparations. What the Hedonovs ate nightly was a mystery, but a consistent one. Even Robert with his dulled olfactory sense timed his boardwalk outings to their hour of dining. The Hedonovs were always jumping and shouting. They took naps in shifts, on the principle that it was easier to join in the revelry than start anew. Devotion to merriment on such a scale meant only one thing: They jumped not only for the thrill of jumping but to keep something terrifying, so terrifying it couldn't be acknowledged, at bay. Of course, after so much bouncing, one couldn't rule out brain damage. As to how many of them there were, it was hard to keep track. The pillars could be counted—the patriarch, Uzh; his two spinster sisters, Bo and El; the matriarch, Klysma; and her deranged brother, Grad—but Klysma's children accrued imperceptibly, blink and there were two more, and relatives in need of convalescence were always arriving for two-week stays—they considered the sea air therapeutic, and America generally lacked for sanatoria.

Before the Hedonovs a man lived there, a Refrigeration Institute friend of Levik's (they'd bonded because their fathers were big-shot factory bosses and huge assholes, Marina had explained). The apartment had witnessed his downfall, as had Frida, whose bedroom was directly above his in a building with no sound insulation. He'd done his best with the place—wallpaper stripped, walls partially gutted, floorboards dug out, doors torn from hinges, ceiling destroyed by water damage. After he'd been taken away (mental institution? prison?), the apartment stood empty for many months. At first it was a shock, a collective shame, a disgrace; residents tried to make use of the building's other wing. Then, simply by not relenting, by remaining destroyed and abandoned, the apartment began the transformation into abstraction, becoming a symbol of something. For a moment it was the building's core, establishing a grid of intimacy around itself. Then the Hedonovs bought the place. It was almost a move against nature, a tempting of fate. Renovation took a year and was rather an exorcism.

But why was Frida still thinking about that man, who'd owned a shriveled-olive Chihuahua with such pure fear in its eyes that, stranded in the elevator with it, Frida would become afraid of herself, as if some force in her might awaken and make her do horrible things to that dog? It hid behind the metal cart without which the man never left home. Of that trio—the man, the cart, and the Chihuahua—only the cart's fate was known. The blue-haired old lady who tended the lobby plants had claimed it for herself, insisting she'd been its rightful owner all along. Four years had already passed, and yet the day of his disappearance grew no less vivid. Frida had been staring at the large swirling snowflakes in her organic chemistry textbook when her mother barged in, screaming, The downstairs apartment is empty, Pasha's gone!

That was it! His name had fallen through the cracks, perhaps not unintentionally. And now it was a simple mistake, confusing the two Pashas. Trying to break through to the surface was the other Pasha, her uncle, but instead she'd slipped out of habit on her old downstairs neighbor. Freud would've been pleased.

But what about her uncle? She had so little to go on, practically nothing of any substance, and yet he loomed so large over the household. He was a mythic creature, a legend. It was impossible to imagine him as the father at a wedding. Dancing? Rejoicing? He slipped out of all the scenarios her mind conjured up for him. Sitting in a dentist's chair, ordering from a menu, stretching a hamstring, filing taxes, trailing a tour guide—not Pasha. Her uncle didn't tie shoelaces or own a cell phone. There was no laundry in his life, though a checkered, yellowed ironing board leaned against the wall behind his desk. The legs of the desk were as crooked as those of his landlady, who had three white hairs sprouting from her chin and at midnight hovered over the charcoal-smudged city astride her broomstick.

Entire seasons refused to contain Pasha. Surrounded by icicles, heaps of snow, and grime, sure, but not sunbathers or trees in bloom. Frida was always hearing about terrible snowstorms, Pasha unable to leave his house for weeks, classes at the university canceled, heating broken, tram tracks iced over. In nostalgia tales of the fair Odessa spring, Pasha didn't figure. Her uncle was stuck in February, unable to fix the radiator because no tool made sense in his large white hands. He could prod some handles, jiggle screws, but the result was that the heating shut off altogether and he huddled beneath five blankets watching his breath while everyone else frolicked seaside or wandered under the birches that had a frail, purebred quality. Pasha awoke with his beard frozen to the wooden boards, bedbugs in the fissures, windows clouded with frost. God forbid he should smile under a clear blue sky. In old photos Frida's family made Odessa look like a resort town. There are cliffs, roaring waters, rustic picnic tables on rough terrain, tomatoes spilling out of their skins, thick sausages, young cheeses, dark bread. Tan faces. White teeth. Men, small to medium in stature, prematurely saggy but with shapely calves, stand around in tiny swimming trunks. Women tower over them. Breasts, breasts everywhere. No telling where body ends and bosom begins. Esther abounds—here she's bending over a table (is she going for the last circle of kielbasa on the plate or to tug a tempting braid—Marina's, perhaps—cut off by the frame?), and there she poses on a boat, hair slapped against her cheek, squinty satisfaction, an ample arm slung over the railing. Marina runs around in white underwear long past an acceptable age.

Pasha chooses not to leave the snow. He wears fur caps with the earflaps pinned, exposing a catastrophic excess of cartilage. Skin strains over nose and ears. His overcoats are as severe as his facial expressions. The sky is low, almost as dark as the shadows under his eyes. The gravity of the Soviet situation is on display, Stalin's legacy palpable in the photos Pasha populates. The Nasmertovs through their documentation constructed an Eden from which they could be evicted. Pasha did no such thing, almost as if he knew he wouldn't need it. Or was this mere hindsight? Perhaps it was Frida's faulty memory. It was years since she'd gone through that box of old photos.

The jumping abated. Frida put her ear to the floor. Uzh liked to plant his seed into Klysma nightly. During this ritual Klysma wailed and pleaded with God, for material possessions or help with their financial situation, which really was in need of divine intervention. It appeared to be a slow night, when it would take forever. Frida could go get a sandwich and easily make it back in time.

But in getting sandwiches Frida got distracted. The kitchen window looked out on the ocean, which had the cast-aside air of a large piece of grandparents' furniture thrown to the curb. Grandparents put plastic covers on sofas so butts and sweaty palms wouldn't damage the fabric, and children sat on the loud, sticky plastic but didn't realize it was a cover, nobody told them, and they suffered, assuming this was just what sitting on sofas was like. The ocean seemed to be inside such a plastic cover, and somewhere at the back there was a zipper that could be undone. But why wax lyrical when Pasha had that angle covered? Outside it was gray and muggy, not at all reminiscent of anything, and Frida sat by a south-facing window, in despair.

TEN

HER MOM HAD GOTTEN HER THE JOB, lest she have too leisurely a respite from medical school, but there was little in the
way of actual work. She sat at the reception desk in a decrepit
medical office with a car-wash vibe, recorded the names and So-
cial Security numbers of the senior citizens who came in, processed their Medicare information, and distributed ten-dollar
bills. The majority of patients never actually laid their impaired
eyes on the physician. This sort of seedy operation would've
been unacceptable from a regular doctor, but Dr. Gamsky was
Yuri, a family friend. Many days of Frida's childhood had been
spent in his lively Manhattan Beach home, playing with his
worldly-wise daughter, Diane, until that abruptly came to an
end. Frida's parents never had to try hard for plausibility with
their stories. If Yuri's beautiful wife, Larissa, went to Africa on
safari and two weeks later Diane got accepted and immediately
sent off to the best boarding school in the country, in neither
Canarsie nor Bensonhurst, there could be no better explanation
for why Frida would no longer be deposited in their Manhattan
Beach home. Once or twice a follow-up question was raised,

whether Diane's mom had returned from safari or if Diane's
boarding school had an address to which a letter and a charm
bracelet could be sent, but then Frida forgot to ask again. She
paid no mind to the fact that Larissa's name was mentioned in a
whisper until it stopped being mentioned at all or that her friend
was, from that point on, referred to as Poor Diane. Only several
years ago, when Diane just as suddenly came back into the picture, seven months along on her dad's doorstep, did Frida's mom
mention juvenile facilities, illegal powders, older men, but in
passing, as if Frida had been in on the situation all along. Pressing for details now would mean admitting to the horrific extent
of her gullibility, so she was resigned to remain in the dark as to
what exactly went down, certain only that the closest thing to a
real safari had been that Manhattan Beach home, and she'd
never even known it.

The atmosphere in the office was particularly tense this
Monday morning. Giant Dr. Gamsky sat in Frida's chair at the
front desk, clutching his forehead. He looked up, his cheek
creased and marked by a cuff-link-size indentation that did little to assuage Frida's fear that he slept in the office. After vigorously blinking away the fog, he said, Look who's finally here.

I'm not late!

He waved her off as if she were being trifling about it and
informed her that today he wanted to do things a bit differently.
Would that be fine with her?

She nodded tentatively.

How are your hands? he asked.

She held them out. I've been told they're small for my size.

He snatched a palm and squeezed. She squeezed back.

They'll do, he said. Forget the old system. This is not a bank, you can tell them that. No more free money. If they want a checkup or a massage—great—if not, tell them to get the hell out.

But the procedure is a medical massage—I haven't been trained.

It's basically the same as what you'd give your boyfriend. A bit more wrist action, if you feel up to it.

But if I'm massaging, said Frida, her throat getting stiff, who's at the desk?

Let's play it by ear, said Dr. Gamsky, a favorite phrase, used whenever he felt backed into a corner or thrust into the realm of the hypothetical. Laborious thinking made him feel like a cat chasing its tail. He wasn't built for problem solving. He stood and retreated to the back. Yuri's standing was an event. Even if he tried to be casual about it, the room underwent a transformation. Whoever witnessed his rising was robbed of breath. He was so tall and hulking, so huge and statuesque. His size was an accomplishment in itself and had probably tampered with his ambition. Why should he strive like the little folk? His presence used to intimidate Frida. Out of all her parents' friends, Yuri had been the most alien. He was representative of the male breed and the only one male enough to belong to it.

She was left alone to stare at the door. Gum wrappers accrued, one for every email sent like a paper airplane into an iron curtain. About an hour later, an old man entered. He moaned all the way to her desk, as if being in pain made him more deserving of recompense.

Very windy out, he said. Where's the sheet?

It's right here, said Frida, sticking a blank pad in front of his nose. But before you sign, you should know that our policy has changed.

Not for me, he said. I'm in a hurry.

For everybody.

Just the money, miss.

That's precisely the issue. Our new policy is that this is not a bank. How about a massage or a checkup?

He peered at her uncomprehendingly. They examined each other's face, finding them odder than they'd imagined. The old man decided to try again. I'll take the ten rubles, he said, making sure to be as clear as possible.

No.

It's my right.

A new policy, Frida said desperately.

I'm a veteran. Do you want to see my medals? They were in his pocket. He had eleven total. Three came in little red boxes, another two were in transparent plastic cases so scratched they were no longer transparent, and the rest were loose. Yet they were all, sheltered or not, in equally deplorable condition. He gave them to Frida one by one, and she looked at them carefully as if appraising with knowledge, meanwhile hoping that this might buy her time and calm the man, who must've had a very large pocket, maybe even had his pants tailored specifically so that the pocket could contain all his medals. She'd been holding the same medal up to her face for a long time. The others were like large, thin coins or copper stars under triangular, striped bands, but this one, which had been in one of the nontransparent plastic cases, looked like a life float with slits, in the center of which was Stalin's profile, which seemed like a decapitated head, a very finely shaped decapitated head, with hair like the choppy sea.

At this moment two more seniors hobbled in wielding Medicare cards. One of them was a woman (never a good sign). They began to feed each other's sense of righteousness and entitlement. Before the two of them even reached Frida's desk, the man with the medals was reporting that Dr. Gamsky was trying to put one over on them. Apparently, senior citizens, veterans of the Great Patriotic War, survivors of Stalinism, weren't very flexible. They used the word *no* freely but didn't acknowledge it when it was used against them. And evidently they thought that doctors in this country just handed out cash. We will report you, they said. The authorities will find out that Dr. Gamsky got greedy and started keeping our bills for himself. The authorities would reprimand Dr. Gamsky and distribute the bills to their rightful owners, who had big plans for them, you could be sure of that.

Let us see the doctor, said the woman.

For a checkup? Frida asked.

For a word.

I'll go back and get him, she heard herself say. Cataract stares bored into her back. The bathroom door was just barely ajar, with no light inside. Frida nudged it with her foot. Dr. Gamsky wasn't inside, but she was, staring at her own glistening face in the mirror. She lifted her shirt—breasts. Farther in, two doors led to examining rooms and one, on the opposite wall, was to Dr. Gamsky's private office. The examining room at the far end was used as storage, but the first examining room was fully functional, at least in appearance, imparting a very necessary sense of hope. That's where Frida went, knocking but not waiting for a reply and finding it empty. A wad of used paper towels lay on the floor like squashed vermin. The bariatric footstool was standing on the counter, and a cabinet door hung open. The roll of paper over the exam table didn't reach the table's edge. It wasn't torn or dirty but was no longer crisp. It was just terribly old.

That left one option. Frida knocked on Yuri's private office. There was no reply. She pressed her ear to the crack—silence. Dr. Gamsky, she called. No answer. She tried the knob, and it gave. What was she afraid of? It was the expression on Dr. Gamsky's face; unfortunately he was only too capable of mustering shame. But the room, which reeked of ammonia, was empty. She peeked into the storage room, dark and dense. This confirmed her suspicion: a hidden door. All this time she'd been wondering what Yuri was doing back there, and actually he hadn't been back there at all.

More seniors had gathered. This qualified as civil commotion. These people had nothing to get back to. They could easily stay in the office all day. Perhaps the only thing more valuable than the ten-dollar bill was the opportunity to band together when it was denied them.

The doctor isn't feeling well right now, said Frida. No one seemed to register this inane announcement.

Nu, said the woman. Where is he?

He said he'd be here in a minute, said Frida. But I'll go see what's taking so long. She grabbed her purse and went in search of the hidden door. It couldn't be very hard to find, as it had to be large enough for Dr. Gamsky to fit through. Her cheeks were burning. She must've been crying. She entered the office and looked around. A shelf of medical textbooks, framed diplomas, a desk stacked high with papers, manila folders, binder clips, a coffee-stained mug—perhaps everything was fine after all. But if everything were fine, she wouldn't be putting her hand on the wall and walking the length of the room, feeling for disturbances that might indicate a hidden passageway. In order to pass behind the desk, she pushed in the chair, but it wouldn't go. She pushed harder. A groan issued from beneath. Frida's heart thumped, and a bubble of icy fluid punctured in her chest, releasing the substance in all directions. She managed to squat down to inspect. At first she didn't understand what she was seeing. Tufts of salt-and-pepper hair, knuckles, cuff links. Dr. Gamsky was folded tightly into the space under his desk. His knees were drawn into his chest, spine twisted and neck bent so that his head rested on his left shoulder, the one pressed up against the back of the desk. A half-empty bottle stood beside his usable hand.

I'm sorry to bother you, said Frida. It's just that the situation out there isn't good.

They've come for me, he said with resignation.

Patients came, said Frida, trying to espy in Yuri's face the barest glimmer of relief.

Those geezers? What else is new? They come here like it's the toilet.

They're demanding the money.

What else do they have to live for?

And they're very upset I'm not giving it to them.

Yuri's chin stirred. Well, why aren't you?

Because you said . . . Oh, never mind! As she stood up, her calves tingled from scrutiny. She pretended to inspect the notebook on his desk in order to prolong the moment, letting her

legs be slathered in admiration. As she took a step away, something tenderly grazed the back of her ankle, and she got the
distinct sense that this something was Dr. Gamsky's lips, that
mix of smoothness and bristle.

Wait, Frida, he said when she turned the knob.

She hurried back, squatted down again, steadying herself
with a hand on the seat of his chair. She checked in with herself
and knew she was prepared for whatever happened. He had that
look on his face now, the one she was afraid of. Was it shame at
his intentions, natural embarrassment at the situation they had
found themselves in, or just an attempt at concentration? That
look would've been fine on anybody else, but Dr. Gamsky was
too manly for facial expressions. Yet he insisted on having them.
She wanted to assure him that there was no need for shame or
embarrassment. Suddenly dizzy, she toppled softly onto the
carpeted floor. Her legs folded under her, calves pressed into
the small rubber wheels of the swivel chair. Her fingers were
tugging at the carpet's individual fibers, or the fibers were tugging on her fingers. Her hair seemed to be everywhere, tousled,
like in the bedroom of a French film. Dr. Gamsky was looking
at her unwaveringly. Overwhelmed by the certainty that they
were about to kiss, that it was only right, Frida leaned in. Dr.
Gamsky's hand, which was the size of a German shepherd's
head, shot outward. Frida didn't flinch. The hand scratched
Dr. Gamsky's nose.

You know, Frida, he said, you should call Diane. The two of
you were such good friends, always running around together,
sly looks on your little faces. Always up to something, weren't
you? And then you lost touch—why?

Was it possible he didn't remember?

That was a long time ago, she said, keeping her face immensely close, figuring that abrupt recoil would be suspicious. We were kids.

You were a good influence on her. All that trouble she got into, who knows, maybe if you'd stayed friends, it would've been different. And now she's living in the pit of Harlem, just as long as it's Manhattan. Let me give you her number. She'd be so happy to hear from you. There are pens up there, on my desk.

The desktop was at eye level—Frida strained to reach up. She tore a thin strip from a yellow notepad, plucked a fat blue marker from the pen holder. Ready, she said, tensing as she took dictation, because just identifying Dr. Gamsky's baritone approximations and translating them into digit form with a marker her fingers barely wrapped around was an incredible feat. Once it was accomplished, read back, confirmed: relief. Underneath the digits, she wrote *Dinka*.

While Frida was handing out bills, a mental reel began to play—jumping on a bed trying to touch a motel's popcorn ceiling, rollerblade racing to the sole intact swing that hung like a last tooth in a ravaged mouth (Frida always won, the reward for which was pushing Dinka as she swung), biting into a blistery hot dog with ketchup-smeared fingers as they sat in damp bathing suits whose rampant itchiness was relieved by the rough texture of the sloping concrete steps overlooking the ocean, gulping down bottle after bottle of peach Snapple and weighing themselves obsessively, the scale reading seventy-eight pounds, eighty-one pounds. Oh, the splendor of those long-gone days. What fun they had! The supply of fond memories was endless, and the painful ones, while also in abundance, had been rendered void by time—Frida couldn't possibly still be angry at the summer-camp snubbing of a ten-year-old, even if it had incorporated some advanced tactics of persecution. When she finally left Dr. Gamsky's office, which was situated behind a large plastic-surgery facility with window-walls featuring ads of stone-faced women whose foreheads were being injected by arm-size syringes, she was clutching the yellow scrap with Diane's number, wondering how so many years had elapsed without an attempt on either of their parts to revive the friendship.

Turning down Brighton Fourteenth Street and heading in the direction of the ocean, Frida quickened her pace, head retracted, as this small stretch was more dangerous to traverse than the Bermuda Triangle, rivaling it in terms of bizarre occurrences, not to mention awkward run-ins. It was a block short of the official border between Brighton Beach and the more prosperous Manhattan Beach, and all distant relatives and no-longer-quite-acquaintances had flocked to this fringe, where they could pay reasonable rents while getting wafted by ritzy breezes. Also, the train was almost out of earshot, not so far away that important service announcements couldn't be heard but at enough of a distance that Grandma didn't lose her dentures every seven minutes. Frida stumbled past tidy strips of lawn, her favorite with a PLEASE CARB YOUR DOG sign, double-parked Ferraris with needlessly tinted windows, the vacant lot that persisted in being a vacant lot despite its prime location, the homeless guitar band playing classic rock hits (mainly "American Pie" on a loop), and took those sloping concrete steps to the boardwalk, resolved to find a bench, overcome her phone anxieties, and make the call. Why shouldn't Diane be happy to hear from her? She'd be overjoyed. Incidentally, she was having a little get-together at her place that Friday. It was late notice, Frida probably already had plans, but she was welcome to join. Plans could be scrapped. Frida's nervousness prior to ringing the doorbell, her stomach cramps, her rapid pulse, would prove for naught. She'd instantly feel comfortable, finding herself in a dimly lit room with beanbag chairs arranged in a rough circle, one empty chair for her to claim, and a carton of red wine (like their parents had at picnics) in the center. Diane was mature, transformed, welcoming. The other beanbag chairs were occupied by youngish intellectual types who exhibited in equal measure Odessa humor, Petersburg interests (sans pretensions), Moscow cosmopolitanism (without the coarseness or hard consonants), and New York transit proficiency; who watched Tarkovsky films and played chess (and would finally succeed in teaching her how); who listened to Pink Floyd and Vysotsky and could recite whole stanzas of *Eugene Onegin* but never went on too long doing so, choosing instead to dance a little, European style, inside the beanbag fortress; who had jobs in the sciences but whose passions lay in art and literature; who got together every weekend in a casual but never obligatory manner and considered this gang, this kompaniya of theirs, a second family, sort of the way her parents considered their kompaniya. If they emulated the model, what was wrong with that? The model was tried and true. And they weren't about to emulate blindly. Adaptations would be made. Think of it as the furthering of a tradition. Into the Vysotsky and Mashina Vremeni repertoire, they'd introduce nineties hip-hop, Uzbek rap. Along with Pushkin they'd recite Nasmertov—because surely Frida wouldn't get the usual stupefied stares when attempting to explain whose niece she was, an excruciating mistake she was determined to repeat whenever given the chance. It was an attempt to bridge a terrible gap, an attempt that invariably proved futile. Within the home Pasha was a world-historical figure grappling with Dostoevskian forces. But the outside world squinted and asked, Pasha who? A poet? As in, they still have those? One reality was bound to triumph to the exclusion of the other. But with the kompaniya she'd just remark offhand that her uncle was *the* Pavel Nasmertov and they'd gape in awe.

And while the kompaniya was exclusive, Frida would be adopted despite her shortcomings. Her new friends would patiently peel away the layers of timidity, anxiety, acne, and fear, revealing—what, exactly? They would certainly know what, detecting deep within her something worthy of being revealed, something deserving of that grueling peeling work. In the end she'd be unrecognizable. In a good way. It would be the true her, fully realized. People would say, She bloomed late. An example would be made of the transformation. Everyone had taken Frida for a lost cause until suddenly, at the ripe age of twenty-five, she did a 360. Or was it a 180? A total turnaround, regardless. Left behind the field of medicine. A clean break. Never looked back. Lost weight and began parting her hair differently, in a much more becoming fashion, though the difference itself was elusive. Perhaps a creative calling should be involved? She'd been one of the top students in her high school's acrylic-painting class. The kompaniya would probably encourage a return to that. They would be supportive, nurturing of the very tendencies the rest of the world tried to weed out. They'd let her borrow money when, painting maniacally, she went broke.

This scenario was countered with one of a lackluster reunion in a single-halogen-bulb kitchen with a faded, old-before-her-time Diane, the pauses in conversation accentuated by a child's wailing in the background—or, worse yet, Diane not faded in the least but as manipulative and snobbish as ever, only more proficient with underhanded techniques of humiliation. It was foggy and blustery on the boardwalk. A gust blew the scrap with the number right out of Frida's clutch, in a direction that was the opposite of home.

LAST NIGHT, SAID MARINA, Baba Fira rode into town on a horse.

Were you happy to see her? Frida asked from the backseat.

Levik chauffeured them down Coney Island Avenue, skirting double-parked halal-meat delivery trucks, imprinting the frank façades of nightclubs and funeral homes onto their retinas. He tensed up when Marina touched on the spiritual realm.

You don't understand, said Marina. You were too young when she died. Baba Fira was always an old lady—desiccated, wrinkled, a fright. From my earliest memories, her back is so hunched that her nose points to the ground. To make it from one room to the next, she pushed a chair in front of her. It took an hour to get from the kitchen to the bathroom, and you can't imagine the sound. But she must've been only fifty at the time. A little later, not much, I somehow got stuck with bedpan duties. The last twenty years of her life, she was practically a corpse. Not a woman you imagine on a horse.

But in the dream she was fine? asked Frida, though the last place she wanted to be was in a car with her parents, analyzing dreams about their grandparents. She put her open mouth to window, as if trying to suck the outside into her lungs.

She was sort of slung over the horse and dangling, like a coat.

You said hello?

I was too busy yelling at you. You were supposed to be accompanying her to make sure she didn't fall, but instead you were home. She rode into Potemkinskaya all by herself.

Frida looked at the back of her mother's head, or rather the back of the headrest attached to her mother's seat, which grew a face and walrus tusks. A moment ago Baba Fira had been riding her horse under the train tracks, galloping past Zuckerman Pharmacy, turning onto Brighton Sixth. The horse, unlike Baba Fira, was large, black, splendid. But evidently the whole time this horse had been riding into central Odessa. Instead of helping her great-grandmother, Frida had been home, a home she didn't remember and couldn't imagine. How did she die? she asked.

Levik ran a red light. She was always dead! he shouted. She never died!

Stroke, said Marina. Do you even have to ask? The answer is always stroke.

What about cancer? said Frida.

Levik dropped them off at the banya and went on his way. He had big plans for the day.

A series of practical steps and formal interactions distracted from the conversation, which had settled comfortably on the subject of cancer—who had it, what kind, coping mechanism (Alla Gabor, breast, happy to get new ones, eating only asparagus puree). A silent rule with discussions such as these was that they weren't returned to. A penny might fall from your pocket and you'd bend down to pick it up, in the process dropping the subject for good.

There was a misunderstanding with the poised Baltic lady who inspected their gift card, apparently issued under old management. Current management used different gift cards. But the management at this establishment changed weekly, and there was always a new Baltic lady to have a gift-card misunderstanding with. When enough fuss was made and Marina's blood pressure reached a satisfactory mark, the situation was suddenly resolved. Bleak smiles exchanged. Marina and Frida put their wallets and keys into a plastic bag and in return were granted keys to lockers. With light steam! said the bloodless Baltic lady, who had a smattering of white pimples on her temples.

For those who have only imagined the scene inside a ladies' locker room, the actuality was a handful of half-squatting women struggling with their locks. The key never fit, and then the key got stuck. There was an atmosphere of stifled panic. Bathroom doors were left flung open, as if the occupants had fled. The floor was wet and contaminated-seeming. A woman came in with hair piled on her crown like a scoop of ice cream about to tip. One side of her bathing suit had ridden up a dimpled buttock, exposing skin that was soaked, shapeless, pinkish, like whale blubber. Women, too, went to great lengths to avoid eye contact.

Marina seemed to think there was a race on for who got to the sauna fastest. The clock was ticking, there wasn't a second to spare. She abandoned Frida to her miserably slow maneuvering and hustled to a clear victory. By the time Frida made it, her mother lay across the top shelf, shutting out the world. Her palms were open, fingers curled, summoning total relaxation. Legs rolled apart. Russet tufts strayed far from the edge of her faded swimsuit (the functional one). She appeared to be making a public demonstration of the phenomenon of gravity, which had healing powers if allowed to work its magic but which the smallest disturbance turned into a force of harm. Frida sat two shelves below, squeezing her knees. Cold wedged deeper than you'd imagine and had to be extracted arduously. This was the seminal moment, when it was necessary to just commit. In the dim corner, someone was panting.

Did he sound at least a little happy? asked Frida.

Damn it! cried Marina.

What's wrong? What did I say?

I got honey in my eye! She rubbed her eyelid and licked her hand. Her feet flew up to the ceiling. Did who sound happy?

Pasha—when you said that I was coming.

My brother doesn't get happy.

Though it would appear that Frida was getting exactly what she wanted, she felt uneasy, perhaps because of the way events had unfolded: She'd voiced a desire to go to Odessa, pretended it was a firm decision, pretended there was no talking her out of it, opposed the pleas of her family, stood her ground, didn't let her father's newly acquired stutter or her grandpa's wildly vacillating blood-pressure readings shake her determination—and when that determination was finally registered, the entire matter was seen from a new light. Of course she should go! It was the city of her birth after all, and her only cousin getting married. Hadn't they been encouraging her the whole time?

But she preferred not to go to the grocery store alone!

Besides, said Marina, I haven't exactly told him yet. After a pause she added, He hasn't been feeling well.

My God, has the man been to a doctor?

Don't be silly. Nobody goes to doctors in Odessa.

Shhh!

As the atmosphere was halfway between sewer and cathedral, it was unclear what the convention was about speaking. A full-blown conversation, evidently, was frowned upon. The process demanded respect. The banya experience was ritualistic, sacred. An air of immense gravity was brought about by the sense that one's ancestors had been heating their bones in the same way for millennia. The banya didn't just offer heat, a good sweat, but a connection to something primal and a purification that went far beyond the pores. They sat in these small, dark, wood-paneled rooms, silent except for labored breathing and the occasional hiss of water on coal, shedding layer upon layer of falsehood, soul grime, dead skin, pretension. To encapsulate, the process was as follows: Sit clutching your red, splotchy knees and counting the seconds if you're a daughter, or lie back and snore occasionally if you're a mother, for half an hour on a shelf in a scorching, oxygen-deprived chamber, leave chamber and jump into a tub of ice water if you're a mother, or dip your toes in if you're a daughter, repeat at least five times in order to be sure you've gotten your money's worth.

A young man who looked like he'd crawled from under the earth's crust, as if his home were amid igneous rock and magma, who may have been made of a single cell blown like a balloon to man size, opened the tiny metal window onto the coals and used a frightening contraption that must've had some alternate, highly specific function to fling water inside. There was a deafening hiss; nothing else happened. He wrapped the end of a towel once over his palm and spun the towel above his head, a naked cowboy with a terry-cloth lasso. Individual nose hairs were set on fire. Further inhales were put off until the lungs took them by force. An oppressive heat descended, intending to stay awhile. The young man sat down beside Marina's feet and began to sweat. The pores could be seen working. They were trained, disciplined pores. Not like those on Frida's legs, which refused to release a drop. The man held an unkempt birch venik like a weapon between his knees.

Who's not afraid? he said, and tickled Marina's toes with the venik's leaves. Her knees flew up. Propped onto her elbows, she peered at him.

Turn over, he said. I'll give you a steam.

Marina looked at Frida, who interpreted the look as, Please help. But it must've had a different meaning, since Marina asked, For free?

The man grinned. For a kiss.

Frida got another sideways glance.

Just kidding. Kiss optional. Like tip. Now turn.

Marina rolled onto her stomach, wriggled about, spread her breasts to either side, and lay still. The man stood over her, cracking his knuckles dramatically.

Your sister? he said, pointing at the splotchy flesh on the low bench.

Daughter. Marina giggled.

I'll do her next, he said magnanimously.

The man's calves, smooth and hairless, flexed in preparation. Heels lifted. The venik, glistening with painful flashes of veiny branch, slammed down on Marina with great urgency, as if her shoulder blades had just gone up in smoke. Then it stayed there. He pressed down using his entire torso (which actually wasn't so large—he had a neat, petite frame). When the venik was peeled off, her back was gushing color, flecked with leaf scraps. But there wasn't a peep to be heard. She simply exhaled.

That's all I get? he said. I must be going too easy on you.

The venik hopped up and down her back like a prima ballerina light on her toes, making good use of the stage, working up the crowd before she really got going. Then it landed with maximal power on the soft underside of Marina's knees. With a noted delay, she uttered a tiny groan, clearly out of sheer politeness. The man bent over to look at her face. Just checking you're alive, he said.

Quite, said Marina, as if she'd taken a sip of tea.

The man was working for squeals, moans, pleas for mercy, and here was Marina half asleep. It wasn't much fun this way. He tried harder and harder to draw them out of her, twisting limbs, beating down manically, to no avail. That Frida was making the necessary sounds, the man failed to notice. His heart was no longer in it. He had to stop and catch his breath, while Frida prayed that a snore didn't emanate from her mother's direction. When he resumed, it was with the efforts of a demoralized man. A few limp swats later, it was all over. The offer to take Frida next wasn't renewed.

Didn't that hurt? Frida asked as they found the only free table in the lounge area, under the flat-screen broadcasting a soccer match, *the* soccer match, some undoubtedly pivotal soccer match on which all eyes were glued. At the surrounding tables, steamed and scrubbed-down Slavs were feasting. Their presence reassured. Frida wanted to thank them for their pre-dictability, but they didn't even acknowledge her existence. They weren't being insulting; it was just that in her place they saw a continuation of atmosphere.

Give me a break, said Marina. The boy had no clue what he was doing.

Marina grabbed the passing busboy holding a stack of dirty dishes up to his chin. He nodded gravely, or maybe just dutifully, to her extensive and improvised list of fruits and vegetables to be squeezed into juices and hurried to the kitchen, situated centrally at the core of the lounge area, itself at the center of the banya, with the various saunas, steam rooms, and massage nooks built along the lounge's perimeter. The staff that went into and came out of the kitchen included everyone from the bowed cleaning ladies who spoke not a single known language to the presumed new banya owner, with a deep subterranean tan brought about by vigorous, overstimulated blood flow, as he clearly spent his days making full use of his own amenities. The kitchen was more brightly lit than the lounge, which in turn was brighter than the dim saunas, creating a light-filtering effect, and the kitchen doors were kept thrown open (hard to say why they were not simply open), so the surrounding air appeared to glow. Marina and Frida, unsure whether it was acceptable to stare into the kitchen, alternately snuck glances, as it was impos-sible not to look, first because the peculiar layout forced your eyes there and second because a long time had elapsed since Marina had ordered and they were beginning to suspect that the busboy had forgotten to relay their request to whoever was in charge of the juicing. It was odd: One moment the kitchen was full of people urgently chopping a single carrot, the next moment the chopped carrot lay on the cutting board with no one to attend to it, and that moment lasted a long time, until the carrot seemed to go limp with indifference, whereas before it had given a distinctly alert impression. The effect of the layout was that the people sitting in the lounge were made uncomfortable (in a not entirely unpleasant way) by basically being forced into overseeing the goings-on of the kitchen, an otherwise private space, but the discomfort actually stemmed from the kitchen's overseeing them. They were in the kitchen, and the people in the kitchen were outside the kitchen. And where, incidentally, was their juice?

It's right over there, said Marina. It's just standing there, all squeezed out, and nobody's bringing it to us.

I hear it loses antioxidants quickly, said Frida. Her head inched back as she stole a glimpse and confirmed.

I'm going to get it, Marina said, and stood, expecting to be stopped. But Frida bit her cheek, and her mother was impelled to action. This she did very slowly, swaying as if slightly drunk. Mere seconds before reaching the kitchen, she was intercepted by a man with blue tattoos across his saggy arms and stooped shoulders and a few on his chest and back, who'd been watching the game so intensely it was a surprise he noticed anything outside the frame. He put one hand tentatively on the outside of Marina's elbow. Marina flashed her American smile and pointed to the juice standing in plain sight on the kitchen counter several feet away. The man's gaze did not follow her finger. He nodded and looked deep into Marina's eyes, said something, and then they separated. The man, whose tattoos were faded and vacant like old stains, sat down and returned to staring at the TV, whereas Marina walked quickly back to the table.

It's coming, she said, plopping into her chair with relief. The waiting resumed. No longer the least bit uncomfortable, they fixed the kitchen with a death stare, until hearing a singsong Here-you-go and turning to find a robe-clad woman, just as relaxed, pore-opened, and glowing as they were, with a tray. She set down a large glass of juice the shade of a young boy's freckles and a large plate of shrimp of roughly the same color. If Marina had been intending to raise hell about the wait, this plate of shrimp confused her into silence. The waitress left, and behind her stood another woman. Frida didn't notice the switch and said, We didn't order the shrimp. The woman nodded absently at Frida, then put her hand on Marina's shoulder and said, Marina!

Oh, said Marina, Milka!

They embraced warmly and naturally, with genuine affection, as if they were old friends. But Frida had never met this woman. Or had she? Milka wasn't exactly a one of a kind; the world wasn't suffering from a dearth. In every train car sat at least one Milka, not realizing just how loudly she was talking on her cell phone as the tabloid she'd been leafing through slid down her stocking-slippery thigh and plopped onto the icky subway floor. The nail salons of Brooklyn were glutted with Milkas. How did those Italian boutiques with abominably overpriced and nonsensical skirt-pants and sweater-jumpers stay open? Thanks to the Milkas. Whose husband had just left her for a not-even-younger woman? Milka's! Who had sued the living daylights out of her ex-husband, ending up with a house on a coveted tree-lined street of Manhattan Beach and two cars in the garage, neither of which she knew how to drive? That, too, would be Milka. So Frida may very well have met Milka before, not once and not a dozen times, and if you took into account how many stories she'd heard about her, Milka was practically family.

Milka wasn't at the banya alone. A woman like that didn't leave the house without an entourage. Today it was just the girls—Irena and Riana, who were outside in the smoking area. Milka had just jumped inside to grab the waitress—they'd been there since noon and had worked up an appetite. Those shrimp do look good, said Milka as Frida popped one into her mouth. Frida nodded, the shrimp's tail sticking out, and bit into the stringy flesh. They *weren't* very good, but when the oil coated her lips, it made her feel wholesome, nourished. Not for long. Soon she realized the shrimp stink was following her. Nothing had the capacity to make her as claustrophobic as a stink. Some people differentiated odors, recognizing scents, aromas, fragrances, and for others it was all a stink, be it overcooked, on-its-way-out shellfish or cherry blossoms in bloom.

It trailed her outside. In the realm of banyas, an outdoor smoking area with enough space for at least four chaise longues was the gold standard. Here it was, the life. Marina already had a cigarette between her lips, her fingers lifted in a tense V shape, ready to clamp down and tug the cigarette from her jaw. Those fingers knew it would be a struggle.

Irena and Riana had taken the two decent chaises and were laid out ideally for purposes of comparison. But there was not much to it: Irena was a snow pea and Riana was a dame of operatic proportions, and yet they were halves of a single being. In theory Frida had zero tolerance for these bazaar-type ladies, whereas Marina, though not overjoyed about it, maintained these relationships and it stood to reason benefited from them somehow. But here Marina yawned and clawed at the chain-link fence so as not to pass out, whereas Frida was mesmerized, leaning in and listening to their discussion, an elaborate analysis of the most horrific car wreck imaginable, which had supposedly occurred a few days ago on Ocean Parkway between Avenues N and H, with a pileup of cars and numerous fatalities. Frida hadn't heard about it, probably because she never watched the news and talked to almost nobody. Riana, who had a lordly air, had witnessed the katastrofa, and you could tell by the way her left eyelid twitched as she described the strewn bodies and purple brains that it really had an effect on her, even though she was making a respectable attempt to be objective and detached in her narration.

Marina suddenly stood upright and said that terrible things happened, but why must we always dwell on them? The women gave dumb stares. Marina tried to elaborate, saying that terrible things had always happened and would always continue to happen whether we dwelled on them or not, so at a nice moment such as this, a very rare moment of leisure for those of us who work like dogs and will probably drop dead long before retirement, it was probably best to think about nice things and try to get a moment's peace.

It's true that we have no control over the horrible things that happen, said Milka, but we have to come to terms with them somehow, don't we? For example, do you remember that hostage situation above the Brighton Starbucks two weeks ago? Well, that seventeen-year-old girl was my niece.

No! Irena said in disbelief, as if that girl couldn't possibly also be a niece. Irena looked as if odd parts of her needed blotting at regular intervals, as if she had to sleep wrapped in a giant paper towel, or not so giant, as she was a tiny woman with no shoulders, just minute protuberances on either side of her neck that should've been pushed back in.

But there are other ways to come to terms with disaster, said Marina, no longer yawning, ways that don't involve rubbing other people's faces into the shit of existence, people who paid an arm and a leg for the banya experience in order *not* to come to terms with anything but to escape, shamelessly escape, the katastrofa that is everyday life.

I see your point, said Milka. The prices here have gotten outrageous. Every time we come, the old price is crossed out and it's plus five. Just once I'd like to see it be minus five.

That'll be the day, said Riana with a solemn expression that seemed to slip from her control.

It was pointed out to Frida that a chaise had opened up by the other side of the fence and made clear as day that she should go lie in it instead of persisting to be a silent presence over adult conversation. Frida looked in the direction of the vacated chaise and shuddered. She wrapped the robe tighter around herself as she lay down and shut her eyes.

She was assumed out of earshot. Conversations were governed by reverse gravity, with the pull created by the absence of the mass. An easy rule to follow would be to never walk out of the room, but it was a touching comment on humanity that people never followed this rule, often leaving rooms for no known reason, as if conceding that it was only fair to give others a chance to talk about them.

Several far-reaching key words alerted Frida to the fact that her situation was being discussed. They were: Pennsylvania, eight hours, Grandma, Indian and Chinese. When Marina updated friends, acquaintances, strangers in line at the grocery store of her daughter's life, she liked to stress how grueling the Lake Erie College of Osteopathic Medicine was. The school, of which no one had ever heard (best to keep it that way, said Marina), was more of a labor camp where the inmates were fed grub and made to work morning to night or night to morning, as it quickly became unclear when one ended and the other began. At this point somebody usually made the observation that if it was really such an immense workload under such inhumane conditions, it was a mystery that the school had a graduating class at all. How did these kids survive?

They didn't. The graduating class was almost exclusively Indian and Chinese, which isn't to say that they weren't humans, only that their will to succeed was unrivaled, or rivaled only by each other's, and the work ethic that had been instilled in them from an early age was . . . all right, perhaps somewhat inhuman. Such an environment was hard on Fridachka, who'd never been particularly good at science or getting up before noon. But she was intent on becoming a pediatrician, just like her grandma.

Enough! cried Frida, sitting upright. Will you please do me one favor and not talk about me when I can hear every word you're saying?

The entire smoking area turned. Her mother and company were farther than she'd remembered, and the pitying looks on their faces made evident that she'd interrupted a discussion that had nothing to do with her. Lying back, she opened her palms the way her mother did, fingers curled. But relaxation was in short supply at the banya, everyone trying to summon it all at once. Frida got up and freed the chaise for somebody else, knowing somehow that it would remain empty for a long time. She issued a quick, formal apology to her mother in passing, though it came out addressed to Milka. The door whooshed to a close, and Marina's fingers clamped down on her cigarette, tugging it from her lips, allowing her to begin.

THE ODESSA INSTRUCTIONS became a favorite pastime. Take your own plastic bags to the market or you'll be charged extra finally explained why every crevice of their apartment was stuffed with used plastic bags. Lists were compiled. Fruits, evidently, had peak seasons. But it wasn't so simple, because her visit fell at the end of August, a transitional time; some summer fruits might no longer be good, and some fall fruits might already be better. I'll explain it again, said Marina, exasperated. The maybe fruits, the use-your-own-judgment fruits, Frida was resolved to avoid altogether. They gave her the names and descriptions of women who sold the freshest produce at the privoz, which deciphered the name of the meat market on Brighton Twelfth. The best woman was Laska. She shouldn't be hard to identify. Unlike the others, Laska was pure skin and bones, and she had an extra-long tooth and a dark, hairy growth across her forehead. But, said Marina, sucking back a mouthful of saliva, she has the best dairy at the lowest prices—of course, more than two decades had gone by, but those women sat there from the time they were little girls in pigtails until their last stroke or heart attack or cirrhosis of the liver. When you find Laska, tell her hello from the pretty but big-nosed girl in the too-short skirts and the too-high heels and the too-low shirts, which was everyone, so stress the nose and that the girl always bought two kilograms of heavy cream and two of sour cream until abruptly in 1991 she disappeared.

Much more important, however—never stay overnight in the dacha alone. Although there's a gate with a lock on it so good you can't open it yourself, there have been incidents. Remember that one time with the metal shutters? How about that other time, in the outhouse? About the dacha we expect a detailed report. You'll have to be a bit sly. Pasha gets upset whenever we broach the subject. The upkeep of his own beard is too much of a responsibility, so imagine a garden. Who knows what's happened to our raspberry bushes? The apricot trees, I'm afraid to even mention. Don't make it obvious that you're inspecting. Be casual, but privately take note. The easiest thing would be to draw out a little diagram, like a blueprint of the place, and fill in what's growing where and in what condition. Do approximately the same with Sveta, her physical attributes, her character. Is she taking good care of Pasha? What motivates her? Is she the take-advantage type he's always been drawn to? How's her cooking, et cetera? It sounds like a lot, but once you're there, it'll come naturally.

For the feral-dog situation, we recommend peppermint spray. Most of the time, they're harmless. They congregate around the trash bins but also wherever there's trash, which is everywhere. Walk fast but not too fast, and don't look them in the eye, and never run. When you go swimming in the sea, don't leave your stuff unattended, not even your precious flip-flops. Anyway, you'll be robbed. Don't ask so many questions. Visit the cemetery to find your great-grandparents' graves, though we doubt it's possible; no one takes care of the Jewish cemetery and Pasha never leaves the city limits, so the tombstones have probably been stolen or overgrown with weeds.

Beware the tram at night when you're walking a wee bit tipsy down the road, not realizing it's behind you until at the last moment, when the horn blows and you manage to jump out of its way, realizing you almost died while the driver waves his fist in the window, though it's his fault for not fixing the headlights.

Ask the taxi driver how much it will cost before getting in. Anyway, you'll be overcharged.

Avoid the ritzy, snooty crowd on the Twelfth Fountain, but walk around there to see the houses.

Comb your hair, for God's sake. Put on a nice dress and lipstick for Sanya's wedding, and smile—after spending half your life taking care of those teeth, you may as well show them off.

Visit the Opera House. It's the most beautiful in all of Europe.

Lie to only one person—the neighbor at the dacha, Galina Malatok. Tell her we're millionaires living in a mansion on Park Avenue, sleeping on sheets made of gold fibers, et cetera. Try to impart the opposite impression on your cousin. What is basically the truth. Downplay, better yet don't mention, all the traveling we do—certainly not a word about the Tuscany vacations. Stay away from Nadia—no one knows what she's capable of.

Eat only in the center of town, and nothing with mushrooms.

Don't get us souvenirs, don't worry about us, we're fine and want you to have a good time and just forget about us, but do get a calling card and call in the evenings—if not, we'll call you.

ELEVEN

SUMMERTIME IN ODESSA was rib cage convulsions, leaden handkerchiefs in pockets, motes of blood in phlegm. Dust consumed the city. The boundary between street and sky was obscured, turned street-to-sky spectrum. People with a cough graduated to a hacking cough, people with a hacking cough advanced to emphysema, those with emphysema hacked their last. It was the land of the ambiguous lung disease, a medley of symptoms that stumped doctors. At least there was always something to talk about, how last night the mucus turned from yellow to green but became less rock hard, how only the right nostril was affected, how it got worse on humid days and better, oddly enough, after a glass of cognac. Going from a wet to a dry cough was an occasion to raise a toast to, sleeping four hours straight a miracle. Then, of course, there was the neighbor with the cough, who put Pasha's own throat clearing to shame. The neighbor's cough shook paintings off walls. The chandelier over the bed began to sway at three in the morning. Every night Pasha was certain that by dawn he'd no longer have a neighbor, but the years passed and the neighbor held out. Daylight had an amnesiac quality. It made everyone optimistic.

Nadia had been a chilling nurse, but to be sick on Sveta's watch was a pleasure. Pasha lay in bed propped up by pillows and Pushkin, wrapped in fabrics with scents ranging from feminine to outright female. Musky velvet, not death, was on Pasha's mind. He was fifty-two. Plenty of doctors hadn't expected him to get this far. Growing up, he'd been surrounded by people terrified of their bodies, people who thought, Well, that was a strange burp, must be something wrong with my large intestine, now it's really the end; who listened to their bodies in the same way that Sveta, gripping the gutted armrests on their descent into Florence, had listened to the noise of the airplane—with absolutely no knowledge of aeronautics but the conviction that nothing operating correctly would sound like that. Multiple generations of Nasmertovs had gone into medicine to conquer a mystery—the gurgles, throbs, swells, and odors that without technical terms, case studies, textbook sterility grew to monstrous proportions and drove a person to madness. Both aunts on his father's side had spent the last three decades of their lives incapacitated by hypochondria; his mother had gone through a germophobic spell that culminated in Pasha's being taken out of second grade and kept home for a year. That year was *almost* worth it for the psychoanalytic juice squeezed from it later on. As a result Pasha resented close scrutiny of one's physical climate. But in his last years of living on Potemkin Square—renamed, after a quick monument swap, Catherine the Great Square—he'd gotten into the habit of checking his pulse on the hour and listening to his lungs for the crackle of accumulating fluid. He'd lost the doomed fatalism that had been his shield.

A steaming bowl appeared on the nightstand, its deliverer dispersed in the vapors. Sveta's fear was to overdote, her goal to be inconspicuous, better yet invisible. She resembled an impossible bird, one that had fallen out of its nest in infancy, landed on the tail of a dead wildcat (thus beginning a lifelong trend of disaster followed by odd luck, and occasionally vice versa), healed well but idiosyncratically, and been adopted into a family of squirrels not without their own issues. When Pasha caught sight of her, he watched in stunned admiration. Throughout his life Pasha had been starved for solitude, devising plans to keep Nadia occupied and out of the house. Sanya, too. How many times had he planted the seed for a hobby that required fresh air, multiple partners, immobile technologies? Now the opposite was true—Sveta left him alone too much, he was always calling for her. It was his own fault: all those years of complaining. He'd made a habit of unburdening himself to Sveta—how Nadia never left him in peace, asked questions with the sole intent of drawing him from his thoughts, interrogated him when he got home, went through his belongings, rearranged his papers, often not in search of anything, her entire mission being to frustrate Pasha and waste his time on a search. In those days it had taken a lot to disturb Pasha's equanimity, but she was up to the challenge. Once she had thrown out (and not into the courtyard bin) his favorite, or most reached-for, books, filled with marks and jottings amassed by repeated readings.

Why would she do that? Sveta had asked, golden-feathered eyebrows twitching in horror.

For the same reason it enraged her when I sat too long at

my desk or got mired in a project—Nadia's a poet herself.
Or she was. When we met, she was being hailed as the next
Akhmatova.

What was she like then?

She was just nineteen at the time, but her poems were already emerging in the best journals, alongside the top names.
Rumor had it that Yevtushenko was terribly smitten with her.
He'd tried to woo her and been ruthlessly rejected. I was just
getting involved in the samizdat scene. The top journals didn't
impress me. But of course I was intrigued.

For you, I would've rejected Pasternak, said Sveta.

Poor Pasternak, said Pasha.

How'd you meet?

We were introduced on New Year's Eve in somebody's
freezing basement—icicles hung from the doorway, and the
heating tube was encased in a block of ice. The Akhmatova
comparison was hardly a stretch. It wasn't just the similar neo-
classical tendencies or preference for rigid forms in their verse.
Like Akhmatova's, Nadia's face was as highly structured as her
poems, as if sculpted from stone. Her nose even bore that lordly
Asiatic bump. She was tall and thin, but with bones like Roman
columns—an imposing presence. She had a deep voice and used
it sparingly. Whenever she did, it was cause for celebration. I
was ready to marry her right then and there.

She sounds just incredible, said Sveta, almost in a whimper.

It was only downhill from there.

The marriage turned sour how soon?

It took no time at all.

But Pasha, why?

Were women who sounded like children attracted to Pasha,

or did Pasha encourage women to sound like children? Whichever it was, he indulged. Initially she liked me because I was her secret, he said. She regarded herself as a public figure and tried desperately to abide by a comprehensive list of what a public figure should and shouldn't do. I was the Jewish kid who couldn't grow facial hair and trailed her every step. She read my unpublished heaps and saw there was something there, but dissuaded me from showing the poems to others. I probably would've come out with a collection a lot sooner if it weren't for her.

If I hate her for anything, said Sveta, it's that!

On the contrary, I should thank her. Regardless, I was very determined, fanatical—there could've been a nuclear disaster and violent revolution simultaneously and I wouldn't have looked up from my notebook. The dynamic was bound to change. It was inevitable. I wasn't going to be her secret for long. In the meantime Nadia began doing chores around the house. She blamed me for the fact that she had no time to write. But I never asked her to be a proper housewife. There was this other girl, Dora. Mama was in love with her, and God knows why this Dora wanted me. She would've made an excellent Jewish housewife. But I didn't want an excellent Jewish housewife.

You never mentioned this Dora. Go on.

I wanted Nadia, with all her moods. I didn't expect the next Akhmatova to iron pants or make borscht. All I required was a clean pair of underwear. Her pregnancy filled me with dread. It was the end for her. She knew it, too, and my theory is that's why she hastened it. Before Sanya she was still managing to compose a poem or two, however painstakingly. Sanya was an excuse to give up. A good excuse, too—he was one of those shrieking, no-sleep, head-to-toe-rash babies.

I've seen the pictures—he's adorable!

A few years later, Nadia's resentment built to such a pitch that she abruptly quit everything that was maintaining the cohesion of our existence as a family. But by that point there was no more writing for her. The worst was when I tried to encourage her. That's the distant past! she'd yell. I sacrificed my potential so that you could recognize yours. Banal, prepackaged sentiments neatly wrapped with a bow on top, like she got them at the resentful-wife store. And when she used them, you could tell how much she was tapping into their universal power. She was destroyed and destructive and had to say something.

What about when *Ancestral Belt* came out? Was she supportive?

The book just confirmed her suspicions about the course our lives were taking. She was inwardly gloating. It gave her reason to be more merciless. It should've been a great time for me, but it was horrible. That was the summer Mama got sick and I went to visit my family in New York, where I met the most beautiful, delicate, birdlike young lady. Guess who.

Sveta, said Sveta. But what you're referring to was our second meeting. The bird lady made no impression whatsoever the first time around.

The period of Pasha's life from meeting Nadia to meeting Sveta had been selected for constant retelling. It wasn't allowed to fade, on the contrary often obtaining an added dose of color. Had Nadia shunned Yevtushenko's advances in Pasha's first narration? From Sveta's exclamations of surprise, horror, disbelief, you'd never guess that this was neither the first nor the tenth time she was hearing the account. Because it was impossible to comprehend—how could Pasha, a poet of genius, a sensitive, intelligent, loving, extraordinary man, have ended up in such a hellish entanglement? It didn't make sense. Pasha was made to revisit the beginning on a regular basis, and Nadia got to be ever more celebrated and beautiful. Hearing this didn't upset Sveta. It shed light on the unambiguous tragedy of Pasha's life. He'd been tricked into marriage!

During the years of Pasha's complaining, Sveta had indeed been taking notes. She was mindful not to repeat Nadia's offenses—there were no inquiries as to Pasha's whereabouts, household duties weren't a suitable topic of conversation, and Pasha's workspace was sacred ground. He could sit for hours, if need be days, undisturbed. He began to detest the isolation of his desk, preferring to work at the crammed kitchen table while Sveta pranced stoveside.

Proximity had to be maintained. They always occupied the same tenth of the apartment, and the apartment was small—no wall moldings or ten-meter ceilings, no Turkish rugs, scenic view, ventilation. The old apartment was on the fourth floor, with exaggerated windows overlooking Potemkin Square. This apartment was on the first floor, or not even. You had to step down to enter. The window (the only one was in the kitchen) looked out at crotch level onto a courtyard whose slabs of concrete had proved inadequate to contain a spoiled earth. It was a ditch.

But the apartment didn't matter! The old apartment had mattered. This apartment was perfect precisely because it wasn't the old apartment, which had belonged to the Nasmertovs since midcentury and in which now resided Nadia and a frequently rearranging group of her distant relations. Nadia had turned out to be not just emotionally needy and mentally unstable but vengeful and greedy. Irrelevant—here was Sveta with a plate of cold, slippery herring and a dill-veined boiled potato. Around the house she wore what could only be called a nightie, terminating at upper thigh. She had schoolgirl legs, skinny with shapely knees. Her thighs were bluish and the inner parts always sweaty, as she was a touch knock-kneed. You wouldn't notice unless you really looked. A shriveled ear poked through her hair. Pasha had grabbed it once at the foggy instant of sexual release, cementing a habit.

Though their affair had already spanned a decade, Pasha discovered that Sveta spent most of her life in this nightie when they convened domestically last November. By all means an incredible surprise. The nightie had a tattered lace trim and stretched-out shoulder straps worn to a thread. It wasn't unusual for a breast to pop out. Sveta's avoidance of bras was as fundamental as her avoidance of complete sentences, black anything, and public functions, and her breasts, though not large, were demanding. They required attention. Basically she was always naked, yet she moved too nimbly and constantly, blurred by motion. The nightie was like a veil being deftly maneuvered. You were never sure if you saw what you thought you saw. If Sveta ever came to a complete stop, the nightie would've been revealed for what it was—a worn scrap of fabric insufficient to cover a child's torso. Pasha had taken it once for a dishrag. He'd wiped his soapy hands on it.

There was really just one problem with the nightie: Sveta smoked. She had crates of long, slender, minty cigarettes. Pasha's sensitive lungs deterred her from puffing away in the house. Not even in February had she bothered to throw something over her alabaster shoulders, softer and whiter than the lightly powdered snow, as she stood out on the porch, sometimes wandering into the courtyard if a friendly cat presented itself, and got her fix. The nicotine's effect was to calm and focus—Sveta was at her most inert when she smoked. The neighbors got a show. On the floor above lived a cadaverous old widower who would've kicked the bucket long ago if Sveta in her nightie didn't revive his pulse on an hourly basis. And to be honest, it was in their interest that he not delay, as he had the more desirable apartment.

Sveta stood in the doorway, telephone in extended hand. Pasha, piled under three plaid blankets, shivered just from looking at her. What a phenomenon it was, the shiksa constitution.

Is it Tochka?

It's your sister.

Say I'm not feeling well.

Sveta covered the mouthpiece. I did. She's insisting.

Pasha took the phone, looked at it for a moment, and pressed it to his ear, conchlike, as if awaiting the sounds of the sea.

Hello-o. Anybody there? asked Marina's voice, which seemed to live naturally inside the plastic receiver.

Where else? said Pasha.

You could speak up. Sveta says you're still not better. It's because you don't take care of yourself.

Sveta's taking care of me.

There was a split second of silence, registered like a pinprick, and a subject switch. Papa's doing fine, she said. He's out for a walk. At first he protests, No, I won't go, I don't feel well, my hypertension, my constipation, leave me alone, it's muggy out, but then he thanks me, So nice outside, the sunset, the seagulls.

Anyway, he wanted me to ask when you're planning to go check on the dacha.

I've been bedridden for a week!

He doesn't mean right this second. He's just wondering if you know when you might—

That man is a broken record.

That man is eighty years old. Besides, you can't deny that you've hardly spent any time there this year.

The summer's barely begun!

It's August.

In my condition, said Pasha, the city's safer. He was coming to dread these communications, in which the dacha was invariably mentioned—when would they be going, how were the raspberry bushes faring, what about Bym, the neighbor's blind golden retriever? The Nasmertovs had been gone almost twenty years, yet their questions grew increasingly elaborate, as if they'd gone on a brief vacation and left Pasha the designated caretaker of their property in the interim. Now they were getting suspicious. Throughout the previous summers, when he and Nadia had resided at the dacha, there had been plenty to report about the state of the crops and the neighbors. This year Pasha had no choice but to lie about his visits. Just as Nadia had kept the Potemkin apartment, she had claimed the dacha, which Esther's parents had purchased with their life savings and considered their treasure, the only valuable possession they could pass on to their daughter. Esther had loved that dacha almost as if it had a heartbeat. Perhaps Nadia had the capacity to feel a measure of shame—Pasha had surmised this when his father called last week to ask why the dacha's landline had been disconnected.

Pasha was a terrible liar, but his father was begging to be duped. So Pasha obliged. The line had been severed during a freak storm, and they had yet to install a new one. Robert was satisfied. No one would doubt Pasha's capacity for procrastination. This meant that Nadia—a woman who barged in on Pasha's poetry seminars at the university to tell him off in front of his impressionable students—didn't have the courage to inform Robert that she was effectively stealing the dacha from them, that from then on in it was to be a rehabilitation home for her cousins. Nadia had never enjoyed spending time at the dacha herself. It took weeks just to persuade her to leave the city. Her cousins, however, were in permanent need of convalescing by the sea.

There's a reason I called, and it wasn't just to nag, said Marina.

That's a relief.

After a momentary pause, she resumed. It's about Frida.

Dad's briefed me.

Marina exhaled. Then gave a lighthearted laugh. So you already know?

That she's—

Coming.

I was under the impression that she was already home. Dad told me she's not so fond of medical school.

She's been *home* for a while. Summer break in this country begins in the winter and ends in the fall. What I meant was that she's coming to Odessa. I hope you're free on Thursday to pick her up from the airport.

Thursday! cried Pasha.

TWELVE

RUSSIAN POETS DIDN'T DO airport pickups. They sent their new wives to fetch long-lost nieces. Sveta was more than happy to do it. She didn't have a car or a driver's license, but she had an industrious half brother, Volk. He took care of things. He made a cardboard sign that Frida passed by four or five times in a benzodiazepine haze before realizing that the emaciated man with the deviant's ponytail and mesh camouflage vest was welcoming her.

He wasn't quick on the uptake. Frida's attempts to relate that she was the person for whom the sign was intended weren't as effective as she might've hoped. Once Volk finally apprehended that the disheveled lady wasn't distracting him from the task but was the task itself, he shook off the shackles of concentration that had been keeping him static and grew animated and twitchy. Apologies began to issue. He was sorry for motioning her away as she'd tried repeatedly to introduce herself; for his poor vision and laziness, as he'd been due to make a visit to the oculist for decades; for his cardboard sign, which was too small and in Cyrillic; for the airport personnel and security guards, who were giving her such awful stares. (Really? All of them?)

Her heart intensified its drum as she charged at the automatic doors separating her from Odessa air, like Moses marching at a sea that didn't split. Momentum brought her cheek up against the glass. Peeling herself off, she stepped back, dumbstruck. Volk whipped out a pocketknife. He inserted the blade into the crack between doors and flipped his wrist, creating a space that his fingers could squeeze through, and proceeded to very unautomatically pry apart the doors. He led her to a woman who was an amalgamation of so much color, fabric, mood, and texture that the eye refused to absorb her as one whole. Sveta leaned against the railing, puffing on a cigarette. She took the apologizing torch. She was profoundly sorry for not waiting inside, she hadn't expected Frida to come out so quickly, usually they detained Americans for at least an hour. You must seem extra harmless, she said. She was sorry for the air so saturated with exhaust—no regulations in Ukraine—and the lack of wheelchair-access ramps. Not that we need them, knock on wood.

A bottle of Coca-Cola awaited in the trunk of Volk's burgundy Volvo. It was practically steaming. From a vest pocket, Volk retrieved a stack of Dixie cups. Sveta Russian-dolled out the cups on the sun-blazed hood of the car, pouring until the brim caught the froth. They toasted in the parking lot. It was a superb parking lot. There was no painted grid delineating individual spaces, and the cars were strewn about as if abandoned by a giant child called to tea. Frida squinted into the distance, gulping her strange drink. It was a syrup made from the fur of an old grizzly, cooked up in a cauldron on the outskirts of town by a lady who mixed cat food into everything she touched and blotted the sores on her ankles with cotton balls that got stuck under her fingernails only to fall into the cauldron that had to stand on the open flame for many a day and be constantly stirred, the last ingredient being a mysterious powder responsible for the torturous effect: With the first sip, Frida almost choked and quit drinking, but a moment later the papillae of her devastated tongue were pleading for another wash of nuance murder.

An alley of lindens led away from the airport like a stitch closing a seam. Volk steered the automobile as if it were half spaceship, half wild bull (it was a stick shift), while Sveta bounced alongside, enumerating the cultural possibilities on offer. In the backseat Frida lay half asleep, clutching the empty bottle and belching in varying volumes and intensities, the loudest of which roused her for a fraction of a second, enough to catch that the Opera House was closed for the season and last week Odessa's only Caravaggio had been stolen. This suited her fine. Ideally all must-see treasures would be stolen, monuments defaced, cultural sights shut down for the season or for renovations or for good. They were distractions from the essential. Where or what the essential was, Frida knew not, but it certainly wasn't an opera house or a Caravaggio.

They were dropped off on a corner that, if a complaint must be made, was a bit too central, open, unencumbered. A large, lively intersection. Discount shoe stores and a fruit stand, determined pedestrians, briefcase collisions, traffic ruckus. It could've been an intersection in any respectable metropolis. Nothing thwarted, secretive, particular. Lest it seem too benign, a three-legged mutt hobbled into the road just as a tram was rounding the corner. There was screeching, a yelp tapered off abruptly. They entered a courtyard that proved soundproof. The street turned off. A faucet turned on. Snores emanated from a shattered window.

On a tucked-away porch, in a low canvas chair, Pasha was hidden behind globular hirsute knees and a laptop. The image struck Frida as ridiculous, and she laughed. Pasha laughed, too, as if something inherent in their reunion, and not in him, was funny, which made Frida stop laughing and cross her arms. There was no outpouring of affection, no messy reunion scene here. For a reunion Pasha would've had to register a separation. His greeting, after his giggle, was brief and casual, as if Frida were a fixture in his life, rather like the floor lamp. Taking her niece in anew, Sveta said, Look how big she's grown! Can you believe how the years passed? Though she'd never seen Frida before today, the lack of a reference point wasn't about to keep her from marveling. If this was an attempt to elicit a proper response from Pasha, it didn't work. He wasn't even capable of tagging on to Sveta's absurd sentiments. Yet with nobody to feel these things, she seemed to really feel them. She was truly overcome by Frida's presumed transformation.

Frida snuck off to the bathroom to investigate whether she hadn't actually undergone one. Perhaps stepping onto native soil had activated, on a cellular level, some dormant capacity, unlocked hidden potential. Or maybe she'd just missed it the last time she looked: Airplane mirrors were too harsh to trust. Here she encountered the opposite problem. Two of the bulbs had burned out, and the amber remainder was moody but insufficient for an appraisal. What she found in the mirror were under-eye bags and an inflamed chin pimple, what she found behind it were pills, pills, and more pills, prescribed for Svetlana Muser and Svetlana Nasmertov. For the weak/sickly/always dying one, there wasn't a single bottle.

He was seated at the tiny kitchen table (a converted sewing table), twirling a matchbook in his fingers. Frida had to stop herself from running out of the house. Grown woman, she said to herself, and took a seat opposite. Gravitas, unkempt leonine facial hair, an aura of solemnity encompassing all past wars, pogroms, exiles, and oppressions, a mild odor of stagnation, a high forehead—oh, very high and very steep and just a bit wrinkled—an intimidating stare, silence. This man didn't apologize. Of course, he had no cause for apology, but this hardly mattered, since under no circumstance would he have apologized. He didn't deal in the petty intricacies of personal relationships. In comparison to the panoramic sphere Pasha was out wandering, Frida was pinned to the present moment.

Do you like chocolate? asked Sveta, hovering over them.

The question was a trick. There was a right answer and a wrong answer, but it wasn't nearly as obvious as it would seem. If secret code, did it have to do with their being female? Frida stared at Sveta, fierce intensity, zero comprehension.

The freezer was open, Sveta climbing inside. Her arms and head were gone, shoulders squeezing. Spit back out holding two cartons like frozen tonsils. Ice cream, she explained. You're welcome to have.

Oh, no, said Frida very categorically, but thank you. Heat tore her cheeks. I'm not really a dessert type of person.

Sveta wished she could say the same for herself. Two happy

bowls were plucked from the dish rack. She scooped vigorously with a soupspoon until one bowl contained a mountain of gooey rich chocolate, and into the other a half spoonful was gently tapped. The mountain was placed under Pasha's nostrils, the anthill Sveta kept for herself, retreating with it into a corner.

Pasha didn't stir. Seconds passed slowly and laboriously. The mountain began to lose height. A puddle formed at the base, particularly around the soupspoon. In the meantime he attended an itch under his beard. Frida gulped, trying to keep back a shameful surge of saliva. Not a dessert type of person? A pure and utter lie! Did Pasha notice her frequent swallowing? Did he notice the ice-cream mountain awaiting him below?

A poet, of course, noticed everything. In addition to five senses sharpened to perfection like test-ready No. 2s, he (in this case) had recourse to a mode of perception that made a mockery of any exam: the sixth poet sense. If the Russian people had to agree on one thing, it would have to be on the existence of this sense—that they themselves lacked it but that someone rare and special possessed it. Into this chosen being they could place their trust. A fatidic capacity was implied, accurate future prediction regarded as the culmination of the cosmic poet powers. But from observing Pasha, Frida would've surmised that he noticed nothing at all, not the pooling ice cream, not the cockroach disappearing into the sugar bowl, not even his own fingers with deep vertical grooves on the nails.

Pasha gave an openmouthed squeak and began to cough, all sorts of mysterious things loosening in his chest. The rings around his eyes went from pale green to lilac to bruise blue and back to pale green. The matchbook dropped to the table and disappeared. The soupspoon was brought to life. The corners of Pasha's mouth were crammed with brown residue.

Don't look so disturbed, he said. I ate my vegetables thirty years ago.

THE DOORBELL RANG. Standing on their doorstep wasn't Sanya but Steve Martin, who seemed just about as confused by his presence there as was Frida. Tall and lean, he was more dashing on the whole than one might've imagined. His wispy white hair was parted on the side, and his large, bland face was made absurd, likable, and distinct by a nose—rarely did one feature carry so much weight. Frida saw him over Sveta's bare shoulder. Sveta had changed into a handkerchief with straps. Her skin was a transparent blue like the sky over snowcapped mountains. Tiny hairs stood on end. Steve Martin saw Sveta's bare shoulder and nothing beyond it. He addressed that shoulder with the question Are you Fridachka? The Russian words contorted his face, pulling it into a strictly Slavic direction.

Who are you? said Sveta.

Not Steve Martin but his Russian variation, Volodya, there on behalf of Avarchuk, the casino king. The explanation satisfied Sveta. Volodya was visibly disappointed when the bare shoulder retreated and was replaced by Fridachka, a staunch adherent of the many-layers policy. His beady eyes had no choice but to look into her beady eyes.

Volodya got to the point, pulling two objects from his briefcase: a cell phone and a thick white envelope. He lifted the flap of the envelope and tilted it to display the contents: colorful bills that would've aroused suspicions of fraudulence in a game of Monopoly. Five thousand hryvnia, to be precise.

That's very kind, said Frida, but isn't it a bit much?

He glanced at her quizzically. It's the amount agreed on. Whatever you don't use, give back to your papa. He'll deal with Avarchuk.

My papa?

Or me. But there's not much in there when you get down to it. You'll see. On Deribasovskaya there are decent shops. Shoes and hats, things like that. There's the seven-kilometer market. Dresses, teakettles. You'll need souvenirs for the folks. A boyfriend, eh? Before long you'll be calling me. Volodya, you'll say, I need more dough! No problemo. As much as you want. They'll take care of the calculations. Your papa and Avarchuk. I'm just Avarchuk's guy. My number's programmed into the phone under Vasya. You call me when you're running low or if you're in a stitch. I mean a real stitch. Not if you need a restaurant recommendation or directions to a nightclub. Not for museum hours either—you look like you'll be wanting some of those. Call only if you need more dough or are about to be murdered. Capisce?

I won't take it, said Frida, pushing away the goods. Tell Avarchuk to tell my papa that I don't need anybody making arrangements for me. I'm sorry you had to waste your time.

Volodya's eyes crinkling. She expected him to try to convince her otherwise, but he just shrugged. As he turned away, a shadow of a smirk passing across his face. Frida wanted to believe that it was intended for her, something like bemused respect at her show of independence. He folded himself away into his white car and sped off. Frida returned to what now struck her as a gnome's home. No one asked a thousand questions about the stranger or made as many remarks about how she'd handled the situation incorrectly. It was usually at this stage of Operation Freedom that she succumbed to a devastating sense of loneliness and remembered the utter indifference of the universe as to whether she lived or died, prospered or failed, which was enough to abort the operation and send her running back into the warm bosom of her family. Now, too, she considered retracting her head into her shoulders, hiding her tail between her legs, changing her return ticket, and ordering a cab back to the airport.

I'll be off to sleep, said Pasha. I've got an old man's bedtime, to go with the old man's body. His hand landed on Frida's shoulder. The moment of truth was upon them. She twisted up her face, straining to channel her chaotic inner existence, her uncertainty, her fear, her lack of footing, which Pasha seemed at last on the brink of acknowledging and shedding light on. He gave two squeezes and said, For tomorrow. Any requests?

The low ceiling was spore-speckled, brown. Water damage: a sinister force spanning nations. She shook her head.

None at all?

She had no requests at all. At last she'd attained such a state. Requests led to anguish, a correlation anybody would recognize. Best to do away with them altogether.

But Pasha persisted. There's absolutely nothing in particular you want to see?

Was this a test? Was the requestless existence she considered an accomplishment actually a failure? To come up empty-handed seemed as unwise as not even making an educated guess on a multiple-choice exam. The dacha, she declared.

Why don't you sleep on it, said Pasha. It's been a long day. Sveta put fresh sheets and a towel on the armchair. Make yourself comfortable, at least as comfortable as possible on that thing. Try experimenting with positions—I'm told there's one in which you don't even feel the metal bar.

JARRED AWAKE BY A RINGING PHONE, Frida sprang upright and rattled off, Mama, don't worry, everything's fine. On the other end, a man's voice shouted in Ukrainian for a steady thirty seconds. People said it was a melodic language, and they were right.

Are you trying to sell me something? Frida asked.

The line went dead.

In her hand was the cell phone she'd so nobly refused to accept. On top of her suitcase lay the envelope full of cash.

Sleeping beauty, said Pasha when she stumbled into the kitchen. Too groggy to say for sure, but she detected sarcasm. It hadn't exactly been a spectacular night of rest. Regardless of jet lag or a foldout sofa through which snaked a metal bar so limber it managed to jab everywhere at once, trying to repose in the room that housed Pasha's collections was no easy feat. At least the icons—countless pairs of eyes embedded in misshapen-as-if-spilling heads, thick globs of boneless babies—could be turned off with the lights, but it was in the dark that the pendulum clocks struck out, not entirely in unison, and proceeded to spend the night in a bravura competition. Toward dawn, in a thrill of ingenuity, Frida had tied her uncle's shoes by their laces to the pendulums, finding not long thereafter that the courtyard served as breeding grounds for livestock.

A man dressed as a pirate sat beside Pasha, directing at her an unctuous grin under an indulgent mustache with upward-tapering tips. The rapacious gleam in his eyes was studied but effective. A white ruffled shirt stretched taut over a barrel chest. He had everything short of an eye patch. And the hat was rather a sombrero. He introduced himself as the foremost painter of Odessa—the most controversial, the least liked, the most talented and underappreciated, the least reimbursed and validated, the most prolific and modern, and had he already mentioned underappreciated? An understatement! Try ostracized and shunned, admittedly not as much as Pavel Robertovich. Your uncle, said the pirate before Frida had finished pouring cold coffee into a mug, is the greatest poet not just in Odessa and not in all of Ukraine but in all of Russia, which is why people hate him. They want him to rot in the ground.

Pasha laughed—spare, dismissive, but a laugh nonetheless. He'd acquired human color overnight and seemed, on the whole, less world-historically solemn.

The coffee wasn't doing a proper job of reviving, perhaps because it was impossible to believe in the power of Ukrainian coffee. If the coffee worked, it would've been a far different country. The only effect was a leaden tongue.

Where's Sveta? she asked.

You're not the only sleeping beauty around here, said Pasha. Thanks for the reminder. He rose and began to fuss. For somebody who moved so sluggishly, an incredible clatter was generated. Everything banged against everything else. Anything capable of clanging didn't hesitate to do so. That Sveta didn't run in, wondering about the earthquake, was testament to the potency of her slumber. Half an hour later, Pasha was finished.

For all the noise, effort, mess, there was surprisingly little yield: a fresh brew of coffee (the batch from which Frida had just taken went down the drain) and a soggy egg mass. These were delicately placed on a silver tray with an undoubtedly rich history and majestically carried off to the master bedroom.

What a mensch, said the pirate. How many men do you know who spoil their wives like that? Women in this country are lucky not to spend half their lives with a black eye. Do you know when was the last time I made breakfast for my wife? I'm really asking, because *I* don't. I'm not even entirely sure what number wife I'm on, or if she eats. And this is a literary man we're talking about, the greatest poet—not just in Odessa, mind you, but in all of the former SSSR!

The pirate didn't stop. While he spoke and gesticulated and let the ends of his mustache stab the air, he glanced intermittently into the corridor to see if Pasha was returning. He needed to be saved from his own performance. At some point Pasha had been gone too long. The pirate destroyed the cracker monument he'd been erecting and fell silent.

Of course, if Pasha expended even a tenth of the effort he does with Sveta to the outside world, the pirate said quietly, who knows, he might not be in this predicament.

Is it dire? asked Frida.

Yes and no—it depends on what he wants.

And what is that?

Do you think Pasha has a clue what he wants himself?

A glass of mineral water would be nice, said Pasha, finding pleasure everywhere this morning.

Treacherous heat notwithstanding, they decided to venture

out for a stroll. There were too many of them, no air-conditioning. The apartment's single window, a porthole situated over the sink, was reminiscent of a jail-cell aperture in that it served a strictly psychological function. Besides, Frida had just arrived—wasn't she curious to take a look around? Mark Twain had been. There was the Opera House, Potemkin Steps, Vorontsov Palace, Railway Station. With every additional proper noun plucked from the air, Frida felt more jet-lagged. Odessa had more obligatory sights than London, Paris, and Rome combined. How could one miss out on seeing the building in which Ilf and Petrov were born, the synagogue that Babel may have once set foot in, the synagogue that Babel would never have set foot in, the Pushkin monument, the hidden Pushkin mementos, the black velvet drape where a Caravaggio used to hang? Luckily, there was time. If it was used wisely, Frida might be able to see a fair amount. The information was contradictory to say the least. Odessa was a backwater town, delusional province, cultural wasteland, Pasha said as much, yet Frida's twelve-day visit wasn't enough to cover everything. A hollow shell of a city, claimed the patron saint himself, but Frida was clearly at fault for not displaying a sufficient measure of curiosity toward it. Was her presence there not curiosity enough?

The pirate, who outside Frida's thoughts went by Tochka, wasn't made for the heat. He promptly began to melt. First his mustache became a viscous puddle that migrated south and poured drip by agonizing drip off his chin, staining the soaked-to-transparency dress shirt, the ruffles of which had wilted. Decomposing eyebrows obstructed vision, making it rather a challenge to ambulate. Nobody was very surprised when he muttered an unintelligible excuse and veered perpendicular on a side street. Pasha didn't appear to notice that their party had shrunk. His heels scraped the pavement. Sveta bounced alongside. Frida craned her neck, occasionally making an affirmative throat sound or venturing an architecture-related inquiry. The answers got lost somewhere. The surroundings were blurred by exhaustion and gastric discomfort (Sveta had made lunch; report on cooking not positive). Frida was cotton-mouthed and angry with herself. The people they passed either looked at Pasha and uttered cordial hellos or looked at Pasha and whispered something to their companions. All signs pointed to the fact that Pasha's eyes were open and functional—he heeded curbs, avoided dog poop (sometimes), paused at stop signs—but he gave no hint of noticing the people who noticed him. Those who greeted him and those who didn't received the same treatment—namely, no response at all, not even an ear twitch. Impenetrably sullen, he scraped onward. Frida shot a pleading look at Sveta. You had to give it to her, Sveta tried her best—she pulled Pasha's beard, tickled the mossy nape of his neck, bit his shoulder, gnawed at his elbow, none of which revived the walking corpse.

They entered a small park, following a narrow, swerving path lined with reassuring oaks that opened out onto a square with a cathedral and a fountain, and Frida felt a swell. I remember this! she cried.

The Sobornaya? clarified Sveta.

Ded took me here. I rode those swings. We fed two sad goats right there by that statue.

Full-scale renovation three years ago, said Pasha. When you left, there was nothing here but a dilapidated cathedral—no swings, no statue, and I greatly doubt the goats.

They did a nice job, though, didn't they? said Sveta. They even put in trash cans. Not nearly enough, but it's a start.

IT WAS THE SORT OF PLACE that required an introducer. Frida could've passed by fifty times without noticing. If asked, she'd guess that in its place was a post office, but this would be pure speculation. Though Gogol Street was rather touristy, the particular door was locked by a visual code, rendering it invisible to nonnatives. Not that inside it was anything special. Tables, chairs, a leathery man dozing with one pant leg slung over the other in the far corner. All cafés had that far corner, which belonged to the people you could never become. Perhaps the only notable aspect was the lack of distinguishing characteristics. No decorative flourishes, no menu innovations. It was like a café of the spiritual realm, everything understood implicitly.

Nobody bothered to take Frida's order. She was still in the doorway when the prominent waiter brought her a giant glass, more of a vase, jammed with behemoth ice cubes, and several glass bottles of Coca-Cola. The others got small glasses, sans ice, filled with any beverage of their choosing. They had vast and varied preferences—black currant juice, kvass, Borjomi water, Tarkhun, an aloe-lemon concoction, bilberry mors—all of which were in need of diluting; for those purposes there were bottles of vodka and cognac. If that sounds like a lot of drinks for the three of them, it's because it wasn't the three of them. The café into which Pasha had led them happened to be packed with his friends—an international group, poets hailing from Petersburg, New York, Berlin, Zurich, Bucharest, Vienna, even Australia. They'd been trickling into Odessa over the past day for the upcoming Conference of Literature, which was just a convenient stop before the main event, a dress rehearsal for the larger, grander, more refined and much-awaited Russian-Georgian poetry festival, Dreams of Georgia, held in Tbilisi, Batumi, Rustavi, and Tskaltubo.

Is that why you're here? Are you a poetess yourself? asked a smiley man with psoriatic streaks across his cheeks.

Oh, no, not at all, not me, said Frida, in a hurry to clarify, as if the possibility of being momentarily mistaken for one were inadmissible, an offense to the very concept of poet, though the way it came off was that it would be an offense to Frida's conception of herself. Everything seemed to fluster her, as if she'd never encountered the likes of it before. She was finding it impossible not to act frazzled in all instances. Or worse yet, disproportionately impressed. But this was just a guise, was it not? She was giving off an entirely wrong impression, unable to locate the correct one. I'm here for my cousin's wedding, she told the man as he fiddled with the saltshaker. Pasha's my uncle.

Evidently Pasha had failed to share this development with Efim, who claimed to be a dear old friend. He turned to Pasha and overplayed his hurt.

Pasha shrugged. My son is thirty-five—

Thirty-two, corrected Sveta.

He already has kids. And I've barely met his bride-to-be, but from the little I've seen—

Efim's hand signaled Pasha to stop. There was no getting around it. News like this deserved a toast.

Frida lifted her vase of Coke and clinked timidly, then enthusiastically, with all across the table. Some people at the other end, having caught only the broadcast announcement, eyed her with interest, taking her, perhaps, for the future daughter-in-law. And how about the son himself? Would he be joining them for a celebratory drink? Where was the lucky young man? Pasha didn't know. Pasha didn't particularly care. The fuss was disturbing. People became strange when it involved news of this sort. Atavisms were activated. Their personalities abandoned them. They lost their cultivated whims and eccentricities, were reduced to elemental humanness. And they became hungry, wanting access. Pasha, instead of rising to the occasion and putting on the proud-father face, sharing an anecdote or two and accepting a pour of champagne, relenting a little in his absolute Pasha-ness, clenched his antisocial jaw and waited out the awkward moment until the subject was dropped and the table splintered into comfortable disunity.

Plates like flying saucers began colonizing tables with fantastic speed and adroitness. Food was not only what clung to the tines of the fork but also what filled ears. The corners of Frida's eyes were salivating. Silverware mishaps, guffaws, the flashing hands of waiters—all were food. A man swayed over a piano, not making music but kneading air. Everything looked scrumptious, yet not entirely edible. No matter what she tried, there was a hint of turned eggplant. It was a while before she looked up. When she did, Pasha was transformed. He'd grown animated and wide-eyed, voluble, dynamic. Flanked by two men, one of them arresting, with geologic features and demonic eyes, an ethnic hat, and an articles-have-been-written-about-me air, the other quite plain, with a puffy pinkish face, large arms, and an ineffable quality—the kind of man to sneak into dreams and tinker with the dreamer's perception of him. Pasha's elbows rested on the table. His lower lip was pronounced, like that of a rabbi in a kitchen, painting. When either of the men spoke, Pasha's eyes lifted to the heavens. He giggled often and abruptly.

The cloud of cigarette smoke thickened. Frida's eyes burned, lungs ached, accustomed to American standards. She stepped outside for the closest thing this city had to fresh air, immediately followed by Sveta with her regenerating cigarette. Sveta gave Frida a look of sympathy, as if they were both suffering quietly through this occasion or this life, and exhaled into her face.

A lady with short orange hair came out to see where Sveta had gone, and in search of the lady with the orange hair came two others, and in a few minutes they were a huddle of gossiping ladies with jarring laughs and warring perfumes. Sveta apologized to Frida because they were being prevented from having a heart-to-heart. Her breath was pungent and the cracks of her lips stained blue. A Mediterranean wind turned the corner. Sveta's unnaturally rigid hair split open, exposing a deformed ear. Frida studied it, mesmerized. But it was quickly returned to its box of hair, hidden away like all things of interest.

Frida's phone rang—could it finally be Sanya, the lucky young man, the closest thing she had to a brother, whose adult voice she had yet to hear? Against all odds she succeeded in a casual allo. But it wasn't Sanya. Once again she found herself being shouted at. It seemed not threatening but somehow informative. Not an ounce of meaning could be extracted. This time she felt that she deserved this treatment and that everybody knew she was getting it. But when she looked around, everybody was gone, the huddle of women dispersed; she stood alone on a curb across the street from a casino. There were no stars or cats, no excuses to linger.

Returning to the table, Frida overheard an unpleasant snippet in which Sveta was pointed at and referred to, in surreptitious English, as the Bride of Frankenstein. Then, during a baffling search for the restroom, Frida stumbled into Pasha being called, and not even with the decency of a whisper, a royal asshole suffering from a Jesus complex. She bent down to adjust a sandal strap. Pasha did have some talent, there was no denying that, but his poetic views were egregiously conservative. There were good poems, but there were too many poems—inspiration didn't visit anybody on such a regular basis. And apparently he beat his ex-wife, but who wouldn't have?

In the bathroom, three flights up and technically in a different building, yawning wives professed with pride to an inability to sleep in planes, trains, and automobiles, enthusiastically enumerating neuroses while a tall lady in a lavish gown vomited into the sink. Squeezing through a narrow, jagged passageway made by the backs of chairs, Frida's butt was pinched. Her response was lethargic. A somnambulist would've about-faced quicker. The perpetrator was the plain man with the puffy face. He recoiled, reddening, but it did no good—slyness was built into the curve of his nonexistent lips. Zeal, for everything, oozed from his pores.

Pardon, mademoiselle, he said, and pointed to the woman for whom the pinch had been intended. Two sensations overcame Frida: horror that her butt was interchangeable with that matronly derriere, and love . . .

Of course out of everyone I had to pick Pasha's future daughter-in-law to harass. He already thinks I'm a creep.

I'm not—

Going to tell? If you want, I can do it again.

That's OK, said Frida, maybe some other time.

Good luck to you. You're marrying into literary aristocracy!

Frida smiled sweetly, but the words left her feeling unsettled in a Shakespearean sort of way, as if everybody were in cloaks and disguises, saying one thing, meaning another.

Unlike all the moths in the light, Pasha stayed in the same seat with his elbows on the table. Frida, in the dual role of Niece and Daughter-in-Law, became a routine pit stop for the poets. One by one they came to tell her in what high esteem they held Pavel Robertovich. Her uncle was the Brodsky-of-our-time, dorogoy drug i velikiy poét (a dear friend and great poet), whose poetry built emotion through a fantastic accrual of detail, whose situation in Odessa was an impossible one, and were he not such an obstinate, principled, intransigent man, he would've left Odessa long ago; that this town had been abandoned by history and didn't need a martyr in the shape of an aging, bearded Russian-Jewish-Christian poet (though it is quite charming when you think about it); that he should've moved to New York or at least Moscow, cosmopolitan cities in which he had friends, readers, supporters ready to help him in any way they could, where he could meet more like-minded people, or at least those with common interests and thicker wallets and an appreciation, no matter how misguided, for what he was doing, for what was essentially his life project; that though ideally he should've made this move decades ago, it still wasn't too late—however, there was no point in telling him this, he simply wouldn't listen, the man couldn't be reasoned with; that in Odessa he had only ene-mies and his tactic of ignoring them for half the year, then launching ferocious, no-longer-relevant counterattacks on his LiveJournal page during the other half was just making these enemies more rabid; that he wasn't taking proper care of himself and looked far worse this year than he had the last (this surprised Frida—her uncle seemed incapable of looking better or worse, as if centuries couldn't touch him); that Sveta should put him on a diet; that he had never before seemed so happy with his domestic situation, and thank God he'd finally gotten rid of that snake Nadia; that a lot of people may be saying things to her about Pasha but not even all of his friends, so-called, had his best interests in mind, and it would be wise for her to listen with a grain of salt; that particularly the Berlin group had to be kept an eye on; that it's not hard to understand why people got so sentimental about Odessa; that in fact it was impossible to understand; that perhaps what annoyed people most was that Pavel Robertovich didn't drink like a real poet; that what possibly irritated some was that Pasha never gave praise, or at least was terribly stingy in that department; that he refused to gossip; that according to him everything fell under the rubric of gossip; that he never met anybody on the other person's terms; that he expected others to read his work but didn't take the time to read theirs; that people were fallible, and such things got to them; that she, Frida, actually bore a resemblance to her uncle, which wasn't immediately obvious but emerged upon speaking to her, as she somehow had the same manner, the way she held her head, and also something in the eye and forehead region.

Frida listened, nodding, neck pain. Having spoken their piece, they asked a single question of her. Learning that she wasn't a poet, not even a prose writer, they returned to their peers. In between these brief encounters, Frida glanced over at her uncle, who kept sitting in that corner with his elbows on the table, and each time he looked a bit altered, enshrouded. Toward evening's end, the café clearing though it was unclear just how quickly as smoke impaired visibility, an older woman with owl eyes and the matronly derriere to which the pinch rightfully belonged approached Frida. Perfectly sober, she took pride in her controlled manner, as if she were a cheetah that had tamed itself. Studying Frida, she said in English that was accented, mannered, and perfumed, Lawyer or accountant?

Neither, Frida said quite proudly.

I didn't think so. Tell me you're a dentist and I'm leaving.

Medical school—just finished my first year.

Congratulations, said the woman, stifling a yawn.

But I'm not going back.

So it gets interesting.

Frida beamed.

Your poor parents—they must be heartbroken.

They don't know yet, said Frida, trying out a deranged fantasy on this ridiculous lady. The heartbreak will come later— first it'll be wrath. But they can't force me back to school when I'm half the world away.

So you're here waiting out the wrath?

I'm getting to know the family.

The woman introduced herself. She was Renata. This was said as if it were common knowledge what a Renata was, in theory. Being Renata was like being atheist or vegetarian. Most people gave their names and their hands; they didn't truly introduce themselves. Renata truly introduced herself. There was a deluge of epithets: poet, essayist, psychoanalyst, wife, mother, mystic, Jew, woman.

Keep going and you'll get to dentist, said Frida.

Are you as incorrigible as your uncle?

I wouldn't know. We haven't exactly been engaging in long conversations—or conversations of any kind, for that matter.

You see the two men he's been talking to the entire night? Does it surprise you that they're the most famous men in the room?

Yes. Nobody here seems famous.

Renata sighed. Nobody was a stranger to her. She dealt in psychological tendencies.

Whatever you're implying, said Frida, don't. I've heard my fill. Those men look interesting.

Those men *are* interesting. What it comes down to is that they're men.

So he's a misogynist as well?

Have you read Svetlana's poetry?

Who's Svetlana?

Your aunt.

Pasha's wife? Sveta? *She's* a poet, too?

A far more modern and thrilling one than your uncle, if you care for my opinion. I'm not alone in it. Svetlana's a prodigious talent, but fully eclipsed by your uncle. It's a shame—all that thwarted potential. Sure he claims to support her writing, the way Picasso might encourage his three-year-old to paint. He's terribly condescending, and she doesn't even notice. She worships him. The trouble with me was that I never worshipped him. I considered him an outstanding poet—his early poems were in a different league from the stuff of recent years—and I happily introduced him to the who's who of the émigré scene. But once I had no more to offer, he washed his hands of me. He stopped writing letters, stopped sending manuscripts. He dedicated a whole collection to me after his last visit to New York, poems I can't bear to reread. There's an openness, a frankness, even a dash of romanticism. I've decided that I myself invested the poems with earnestness. Pasha would like to be an earnest man, but he's not an earnest man. Perhaps that's a central conflict. He's not earnest, nor is he full of faith. You know what he's full of? Himself. But don't be lazy. Read your uncle's poetry, especially his first collection—you may find it interesting—it's about your family after all.

Renata paused, her gaze caught by someone behind Frida. She lowered her lashes, melted into a demure smile. Frida was left alone, sitting in a warm seat over someone's half-chewed shashlik and lipstick-rimmed wineglass, trapped in a hot, airless rage. Why would Renata just assume that Frida hadn't dabbled in her uncle's canon? And how come her parents never told her that Pasha wrote a book about their family? Why hadn't they given the book to her or asked if she was interested in taking a look at his others? Did they consider her devoid of curiosity? Admittedly, she'd never inquired. When a poem was mentioned or news came of another collection to be published, Frida was seized by an urge to plug her ears and vacate the room. She preferred to be kept in a state of ignorance. Her body resisted the information. In fact, she knew exactly where Pasha's books were: slumped against each other on the top shelf in the corridor of their apartment. At any time, with any passing whim, she could've taken one down. Instead she'd been collecting excuses and justifications in order to support the theory that she was being willfully excluded from his readership. She had it all—the hurt feelings, the accusations—but there was no one to tell it to. Pasha certainly didn't care whether his American niece had taken the time to read a single one of his collections. His blatant indifference made any theory of willful exclusion laughable. She could've read the poems but hadn't. The willfulness was entirely on her end. Her surface apathy hid a deeper ambivalence, eschewal, restraint. Dig through those layers and reach a bedrock animosity. Frida felt only more confirmed in that stance. Why make an effort when there was no chance of its being reciprocated? But was she really looking for reciprocation from Pasha? No, she wanted it from her family. The rules that were writ in stone for her didn't apply to Pasha—he didn't reside within a block radius of the family headquarters, didn't consult on every minor decision, didn't put in the mandatory quality time, either of bonding or household labor, wasn't a doctor, wasn't even a Jew! And yet he got away with it. Not only that, he reigned supreme. *They* consulted him. He'd won. Was this fair? How could Frida not be resentful? Although the fact of the matter was that those rules from which he was not exempt must've once applied—he'd just had the resolve to struggle against them. I should read the poems, thought Frida.

Efim was still twirling the saltshaker.

This is only the beginning, he said sadly. It's a steady degradation from here on in. Most of these guys won't be sober again until they return home three weeks from now. Then they'll start chronicling in extensive detail their experiences on Live-Journal, finding they all remember things a bit differently. They'll launch internet battles, terrorize with comments, go on unfriending sprees.

You don't sound like a poet, said Frida.

I'm a computer programmer, he said.

She refrained from asking the obvious question, soon answered when a bullfighting aficionado slapped Efim on the back and said, Hello, good man, I'm glad to see some things never change—your wife is still the life of the party.

I'm surprised Pasha's not going to this Bulgarian carnival, Frida said to change the subject, as that comment had visibly diminished Efim's spirits.

It's Georgian, and what do you mean he's not going?

We leave Monday, said tipsy Sveta, trying charmingly to pull together and not sound tipsy in the least. Did Pasha not tell you? He must've forgotten to mention it.

What about the wedding?

As it stands as of the present moment, we fly in the morning after the wedding, but not to worry, I'm about to fix that. It's all my fault. Pasha's lousy with dates. I should've known not to trust him with tickets.

But—said Frida.

No, said Sveta.

Then maybe while you're away, I'll stay at the dacha.

The dacha's gone, said Pasha, evidently tuned in to the conversation. It's gone. Finis. Poof. Please pass that along.

THIRTEEN

PASHA HADN'T BEEN INVITED to participate in the Odessa Conference of Literature. Not only did they not ask him to give a reading, instead scraping the bottom of the barrel for the few local poets not yet too far gone along the path of drunken incoherence or drunken vulgarity and incoherence or, the most terrible of all, of sober attempts at meaningful and/or innovative poetry, but they—the organizers, whom Pasha didn't mention, perhaps deeming it too obvious, were those very bottom-of-the-barrel poets themselves—didn't even invite him to take part in any of the marginal events, the festival fluff, which was how Pasha knew, though of course he would've known regardless, that he was being subjected to purposeful banishment. To put it simply: blacklisted.

From the acute pang and magnitude of hurt accompanying his exclusion, it would seem that this hadn't happened last year. Because Pasha didn't hold grudges, the wounds inflicted on him were always unforeseen. Scar tissue never formed. And he'd used the year to convince himself that it'd been a genuine blunder on some novice organizer's part. Worse errors were known to occur in Ukraine. Someone could've easily forgotten to enter his name into the schedule just because he was too obvious a candidate for every single slot. The human brain had a funny way. A more probable explanation, he knew, was that they'd been teaching him a lesson. In that case the volumes of Google-able backlash from nonlocals should've taught a lesson in reverse.

At the conference he had spies. He didn't have to ask—they volunteered their reports. His name circulated at public panels and during interviews, but most frequently in the gossip realm he so opposed. The volunteer spies had a great deal to disclose and did so with relish. Pasha was grateful. Motives weren't questioned. He developed an addiction to their scoops, collecting evidence of victimhood. These purported friends were like drug dealers providing a steady supply of slanderous material. Pasha didn't differentiate—a trivial scrap of spiteful blather from a notorious drunkard affected him no less than a six-thousand-word, vitriol-spewing, undigested work of so-called scholarship by a prominent critic in a widely read journal.

Pasha sulked around the house, not amused by Frida's equally sulky accompaniment. She treated the moping of others as a challenge—could she mope to match? Several worries were on her mind: that it was already Saturday yet she was no closer to whatever miraculous intervention on the part of fate she'd been hoping for, that tomorrow she'd be faced with the decision of whether to accompany Pasha and Sveta to church or remain loyal to her condescending attitude toward all religious observance, that the day after tomorrow Pasha and Sveta were set to depart for their festival, and that Sanya hadn't made the effort to see her on any of these days.

To escape the gloom, Pasha went to make the rounds of the corner marts, groceries, and shops on a fruitless search for a particular brand of Georgian mineral water, which he claimed was the only tonic for the gastric tumult that caused him to visit the bathroom as often as he checked his email for updates.

Can he possibly be *this* naïve? Frida asked once he'd gone, seizing the opportunity to reason with Sveta, who sat Indian style in her nightie on the living room floor, working on a watercolor. I mean, Frida clarified, he's not an idiot. Doesn't he realize they'll keep doing this to him as long as he refuses to build defenses or change his ways? He makes it fun for them! Why won't he just tell them to go fuck themselves? They're nobodies! Instead he acts all wounded and helpless. How can he still be surprised by this bullshit? More important, how can he still bear to live in this city? If it's so miserable, why won't he budge?

Sveta spilled water onto the canvas. Frida gasped. Sveta's hand had twitched, and she'd spilled too much. But after appraising, Sveta tipped the jar again, spilling even more. It's not my job to analyze, she said. Dropping her paintbrush, she looked Frida in the eye. The wife of a poet, she explained, has three responsibilities: to feed him, to believe unconditionally in his genius, and to leave him alone. These posed no difficulty for her. Her ex-husband, Artem Muser (Hungarian parentage), an eminent philosopher and bassist for the rock group Rote Goat, had also required the three, though with each passing year addenda had emerged. The second principle was key. As long as she'd believed in Artem, the rest was a pleasure. But somewhere along the way, she had lost her faith. Don't get me wrong, she said, Artem is great at what he does—he's a success by anybody's standards. But a genius is a genius. Would his philo-sophical oeuvre be contemplated a century from then? Would the music of his band be moshed to? The unlikelihood of either never bothered him. He was cruising. He'd built a solid reputa-tion and was reaping the rewards. Ranked among the leading philosophers in the country based on a sensationalistic doctoral dissertation, he was happy to sit on panels about Schopenhau-er's toilet and be told by the sleaziest department chair imagin-able that out of all introductory courses his was the quickest to fill to capacity. And it was enough that his band played the an-nual Ukrainian heavy-metal fest. Occasionally they gathered a good crowd in Kiev.

Sveta, however, had expected more. She began to regard Artem as a regular man—gifted, endowed with a strong will, but nothing extraordinary. And feeding a regular man was little pleasure. In this new light, a few other trifles had come to her attention: Artem was a shameless philanderer, never asked a single question about her existence, and mentioned her "barren womb" regularly. These revelations had coincided, quite fortu-itously, with the arrival of Pasha.

Your uncle is a genius the likes of which are distributed over time and across the earth with an exceedingly spare hand, said Sveta. I was sure of this from the very start. Sveta's gaze went coy. Do you want to hear how we met?

Frida nodded, her foot going numb.

It was actually in New York, and I probably shouldn't be telling you this, but it was a July evening in '93. My husband had dragged me to Renata Ostraya's party. I really didn't want to go. They'd had a brief thing, but that wasn't the issue. I'd lost my appetite after a weeklong flu, and for me Renata's parties were strictly about gastronomic potential. Unable to partake, I was forced to interact. For an hour or two I nodded beside Artem but was drawn back to the table. Its proximity comforted. Instead of sampling dishes, I sampled conversations, overhearing fragments, rarely of interest. That's how I spotted Pasha. A group of men were having one of those rambling discussions about everything at once. They were impressed with one another, this was clear. But they were standing by the table and popping pigs in a blanket into their mouths. I began to eavesdrop, my attention entirely given over to the gawky man with the unkempt beard—he wasn't like the rest. He was different. I was just standing there when one of them, a chubby man with a pink face and no eyebrows—you saw him last night, Andrei Fishman—turned to me and said, Want to join in, or are we blocking the sausages? Stupefied, I'd said, Sausages. So what did Andrei do? He took a pig in a blanket from the pile and said, Open up. Can you imagine? I was mortified! He was dangling it in front of my nose, but my jaw was clamped shut. Nothing could've pried it open. That was when Pasha stepped in. He tilted back his head. He opened his mouth.

In telling the story, Sveta claimed she knew right then. Her fate had been disclosed. Weeks later she ran into Pasha in Brooklyn, and the coincidence didn't surprise her, not least of all because she'd been hanging around Brighton bookstores for days on end in hopes of bumping into him. By the end of the year, she'd convinced Artem to apply for a professorship at Odessa State University, and the rest was history.

But the problem, for a long time, had been quite literally in the telling of the story—namely, that it was forbidden. Odessa was small, and Pasha's renown had been steadily on the rise throughout their affair. (Artem lasted two years in Odessa—when he left, it was on his own.) It was as if the city were shrinking and Pasha expanding. When Odessa was unsure about anything, it turned to Pasha for his input. No matter that it was never to the liking of the public. His voice regularly flowed from the radio, and his stooped figure freely ambled into and out of the local TV stations. As long as he was with Nadia, Sveta couldn't shout from the rooftops about their love. It was ironic—his wife had wanted to keep him a secret but couldn't, and now Sveta had to keep him a secret but didn't want to! She could tell only her best friend, Korina, and, post-divorce, her mother. Her best friend and her mother, two women Pasha was sure to find unbearable, were made to sit through countless iterations of the story.

He wasn't about to leave Nadia, said Sveta. For all the drama in his life, Pasha will go to any lengths to avoid confrontation.

It took a long time for the inevitable to happen. At first Sveta had lived in dire fear of a run-in, then she'd desperately tried to psychically summon it, and by the time it actually occurred, she'd resigned herself to the fact that a cosmic force was against it, probably for the best. She'd been sitting with Korina at one of the wobbly metal tables outside Klara Bara, a café nestled in City Garden. The park was roughly the size of a city block yet had been laid out in such a manner that even natives lost their way there. This space-warp effect was useful to criminals, who fortunately had pieties and stuck if at all possible to the purses and wallets of out-of-towners.

Despite the heat, a cashmere shawl had been draped over

her friend's shoulders. Shawls were made to be fiddled with, but Korina took it to the extreme. She was rattling off her non se-quiturs and taking calculated sips of her cappuccino, oohing and aahing. She calls herself a life connoisseur, said Sveta. It was a struggle. In those days I was still trying to mimic her sips. Suddenly Korina froze mid–shawl toss and said, Don't turn, your poet's here. Pasha walked by—no hello, nothing. He was trailed by Nadia and Sanya and a morose girl who was Sanya's girlfriend. About ten minutes later, he emerged from the café with the most unfathomable expression on his face and intro-duced himself formally to Korina. What a pleasure, and I've heard so much about you (if Korina only knew . . .). He made this altogether genuine effort to engage a woman among whose wis-doms was that a Virgo and a Cancer should never mix except for *in the bedroom* and who saw logic in wearing a crucifix, a kab-balah bracelet, and a bindi simultaneously. Sveta had kept up the friendship not least of all because she'd needed someone to listen, without growing weary or skeptical, to the legend of Pasha. But here was the famous poet, her illicit lover—in a stained, oversize polo with golf clubs on it, his left eyelid thick and oozing, clumps of dried food lodged in his gray beard.

So what did Pasha do? He squeezed my fingers under the table and went back to his family. As he walked off, I remem-ber, Korina gripped her straw and said, That man is *terribly* libidinally charged.

So what did I say? I'm going to leave him!

And I did, said Sveta, experiencing a resurgence of pride. Your uncle, who isn't the most proactive man, was forced into action—or rather into pathetic, hushed, late-night beseeching. He was a very disoriented gift giver (one week I got antique ivory incense canisters, a bag of cotton balls, anal beads, and a used toaster). None of that worked, so he tried anger and silence. Then, finally, after two months, he moved into my place.

What about Nadia?

What about her? said Sveta. She was put on suicide watch. But she'd never do it! I said this to Korina at the time, and I was right. At long last Nadia has reason to live—to make sure that Pasha gets no peace. Her goal is to take away the little that he has and torment him by any means, the more trite and disgraceful the better. Nadia has no qualms about being perceived as a hysterical, deranged old shrew. And do you know what Korina replied? She said, What else would you expect from a Scorpio?

Sveta laughed to herself. Too bad Korina's no longer here, she said wistfully.

She *died*? said Frida.

God, no! An older man appeared, she was offered a position as a radio host, then the offer was rescinded, but not before she made the move to Lvov.

PASHA DIDN'T FEEL GOOD about leaving Frida alone and unentertained—though was he really a viable means of entertainment? Dreams of Georgia was the highlight of his year. Fifty-one weeks of isolation were made tolerable by it. Socially ravenous on arrival, starved for acknowledgment, by festival's end he was sated not only for the time being but for months. To refuel was imperative; a guilty conscience wouldn't deter.

The morning of their departure to Tbilisi, Frida was awoken by a hushed phone conversation (loud conversations rarely woke anybody), Pasha's voice leaking from the kitchen. Nu, nu, he said, followed by a pause. Aren't you being rash about this? When Frida's feet stirred—they were in the kitchen—he hastened the conversation to a close. If you say it must be so . . . But I beg you, give the matter some time, let it sit, and then see how you feel— Fine, I won't, good-bye.

A fly came down the pockmarked runway of Pasha's nose, resting a moment on the tip before resuming its frenzy of flight. Frida opened the fridge, contemplating the interior as if it were a composition made with artistic intention. She pretended to chew something and swallow. She wiped her palms on her shorts and looked out the window onto a dull courtyard that resembled the inside of the fridge.

The engagement is off, said Pasha.

Frida shook her head.

Sanya and his lady friend had an argument. They came to the conclusion that they shouldn't be getting married.

I thought she was pregnant, said Frida.

Pasha shrugged. I don't think she's pregnant, he said.

So it's that simple?

It's as simple, or as complicated, as one chooses to make it.

Really? thought Frida. How horrible. She opted to disregard that sentiment or put it aside for future analysis, suspecting that it had only the ring of truth. Does Sanya even know that I'm here?

Her question seemed to pull Pasha from the depths of thought, interrupting an unrelated contemplation of something ineffable and solemn. But was it possible to always be pondering the very nature of existence, and if it was, didn't it constitute some sort of disorder? In response to Frida's question, he nodded sadly. Sanya knows. He wants to take you out on the town, show you the nightlife scene of Arcadia. That's Sanya's meadow of expertise, as the Americantsi say.

Right now? she said, alarmed.

Pasha was tickled. Now have some breakfast. Tomorrow night.

Was Frida supposed to feel grateful at the offer? Was it meant to smooth over the fact that her entire excuse for being there had just been pulled out from under her? Assumed in the Arcadia offer was an utter lack of will on her part. Regrettably, the offer aroused a spike of positive feeling, which was by its very nature cowardly. It counteracted, it completely destroyed, the daring intensity of the rage that had just started to build. Sanya wanted to take her out to the nightclubs—well, she desperately wanted to go. Where else would she accidentally step on the foot of her future husband? That her forays into the nightlife scene of New York had been disastrous, mostly in a quiet way, pointing out a chronic inability to relax and have a good time, was irrelevant. By predisposing herself against Sanya, she'd only be harming herself. Why not try instead to empathize? Her cousin must've been devastated. He was embarrassed. Filled with grief and shame. He thought he'd found a life partner, not a simple pursuit in Odessa. The girls were gorgeous, sure, and liked a good time, but life-partner material they weren't. Neither were they the least bit eager to settle for a man who didn't own a yacht or a foreign passport, preferably both. If they did happen to settle, their bodies intuited the capitulation immediately—whatever crazy biological force had been keeping every part firm, distinct, and perky relented, letting all those parts slacken, merge, and collectively expand. Undoubtedly Sanya had been relieved to find a suitable bride and now experienced catastrophic disappointment. Aside from that, he knew that Frida had flown in for his wedding—to call it off so close to the date would've been mortifying for anybody. It became clear why almost a week had elapsed and Sanya had yet to make an effort to see her—he'd been undergoing great emotional upheaval.

Did he give a time?

He said he'd call an hour or so beforehand, to give you a chance to get ready.

IT WAS PAST NOON WHEN SVETA staggered out of the bedroom in her clingy, sweated-through nightie, looking as if she'd just regained consciousness after a frying-pan whack to the skull, which probably wasn't far afield from the effect of her pharmaceutical concoctions. Pasha had forgotten to make his silver-tray delivery, and it became evident that the treatment was hardly a luxury. Sveta knocked into the edge of the table in the corridor, sending the landline flying—batteries, plastic, not that she noticed. Pressing the heels of her hands into her wounded hip, she bent in half and yowled, then continued groping her way to the kitchen. Somewhere she found a kiwi. She ate it like a soft-boiled egg, peeling the top half and using a small rusty spoon to scoop out the flesh. By then the coffee was in a mug whose handle Pasha fitted over her hooked finger. She took it down in a single gulp. Sense returned to her gaze. Her hands jumped to her head, finding that her hair was still pinned back, ear exposed. Frida sat across the table pretending to leaf through something black and white with varying font sizes and interspersed images. Sveta was about to run out to preserve her dignity but then realized that the little dignity there was to preserve didn't merit such effort. She sighed and tapped the mug's rim, signaling for more coffee.

But before it was poured, she was rushing out, screaming, Our flight, our flight! It was that afternoon, in just a few hours, and they weren't packed, and Volk said he couldn't drive them and there wasn't a chance they'd make it. Not surprisingly, Sveta had a frantic style of departing. No one in the family was capable of even finding a partner who knew how to depart with grace.

Pasha followed into the direction of the drawer banging, unzipping, torrential toppling. That he hadn't packed the bags on his own or arranged for a ride to the airport or simply woken Sveta at an hour when she could do it herself without having a conniption—none of this was mentioned or seemingly even thought, except by Frida, who needed to remember that this was none of her business and she must stay out of it. But stay out of it where? Not sure what to do with herself, she found herself staring at the bookshelves in the corridor, about to pluck one of Pasha's poetry collections from the stacks but picking up a stat-uette instead, placing in her palm a turtle with a globe-size tu-mor on its shell. Meanwhile, in the nearby bedroom, Pasha attempted to calm Sveta with the good news that now there was one less thing to worry about. A major hassle had been averted. Sveta's curiosity was piqued (the toppling momentarily abated). Pasha explained that it was no longer necessary to change their return flight—because the wedding was off! Sveta admirably discarded the packaging in which the news was delivered. Chto, she said, and in her chto could be heard every nuance the news suddenly brought from black depths into plain sight. She had

Frida in mind when that chto was uttered. But then their bedroom door closed, no more was heard.

They emerged an hour later dressed as members of a pastoral
polyamorous cult, lugging two suitcases and three lumpy duffel
bags. The bedroom was the giant suitcase they'd decided to leave
behind. It looked like the scene of a pogrom. Hesitating as to
how formal to make this farewell, Sveta was about to say something genuine and heartfelt when three loud honks resounded.
Disturbed more than most by noise, she ran to the door. Parked
out front was her glamorous friend Ada—embarrassing on most
occasions, heaven-sent in emergencies. She hopped out of the
quivering convertible in order to assist with their bags, which she
did with wondrous ease despite knee-length patent-leather boots
on a six-inch heel, adapted for the season by the presence of air-
vent strips along the calves. As Ada leaned in to plant a smooch
on Pasha's cheek, Frida swung shut the door—alone at last!

The convertible's *vroom* was still echoing when the lock
turned. What'd you forget? yelled Frida. In marched Sveta's
half brother, Volk, followed by a wobbling wife of the minia-
ture hormonal variety, and their kids. Frida's face muscles betrayed her.

They didn't tell you? said Volk.

There's no communication in this household, said Frida.

We're here for the week.

The family had left their home in the suburbs to come to
the city and sleep in Pasha and Sveta's windowless bedroom—
this was their idea of a vacation. The room it took Sveta an
hour to destroy took the wife three to return to order, a ratio
that likely had broad applicability. The children moved in a

multisonorous cloud of elbows. Primarily at home in the court-yard, they occasionally swooped indoors. The wife retrieved a frozen hunk of meat and began slamming it against the counter's edge. The fact had to be acknowledged, circumstances were deteriorating fast.

FOURTEEN

VOLK'S WIFE CAME equipped with a nose and used it to sniff at fishy situations such as this. They'd planned their city vacation months ago, after learning that Pasha and Sveta would be going to Georgia for some writers' congress or other. Sveta had boasted of her travel plans to her brother, and later that evening over a steamy mound of buckwheat Volk had good-humoredly poked fun at his sister's jet-setting lifestyle to his always-thinking wife, who'd said, Volky, you know what this means, don't you? Volky rarely did. A city vacation, of course! The wife masterminded, Volky arranged. An empty house had been promised. Instead they got Pasha's American niece, Frida, who sat unmoving in the living room. The wife suspected that the girl had been planted there to make sure they didn't do God knows what with the apartment and to report them if they did, in which case they could be sure to never have another city vacation again.

The wife journeyed from the kitchen to the bathroom, as this was an opportunity to pass by Frida's station. Having taken a good look, she went to deliberate over the toilet seat. Her impression was that Frida didn't look like a spy. But back in the kitchen, the suspicions returned. She took a vase of wilted carnations from the corridor and brought it, along with a cloud of fruit flies, to the living room, setting it atop an already overloaded coffee table. Frida's gaze bounced from the wife to the vase to the wife. Thank you, Frida muttered. The wife noticed a photo album in Frida's hands and left satisfied. But something still didn't sit right.

Over the course of the morning, Frida received stale flowers, fresh towels, and plenty of unnerving stares. There was minimal verbal accompaniment. A malfunction seemed to occur when the wife ran into the room, looked square at Frida, and ran out. A minute later, more composed, she peeked in to see whether Frida had worked up an appetite—odd phrasing, as Frida had hardly moved all day. Frida shook her head in what was presumably a universal gesture. A plate of plov appeared on her lap. The wife was on her way out but plopped down on the sofa instead.

The remote control was nearby, but the wife's arms were short; they couldn't quite make it. Frida was determined not to help. The wife was determined to prove her helplessness, groaning and grunting as she fruitlessly reached. Frida refused to be drawn into this ridiculous drama, the wife refused to get up or even scooch forward to get the damn piece of plastic off the coffee table. After much ineffectual strain, she emitted a sigh of defeat and fell back onto the cushion. Resigned to life without television. This was horrible. Little was as depressing as the wife sitting on the sofa deprived of entertainment. Unfortunately she couldn't also turn off her need to see. Her gaze began to scale the walls, crammed with icons of the Virgin. If she were to become entranced by the icons, Frida was in danger as well. Remote snatched and thrown at the wife, who accepted the device with only a touch of exasperation that it hadn't arrived sooner.

Two women sat across from each other in an intimate kitchen setting, their flabby elbows propped on a crocheted tablecloth on which stood, ideally spaced, a gorgeous blue porcelain tea set, cups too tiny to hold any reasonable amount of liquid, fulfilling the nobler function of evoking distant epochs when objects still had value. These were hefty broads, keen to gossip. With chins drawn into their chests, they peered out deviously from under hooded eyelids while tossing around names that in a country of roughly fifty million meant nothing only to Frida. Once a name was thrown into the air, the unfortunate person to whom it belonged became an invisible patient lying on the table amid the fine china and a dissection began, lasting as long as it took to get to the source of all rottenness. The finer specimens really made you dig. There didn't seem to be more to the show's premise. Commercials were few but potent. Frida tried to avoid looking up, as the TV was now the wife's domain and Frida intended to not get tangled up in the wife's business. The screen, clearly, was a trap. So she stared at the massive photo album in her lap, selecting a page at random. It was toward the beginning—the obscure part of every good photo album, where the relationships on display were at their most abstract. Pasha took this obscurity to the extreme. Most people's albums began with their grandparents and ended with themselves in the present or the recent past or their children. Pasha's album ended with grandparents and began with inconceivable likenesses. Here was a photograph of a man, yet the photograph didn't look like a photograph and the man didn't look like a man. It looked as if someone had used a soft graphite pencil to sketch the shadow of a ghost caught in a dusty mirror, then tried to erase it with one of those hardened pink erasers on the pencil's other end, and buried the sketch in a courtyard's piss-soaked soil until it was dug up by Pasha, who didn't bother to clean it off before sticking it into the album. The man was ultra-dead, all the people who'd ever seen the back of his head or heard him hum were dead, and this lack of ties to the wet cement of time was felt deeply when looking at his face. Or trying to look and failing, since a composite image never formed, there was no man to be seen.

That's a pretty top, said the wife.

Frida looked up when spoken to, a bad habit. The wife noted Frida's confusion and pinched her collar to show what she meant. Your top, she said, is pretty.

Frida looked down at her long-sleeved gray T-shirt, the one she'd been sleeping in, which contained visible traces of many of her previous snacks and was sprinkled with crumbs from her latest one, and the heat rushed to her face.

Is that a typical American top? asked the wife. Once again registering Frida's confusion, she elaborated, Are those the kinds of tops that the young women wear in the States?

Yeah, said Frida. Then shook her head, No. They wear lots of different kinds, she said, an infinite variety. No such thing as a typical top. That's why America's known as a free country. She wasn't sure why she was taking this tone or whether she was being sarcastic.

And you have Baby Einstein, said the wife.

Yep, said Frida, hoping to leave it at that and not stir the insanity brewing underneath.

Here they'd never think up anything like that, said the wife. And it shows, you know, upon the quality of our youth. Savages! Little liars, hooligans, and thieves! Whenever Volky or I hear that somebody's visiting from abroad, we don't ask for denim jackets or air conditioners or even fancy phones, we ask only for Baby Einstein. The wife paused and gave a stare of significance. When we heard you were coming, she resumed, we asked Pavel Robertovich to ask you to bring the Baby Einstein for us. They're always coming up with something new, you know.

Frida's eyes lifted in contemplation, as if she might suddenly remember about all the Baby Einstein products she'd hauled in from the States. The wife read Frida's thoughts and narrowed her focus on the bloated suitcase in the center of the room (still packed, of course, just herniating a few garments). The moment of hope was allowed to take a breath.

I would've, but Pasha never mentioned anything.

The wife's attention remained fixed on the suitcase. He never mentioned it? she repeated, absorbing her disappointment gradually, in doses.

Not a word, said Frida.

Well, Pavel Robertovich is a busy man. He has many important things to think about. And who are we to him?

Pasha's a little absentminded, said Frida. There seems to be a consensus about that. If you want him to do something, you need to provide constant poking.

We reminded the both of them not once and not twice. Volky and I keep to ourselves, we don't impose. But when it comes to Baby Einstein, we're not shy. They really never said anything about it to you?

Frida shook her head, noting the regression, a bad sign. Of

course, if I'd known, she said, I would've brought it for you. And next time—

So you don't have it? said the wife.

No, said Frida.

The wife wasn't devastated, another bad sign. She wasn't devastated not because she was a rational adult who could handle such news but because it still didn't register, or perhaps she didn't believe it.

The door flew open, and a boy ran in, inflamed knees like grapefruits being lurched through the air, hands cupped tensely over something. He screeched—the sound came from his joints. Other boys followed, dashing after the first, screeching at their own particular frequencies, little Einsteins in training. The last one, chubby and asthmatic, probably with a rash somewhere, caught Frida's foot and went flying, stumpy arms akimbo, past the sofa, slamming the entirety of his weight into one of the grandfather clocks. The compound wail of the boy and the clock set something off in Frida. She was gone.

AFTER SHE'D LEFT the courtyard behind, there was a lapse of several blocks. She hurried blindly, inserting distance between herself and the apartment, the icons and clocks, Volky and his wife on their precious city vacation as they kept referring to it, with no intention to seize the day and take advantage of the actual city. Was Frida one to talk? She had yet to stray from the half-mile radius of Pasha's initial tour. She kept to the same side of the street, used the same crosswalks, passed between the same two paint-chipped colonnades, all the while noticing helplessly the rigidity with which she navigated.

The people on the benches in Sobornaya Square were ancient. It was hard to imagine them ever going home, and it didn't help that the city had a fondness for the sitting statue. Leonid Utesov was sunning himself beside an old lady not at all averse to a distinguished bronze arm around her papery shoulders.

Crossing Preobrazhenskaya at the frenzied intersection where public minibuses convened in a chaotic grid-central huddle, Frida was blasted by their ferocious heat. She continued, coughing, along the gated perimeter of City Garden. Go inside, an inner voice instructed. Enjoy your life—explore! But the tangle of shrubbery was too thick, the trees screened out too much daylight. Hadn't she been warned about this park? Under no circumstances go in the vicinity of City Garden! It's the scene of gruesome murders and frequent robberies, and let's not get started on the rapes. Or had that warning been tacked onto Park Shevchenko? One of them was a beautiful park, ideal for a stroll on a warm summer day such as this, and the other was where practically every Ukrainian female had been robbed at gunpoint, molested, viciously raped.

Sabaneev Bridge was also called Mother-in-Law Bridge. Prince Vorontsov had it erected after building his mother-in-law a house across a now-nonexistent river from his palace, a bridge that in the past few decades had acquired the tradition of newly-wed lock-hanging. Sveta's chirp, Pasha's rabbinic profile. Were they having fun in Tbilisi? Were they at least a little bit worried, racked by guilt, having left Frida to fend for herself in a foreign city?

Two guards stared her away from a synagogue freshly painted or long untouched. Walking away was like cutting short an encounter with a prissy friend, an only child who'd been pampered from a young age, but probably for good reason. Cobblestones carved breath. Past the cream-puff-pastry Opera House and the gardened-off Literary Museum, down the quaint urine-dribbled steps to a narrow street at the tapered end of which was a cliff.

Nearby, construction workers were taking a lunch break. She yearned to feel disgusted at their ogling, if only they weren't so engrossed in their sandwiches. She went up to them and asked a question. A gaunt boy gave no-nonsense directions while twisting the cap off a two-liter plastic bottle of beer. A couple of empty bottles lay at his feet, still frothy around the edges. His eyes were eerily striking, like toxic sunsets over polluted waters.

SHE FAILED TO NOTICE the proper things. Was everything smaller than she remembered—or was it supposed to be larger? Less daunting and serpentine or only more so? By the time she remembered the duty to make such observations, the window for them had closed—size was no longer relative or meaningful but an inarguable fact to be accepted at face value. The skyline was in disarray, everything in halted construction. An engine revved, releasing the smell of shashlik. The rusted gate wore a shaggy coat of ivy. Frida got down on all fours on the narrow dirt path and pressed her cheek to the ground, trying to get a peek through the crevice under the gate. There was no sign of life from within. As she was spitting out dirt, the ridiculousness of the enterprise dawned on her. It was as if she were taking orders from some behind-the-scenes charlatan who regularly guided foolish young people through these kinds of missions, from which they left empty-handed and only more spiritually bereft than before but convinced that their arduous floundering and grasping meant that something had been accomplished too great for their own comprehending. Frida collapsed and curled up in a ball. Think, she implored herself. Make a plan! But she was tired, tired in a new way. There was no end to discovering the subtleties of exhaustion. Or did they all fall under the rubric of self-pity? Relief came in the form of some shade. The sun had been taking a vicious afternoon angle.

The shade had voice—deep, resonant, husky. Get away from my dacha, it said. Find someone else's gate to sleep on! That's right, young lady. Shoo!

Frida looked up and was instantly recognized. It was a much-needed affirmation. Not only was she recognized, her presence induced an uplift of mood, a heightening of tonus, a surge of joy—it was treated as a stupendous surprise. The bloated yet mousy, yellowish gray woman overhead gasped and cried, Frida, it's you! I don't believe it! My God, let me get a look at you! and a succession of many more delicious exclamatory platitudes that occasionally were the only satisfactory response. The bloated lady was Nadia, but by the time that thunderbolt struck, Frida was already experiencing great surges in return, overcome by the desire to burrow her nose into the dark, glistening pocket of Nadia's neck.

Bozhe moi, bozhe moi (My God, my God), Nadia repeated. It was as if Frida belonged to the top tier of guest, was the most special visitor. Any visitor would likely fall into this rank. The loneliness on Nadia's face was glaring. The spools of golden sunshine would've freshened a corpse but did nothing to Nadia's sewer-lady pallor. An entirely new face would be needed if she ever stopped living in a state of unvarying solitude. Bending down, she picked Frida up off the ground. Frida's spiritual flailing felt proportional to Nadia's physical effort. Come in, said Nadia, rummaging in her bag for keys. Her stooped figure labored over the giant rusted lock. She let out an exasperated groan. It wouldn't give, defying her fitful attempts. She paused for a few gulps of air, pulled a crumpled handkerchief from the pocket of her frock, and blotted her forehead. With renewed vigor she attacked the lock.

Frida said, Do you want me to—

Talk when inside, barked Nadia, jiggling violently.

I can come back another time.

Nonsense! The grimy metal cracked. The lock popped open and was tugged out. Nadia gave Frida a nudge inside and shut the gate behind her.

Frida had been worried that she would feel nothing at the sight of the dacha, no connection, no recognition, but she wasn't prepared for the fact that there would actually *be* nothing. The dacha was demolished. The entirety was in ruins, as if leveled by a tornado. It struck the eye no longer as a single entity—a house—but simply a mound of rubble.

Hungry? Thirsty? After determining, with relief, that Frida was neither, Nadia explained that her legs weren't what they used to be.

I'll leave you to rest, said Frida, backing away.

Stop with this utter horseshit! Nadia screamed. Noticing that Frida blanched, she softened and said, An old lady could use some company every once in a while. And it has been a while, hasn't it? This is your dacha after all. I apologize if it's a bit dark inside. There's no circuitry, as of the moment.

A lack of circuitry was no surprise, but the existence of an inside was. How could this heap of boards and debris have an interior? But one of the more upright boards served as a door, through which Nadia's stocky frame just barely squeezed. Inside, it was narrow, bare, dark indeed. Several mattresses were distributed along the floor, stripped of bedding, iodine-stained. The last mattress was propped by a cot, and Nadia threw herself across it.

I'm sorry it's not all that tidy, she said quietly. As it happens, I have no help from anybody on this earth. My cousins, who are very sickly from Chernobyl, come and go as they please. Nadia laughed. You probably don't have a clue what I'm talking about. Chernobyl was—

I know what Chernobyl was, said Frida with irritation, though while she said it, a fear shot though her that she'd be tested on the subject and fail horribly, like in a dream, mixing up Chernobyl with the Triangle Shirtwaist Fire or the *Titanic*.

A free sanatorium is what they take this for. They're sensitive to light, to heat, to moisture in the air, to feathers, citrus fruit, drafts, the least echo of music. I'm not the picture of health myself, but to compare . . . I manage the best I can. But I wasn't expecting you so soon. Otherwise I would've been prepared. I intended to have the renovations done by your arrival— you'll just have to take my word on that. Nadia lay as if the sea had washed up her body, as if she didn't have access to the biological pathways to wiggle a finger, and her voice was the result of some stirring and rustling deep within this senseless flesh. Now, tell me, she said, how are your parents?

Frida was suspended in the air by some highly delicate balance of forces, which could be thrown into disproportion by the least insensitivity on her part. The tiniest wrong move and she'd drop onto one of the iodine-stained mattresses, where for all she knew the cousins lay napping or telepathically chatting in irradiated invisibility. What to do? She took a breath. Her palms were planted in the burnt-orange stains, and her bare feet (she must've removed her shoes in an uncharacteristic display of politeness) were ankle-deep in dust. Ragged strips of sunlight divided the floor, serving as the gelatinous substance in which dust particles became lodged.

My parents are fine. They say privet.

Your mother was like a sister, whispered Nadia. And how is Robert Grigorievich?

Fine, said Frida. Getting older.

Aren't we all! Robert Grigorievich is an exceptional man in every sense, but time makes no exceptions. Not even Pasha is spared, though I do believe he still isn't convinced of that himself. But none of this unpleasantness. I remember you as a little fat dumpling, a little nasty fat dumpling resolved to not make life easier for anybody. And now am I to believe that the dumpling I remember so well has transformed into a young woman with an American accent and such an interesting top? And I must say, you really do resemble your uncle. But just look what Pasha did to me! Who could've known? Who would've predicted in a million years? Yet nobody on this earth feels a shred of sympathy for me.

Don't stir the darkness, thought Frida. Keep perfectly still.

Except you, said Nadia. You feel sympathy for your poor aunt, don't you?

Frida nodded.

As for the renovation, said Nadia, dropping an octave to the universal business baritone, I'm currently in the process of dividing the dacha in two. The part we're in right now will be yours, and the other part will be mine. It'll be exactly as it should.

Oh, thought Frida, so it's a betterment process. She should've known that this was the case—in her own neck of the woods people acted impulsively, with little or no foresight, the result being fits and starts on every block. If they came upon the means to accomplish the first step of their Grand Plan, they didn't hesitate to do so, trusting momentum to carry the rest to fruition. When the funds ran out, no one bothered to clean up the mess. In Brooklyn the guiding force, however disguised, was creation, whereas here it wasn't so obvious.

I wanted to have the renovation done by the time you got here, continued Nadia, but who knew you'd be so quick? I was expecting the opposite problem. I figured I had another eighteen months at the least. But it's all for the best. Truth is, I'm weak. There's not a soul to help me.

What about Sanya?

If I can give you a piece of advice: Think twice before having a son. It may seem like a good idea at the time, but it never pans out. If you're looking for affection, a bit of understanding, support in your old age, a son isn't the way to go. Do you think Sanya would take an hour out of his day to visit his ailing mother all alone in the world? A helping hand he is not, never was. But the fact of the matter is, who needs him? You look sturdy enough. I can tell when someone eats her spinach. As you can see, there's no shortage of beds. Just pick the one you want, and I'll get some fresh linen.

That's very kind of you, muttered Frida, but I don't want to be any trouble.

Pooh! What kind of trouble could you possibly be?

The mattress nearest the entrance had almost no iodine stains; it was the most sunken in the center, as if a meteorite had landed there a few million years ago, but one couldn't expect to have it all. The offer was, in many ways, a godsend. Spending another day in that apartment with Volk and his family was unimaginable. So was the idea of going back to Brooklyn and, in two weeks' time, packing her bags to return to school for another year of somnambulating around a space-alien campus, snoring through amphitheater lectures, wallowing over the toilet seat, overhearing snippets of conversation about the awesome things her peers did with their preceptors, such as handing a needle during a paracentesis, how one person studied for forty hours straight but the other was already prepping for her Step 1, and shrugging it all off until finding herself alone at daybreak in her cell with the Krebs cycle and a bunch of amino acids or cranial nerves and anterior compartments of the leg. Another year couldn't be endured. Yet staying on with Pasha and Sveta wasn't an option—even if she wanted to, they wouldn't have it. Then she remembered about the veranda, which was no longer a veranda—you couldn't do such an injustice to the word. Because however highfalutin the word was, what good would it do to let the hot air out of it? The area of space in front of the dacha heap was no longer a veranda but a tattered cot under a chipped concrete awning with a tilt. Torrents of rain would enclose whoever lay there within transparent walls. She'd sleep out in the fresh air, with the porcupines at her feet.

Then you'll probably need an extra blanket. Because—don't
let the daylight fool you—at night it gets quite chilly. The bedding was in an outdoor closet near the outhouse right around
back and sort of diagonal. Be a dear, said Nadia.

Gray muffled light was like a sticky net out of which it was
impossible to break free. It was sobering, neutralizing light. The
gate through which they'd passed already looked like a different
gate. How had she even recognized this dacha as her own? Looking around, she recognized nothing and couldn't even say for sure
from which direction she'd come. But she knew where she had to
go: the closet. There was patchy shrubbery and twigs, powdery
piles of dry leaves, a partially duct-taped hose spitting up bile,
some wild berries trying to establish secret niches. Things were
either dying off or scheming for diabolical proliferation. This was
a real plot of land, instantly invigorating. Getting sheets and a pillow, when it involved stepping over malicious plants, shaking open
the rotted door of a death closet, and watching slinky spiders and
billowing centipedes scurry creviceward, wasn't a chore but an ultimate test of will and character, and by succeeding, by making it
back to shelter with sheets and a pillow, a victory of no measly significance was secured. No challenge was beyond her. Only she'd
forgotten the blanket and towels, and a pillowcase wouldn't hurt.

By the time Frida made it back with every unfitted scrap of
starchy cotton a person could desire, Nadia had drifted off.
Breaths were being sucked in and held captive in that ossified
chamber for disconcertingly prolonged stretches. In the dank,
medicinal room ripe with a scent of old saliva stood Frida, holding everything, unable to move. Should she put the linen down,
where, and then what?

She reminded herself that just a moment ago she'd felt great success and certainty. Now her arms ached and she was coughing into the linen. All of a sudden, it came into perspective: She'd gone to be disappointed. This must've been her actual reason all along. Disappointment had become necessary in order to forge ahead. Several times in one's life, a good sobering was required, and that's what this trip was—a blatant disappointment that would serve as an electric charge to zap the elements back into motion, realigning the facets of her life that had been allowed to slacken into disrepair and stagnation. It was like her mother's favorite anekdot about the lady who goes to see the rabbi and complains that life is so terrible with her slob of a husband and the crying children in a tiny apartment with such neighbors you start to think it might be better to be homeless, and the rabbi advises the lady to get a goat, so the lady does as told and not a week later is back to see the rabbi in a far worse state, complaining that the goat makes a mess and eats their food and stinks up their place and bleats all night long, to which the rabbi says, My dear Rivkele, as I see it, the solution to your dilemma is only too clear—you must get rid of the goat!

Frida returned the linen to the closet and decided to forgo the not yet urgently needed services of the outhouse (one test of will and character a day being plenty), then tiptoed past a tree stump bearing the strangulated markings from their old mesh hammock, to the gate, where she found her prayers answered— the lock had indeed been broken by Nadia's metal-bending fingers. It dangled, sad and limp, scary no more. Escape was imminent, which made it infinitely less desirable. A mental photograph was in order (her parents' camera, memory stick, and charger remained lodged in the sock-cushioned core of the bloated suitcase, through which Volk's wife was currently digging). Frida turned to take in the dacha one last time, but the scene was already jumbling, blurring, rearranging. Her mental photo would end up atrociously underexposed, a photo foremost of darkness, of a gritty, inexact darkness that could roll over vivid three-dimensional worlds and crush them. Luckily, her parents, who boasted a fine medley of hobbies, would never get to see the result and criticize her retina for being set on the wrong shutter speed or her laziness for not moving a few feet left to catch better natural light.

Frida was out of there and fast. No choice but to trust her feet to deliver her to the spot where the tram had dropped her off. Cicadas transmitted a dangerous electrical current to either side of the narrow path down which she was hurtling in an attempt to outrun, not least of all, their panicky buzz. She turned a corner into what she kept fingers crossed would be the wide, dusty alley tenderly called No Name Alley that opened out to the road with the tram tracks, but ended up deeper in the maze on a still-narrower, craggier path. In the distance a dog's bark was put out like a fire. Helicopter sounds drew her gaze upward. Overhead weren't the black, barbell-shaped things that carried presidents over the waters of Brighton Beach but nothingness, the sky a groovy blue-white tie-dye generator, building to something and collapsing, self-consuming, spinning, and dissolving. Orient her it did not. Through a gash in a fence, she saw wet laundry on a clothesline, flapping wildly. Was there a breeze? Gravel crunched under her feet, sending shooting pain because those broad, veiny feet were bare—oh, no, how had she forgotten? Nadia would wake to Frida's beat-up Keds but no Frida. Such a misstep was hard not to read as a bad omen.

Leaving behind something so personal was unwise; Nadia was sure to have a rich knowledge of black magic.

No longer was it gravel, concrete, or cool, looping weeds being driven between Frida's toes but sand, and the green shards from smashed bottles that went with it. She had bumped into the Black Sea. It was nice. Either today was Saturday or the stories were true and every day was Saturday by the sea. The crowds were thick and boisterous, shuttlecocks shared the airways with dragonflies and bright yellow wasps, beer cans sweated into swarthy clutches, prepubescent boys with punched-in chests ran around recruiting people for a ride in their hydrobikes. *This is the life* was written in smug ink on every aired face. A girl in a cobalt bikini held a glistening ear of corn-on-the-cob while an old woman with a cart hobbled away a few hryvnia wealthier. The girl's pinkie jutted, an antenna straining to transmit a weak signal of femininity. Gripping both ends, she leaned forward so that the lost kernels would land in the triangle of sand between her splayed legs and began a very methodical process of rotating the cob while clamping and unhinging her jaw.

Frida's feet hurt. She stuck them into the frazzled end of a milky wave and tried to feel something, quickly realizing she should've made use of the outhouse. What was largely speculative twenty minutes ago was now an emergency. She could go into one of the indistinguishable cafés lining the beach, but her pants were off and she was running. The water was up to her neck, and relief was not to be measured in milliliters.

Some kind of childish force overtook her, dragging her to the bottom of the sea, turning her upside down into handstands and underwater somersaults, as if she were stuck in a washer-dryer, tumbling forward. The machine had been fed only so many quarters, and at some point the propelling force abated. Frida continued splashing around for a few minutes before the atmospheric change was noted—it had grown darker and more silent. She had just popped up from yet another exploration of the oddly fishless depths and thought the seawater had plugged her ears. She stuck in a pruned fingertip and shook. Nothing dribbled out. It was an eventful quiet, like the hushed voices and mincing footsteps that had nightly navigated the corridor outside her childhood bedroom door. And the darkness—could it be dusk already? Could it be rolling on so unevenly and suddenly, in such odd clumps? Frida was facing the horizon, and instinct turned her head to the right in search of the pier and the setting sun, but there was only a thicker pile of altered atmosphere, dense murk. This wasn't Brighton, however. When in a certain mood, Marina liked to proclaim that Odessa was inferior to Brooklyn only in that it had a north-south as opposed to an east-west beach, meaning that if you intended to tan properly—and why wouldn't you?—by day's end you'd be facing not the glorious sea but the trash cans, café drunkards, smog off the city's skyline. Aha! But having turned around, Frida still failed to locate the sun, instead finding that the beach, just a moment ago populated by the malnourished and seedy, the youthful and sluggish, the elderly and exhaustingly vital, was almost entirely cleared. Food wrappers and trampled sand. A chaise longue tipped on its side. The remaining few were bent over, stuffing haphazard handfuls into giant straw bags before scampering off. The backs of their knees were heartbreaking. Frida thought she saw a bowlegged man squat down and in a single jerk snatch her stuff, which she'd left in a deflated heap begging to be snatched. Wait, she yelled, young man, wait! But why should the man, who wasn't at all young, do that? The bowlegs were perfect for getting over a jetty. Her muscles turned leaden. The sky, too, seemed to have turned to lead. This low, oppressive ceiling was bound to collapse. Almost with relief she realized how dire the situation was, how inexorably dire. There was no one around. Odd objects were being hurled by gusts, rebounding off metal clouds. Birds—tiny seagulls—were flying low and fast. All was lost. She heard a rumble, felt a drop.

It lasted several minutes and was more of a drizzle. Then the clouds parted and some rays dropped down, weak ones, as it was getting late.

People spilled out of cafés, emerged from behind corners, out of potholes and ditches, returning in throngs. You'd think they were made of sugar, thought Frida, to be so afraid of a little rain. A chill in the air was taken advantage of by young men, who eagerly wrapped themselves around any pair of bare shoulders in the vicinity. Shivers convulsed Frida's own shoulders, on which every hair stood at attention, yet she didn't pick up her pace as she waded out of the water, taking steps with deliberate slowness, afraid of what she'd find on shore.

She had no money (stolen) but she did have pants (discarded), which was more than could be said for most of the girls boarding the tram. Young women in this city evidently commuted free of charge. Though the term *commute* implies obligation, routine, dreariness, whereas these women were composed of light particles that simply floated (or took the tram) from one location to another, likely never to revisit the same place twice, not least of all because these women had the memory spans of cats and approximately eight minutes after arriving at their destination would have forgotten all about a point of origin. Frida's free ride wasn't the same as theirs—they got by on their shapely, tanned legs, she got by on pity. Though the truth of the matter was that the tram conductor had long ceased admiring legs or feeling pity, now interested only in finishing up his shift and getting back to his homing pigeons.

THE WIFE STOPPED GOING about her business (a crossword puzzle) in order to relay a message. She wanted to exude contentment but was sweating buckets. The city was taking its toll, and she hadn't even gone outside yet.

A message for me? said Frida in alarm, seeing before her eyes, in rapid succession, a mushroom cloud, the scene from *Terminator 2* when the children in the playground disintegrate, a tidal wave with claws in the style of Hokusai, a many-car pileup, and a collapsing skyscraper. She took a few steps into the kitchen to sit down, overcome, suddenly, by exhaustion.

The wife's attention was drawn to the floor. Stop right there! she screamed. Look at the grime you're hauling in here! Where are your shoes?

By the time Frida had managed to mouth, I lost them, her feet were planted in a plastic tub of warm water while a pungent mop made concentric circles around her.

Yes, said the wife, a message, from Aleksandr Pavlovich.

Sanya came by?

He called. Asked to speak with his father. There's a forgetful gene in your family if you ask me. Then he said that he also wanted to talk to you.

He could've called my cell—Pasha gave him the number.

He said he tried. A man answered and shouted at him.

That can't be, said Frida. The wallpaper's domino pattern began to blur and the wife's face to rearrange like a game of Tetris. Frida was suddenly aware of the universe, in all its strangeness and inescapability. You run one way and it's the universe, the other way and universe. The wife was supporting her elbow when she came to, having realized that after putting on her pants post-swim, she'd no longer felt the cell phone's hardness in her back pocket. Of course this didn't rule out the possibility that she was being followed.

The wife, who proved to have very large teeth and hazel eyes with velvety lashes, didn't require an explanation for Frida's little spell, preferring, in fact, *not* to have one. Frida was now standing upright and no longer draining of color rapidly, which the wife took to signal the episode's end.

He probably wanted to say that he's going to pick me up, said Frida. Did he give a time? I have to get dressed! What do I wear? I'll be late. Should I meet him somewhere, or is he on his way here?

None of this, said the wife. The wedding's back on. That's what he called to say. Now, if you ask me, all this back-and-forth, it doesn't bode well.

Sanya had reconciled with Nadia—yes, just like the mother, a particularly common coincidence nobody was adequately disturbed by. This joyous news came, however, with a downside: Sanya wouldn't get a chance to see Frida prior to Sunday's event. The couple had decided that there was too much noise around them and that in order to start their marriage on the right footing they needed quality time alone before the nuptials, something that just wasn't possible in Odessa, which might seem like a big city to a foreigner like Frida but was actually a village where going out for eggs meant that in exactly three and a quarter hours Olga Nudnaya, who had Gypsy blood and lived on the opposite side of town, would call to ask what the matter was, as there were bags under your eyes and you were wearing the same shirt from yesterday. Besides, Sanya was something of a celebrity, not just as his father's son but on his own merit as filmmaker and bon vivant. The news of the wedding's reinstatement was sure to spread like wildfire. They were off to Yalta for a few days to bask in the Crimean sun and get a dose of the savage Tatar spirit, and lamb. Frida would have to take a rain check on Arkadya, which he'd make good on if she was still around when they got back from their real honeymoon, a month of island-hopping in Greece.

FRIDA CALLED HOME. Her mother picked up and failed to sound sufficiently enthusiastic.

I'm very enthusiastic, said Marina, it's just four A.M. on Tuesday.

Aren't you worried about me? Don't you care how I'm doing?

I was trying to give you your space—

Well, if you care to know, I've been robbed! Frida's face grew piping hot, and her mouth twisted open. There was a brief pause as the pressure built inside her head, climbing steadily until with a rubbery croak all that air was released, alongside a deluge of mucus and tears.

Change your ticket and come home this minute, said her mother.

Frida whimpered for a little longer, then stopped abruptly. Please don't give me orders, she said.

What did they take? Are you hurt?

Only my cell phone and some of the stranger's money.

What stranger? Fridachka, come home. Take the knife out of my liver.

Frida took an exasperated breath. I'm fine, Ma. In fact, I've never been better. I only called to say hello. But now I need to be getting back.

Wait—tell me more. Have you been to the dacha? How are the raspberry—

I can't talk! I have to get back!

Get back to what?

To sitting in Pasha's bathtub fully dressed. She stretched out her legs and lay back, finding herself under a zigzag canopy of Sveta's tiny, lacy delicates, which had been squeezed aggressively and hung to dry. Pasha was, after all, a sensualist. Packaging made a difference to him. You could tell by one glance at Sveta's shoe rack. There wasn't a single sensible pair—but there was nothing sensible about these people. What so infuriated Frida about this place was that the rules of proper living were neither enforced nor acknowledged. And yet the feeling she'd had at the dacha, that this trip would serve to realign the facets of her life at home, stimulate the machine into motion, was gone. How convenient if that'd been the case—she'd go on battling anatomy textbooks, look back with fond bewilderment on her visit to Odessa, and that would be that. Trying to become convinced of the rightness of this outcome was useless. She already knew what had to be done.

She had to miss that flight. By the time the thought was articulated, it was too far along to be dismissed. There's a delay, thought Frida, between the lurking forces that brew into events and the events as they unfold for our viewing pleasure, like the universe equivalent of the delay between the windup effort and the automatic chatter of a pair of mechanized plastic teeth. She'd often been accused of not having appropriate reactions, of being zatormozhenaya, existentially blocked, an important word lacking a proper English match; perhaps it was because by the time events actually occurred, they already felt old, as obvious and inevitable as memories, and to react to them adequately required some showmanship. Those resistant to acting, if not biologically incapable of it, were deemed zatormozheniye. But the fact of the matter was that if enough attention was paid to those lurking forces, very few events couldn't be seen coming from miles away. Therein lay the danger of the delay. It cast a shadow that could be interpreted as fate—but there was no such thing. She wasn't fated to forget about medical school, to stay in Odessa; to stay was her choice, and most probably a stupid one. If it felt inevitable, it just felt so, the illusion of destiny. When the decision to throw her future down the toilet didn't pan out, she wouldn't allow herself solace in the thought that at least it was meant to be so, and therefore she couldn't plunge headfirst and then pray, relying, as the Brighton Beach real estate developers did, on the higher powers to take care of the rest. She knew all too well what the end result of such heedless faith looked like—crumbling stucco, torn plastic, exposed innards, weathered rot, and eventual collapse. If she was to go through with this, really go through with it, she needed resolve, tenacity, and, more pointedly, a purpose.

Tired of studying the frilly hems and see-through patches of Sveta's underwear, she looked down and found herself clutching Pasha's book—she must've grabbed it off the shelf on the way to the bathroom by reflex. She brought its spine to her nose. It smelled of dust and purpose. This insensible man was it. Who better to write Pasha's biography? Someone would have to do it, and considering Pasha's wealth of enemies, his radical—at least by the day's standard—sense of privacy, his intolerance of gossip and insistence on historical accuracy and precision, it was in his interest that his niece be the one. She'd need to buy a tape recorder, a marbled notebook, a pen. She'd interview mercilessly. It would be eight hundred pages, a scholarly tome examining Pasha's life, analyzing every one of his works and wives.

But she didn't know the first thing about biographies. Where did one begin, especially with a story so tangled from the very start? The great Russian poet Pavel Robertovich Nasmertov, who wasn't really Russian considering that he'd never lived in Russia proper but in Ukraine, only don't *dare* call him Ukrainian, and furthermore was Jewish, which in Russia qualified as a separate nationality if not species, though he wasn't really Jewish, having converted to Orthodoxy, was born on November 20-something in the year 1950-something in Odessa, a city where he'd lived his entire life, although hadn't he actually been born elsewhere, and neither could this still be considered the same Odessa, as what remained of the city was a shell of its former self, full of recent transplants and ruthless hostility to the Poet who'd remained? (It would probably be necessary at this juncture to mention that practically the entire Jewish population had relocated to Brighton's stinky hub, without making it too obvious that she believed that old Odessa's greatness lay solely in its Jews.) Frida had never been diligent or thorough. Facts were nothing but a nuisance. She'd have to defer to her uncle on many complex matters. Would her temperament allow her to take dictation? And would she be able to swallow her personal feelings and opinions in order to pen an objective account? But she was getting ahead of herself—in order to put aside personal feelings and opinions, she'd first have to figure out what they were. The effort struck her as nothing short of impossible.

A not-terrible place to get started, however, was the poems. The poems! Here they were, sitting quiet in a worn jacket. Just as she cracked the cover and began to make fumbling attempts to decipher the Cyrillic, she was reminded by a wild banging that she'd been camping out for over an hour in a very prime location, to the great frustration of the rest of the household. Volk, it's true, had been created to survive in the desert and went for days without an ounce of water coming or going, and the children could relieve themselves in the courtyard, but the wife had given birth to those children and wished that one day Frida would discover what that did to a bladder.

FIFTEEN

IN THE LAND OF GEORGIA, the poets were sporting fresh tans and new necklaces as they arrived from a day trip to the seaside town of Poti and were distributed among the forty-nine floors of Hotel Skyscratcher, which compensated for its location on the frayed hem of the outskirts of Tbilisi with an Olympic-size swimming pool and three Ping-Pong tables, though only the negligible poets from Bulgaria were intent on making use of them. That evening a banquet was held in their honor in the airy palm-tree-lined lobby, and it somehow never ended, perhaps because the poets kept eating and drinking until it was time for the staff to set up for breakfast. The banquet turned into a permanent fixture, as the hotel manager, a short young man with mischievous eyes, seemed to understand that poets couldn't be expected to abide by regular mealtimes, getting hungry at all hours of the day and night. Some smoked fish, suluguni, dwarf cucumbers—nothing spectacular, but better than nothing. There was a late-morning scuffle, however, in the course of which the electric samovar was knocked over and scalding water flew everywhere, burning the scrawny bald poet who'd been shoved into the impressive machine. The nearest hospital was hours away and technically in a different district, so he was taken to the hotel manager's brother-in-law's father's house, whose basement served as a private clinic. Nobody knew the poet's name, but everybody agreed that he had it coming. Since the festival's opening, he'd been laughing deliberately at inappropriate moments and chewing loudly throughout the readings and performances, asking baffling questions during the question-and-answer portions, and behaving very coarsely with the poetesses and poets' wives, who didn't seem to mind. The elderly woman who accompanied him everywhere, assumed to be his mother, disappeared with him. After the incident the hotel threatened to remove the banquet, since perhaps it was a bad idea to have so many hot-blooded poets congregating in the lobby at all hours, eating spicy foods and washing them down with spiked tea. But the poets didn't want to be so inconvenienced as to have to find another venue to fit the whole lot of them, especially considering that for miles around there was nothing but barren, scorched earth. They promised to be on their best behavior and leave large tips. They'd developed a deep fondness for the lobby. Every corner of it had been claimed. It was divided into thirty-two sections, which was the number of countries represented that year in the festival. Of course, none of them stayed in their own nation's section, or even visited, but they knew it was there in case a return became necessary.

About eight hours after the first incident, there was another, a skirmish among the Romanians, who were surprisingly active this year and producing stellar work (that made you want to slit your wrists). This time the injured included an elderly Georgian waiter who happened to be the disabled uncle of the hotel manager. Everybody kept saying disabled uncle until the two words merged, but nobody mentioned disabled how. The banquet was cleared. The problem was that there were so many of them. The number of attendees had more than doubled from the previous year. No longer was it exclusively poets—dramaturges, translators, editors, publishers, and journalists were now welcome to take part, and had anybody ever heard of a translator turning down an invitation? In the months leading up to the festival, an additional effort had been made to attract young poets, because apparently it was very important that the younger generation of writers feel connected to a long-standing tradition and not just, as one coordinator put it, stew in their own juices, but the suspicion was that the festival organizers wanted nice photos of good-looking people to display on the festival's website. Writers in general weren't the most attractive bunch, but in the previous years the average age of the participants had been sixty, and not the new sixty; both on the stage and off and everywhere you looked, it was just old-fogy poets who either never showered or had sweat-gland issues and smiled black, toothless smiles, and even they were moved to a quick bath or a shave or an appointment with the dentist after clicking through those pics.

A few poets took the organizational effort upon themselves, trying to ensure that a new venue be found and agreed upon by all, a place that would preserve the collective unity but still have a casual atmosphere and enough space for people to wander around and not feel the pressure to interact constantly, and which would have those dwarf cucumbers cut into halves and peeled. Basically, they wanted to find another lobby banquet.

For some reason they started collecting signatures. They were very much against what seemed to already be naturally occurring—namely, that after the scheduled events of the day ended, different groups went off into different directions, because in the previous years when there had not been so many of them, they had done everything together, and they believed that the entire point of such a festival was to make new friends and contacts, not just stick with those you already knew. They were sad, lonely people, engaged in a noble, if impossible, pursuit.

Pasha and Sveta were, of course, relieved only now that they and their group, mainly poets from New York and a few from Moscow, could use their three remaining evenings in this locale to wander off in their own direction (or call a car service and pay a surprisingly reasonable fee to get to downtown Tbilisi—if they'd known it would be so reasonable, they might've tried it sooner). Wherever they went, others somehow sniffed it out and followed, feigning coincidence. They were the cool group insofar as there was still such a concept, and naturally there was, which didn't matter much but was amusing to realize. Really, everything was going wonderfully. The weather was superb. There had been a misty rain in the beginning, just when they had gotten there, but it quickly dissipated and the sun came out and hadn't left their side since. In the outdoor market in Poti, Pasha had bought a traditional Georgian vest and was wearing it daily. He felt he had reached the apex of maturity and could do something silly like wear a Georgian vest over his mature belly, a vest with colorful silk patches, exaggerated lapels, and tassels destined to be dipped in Tkemali sauce. In Pasha's case maturing proved to be the opposite of what may be expected—it was the progression from seriousness to silliness, from rigidity to looseness. Nevertheless he would undoubtedly experience a pinch of regret when looking through the festival photos. Without realizing it he was wandering into everybody's background, and that ridiculous vest made him extremely discernible, regardless of the degree of blur. The photos would be posted widely on the internet, both on the official festival website and on individual blogs, announcing Pasha as a fat man with a smug smirk in a pompous vest and thereby alienating even those he hadn't managed to alienate personally. And if that didn't do the trick, there was the unfortunate quote he gave the not-unattractive journalist covering the festival for *Znamya*. A slender blonde with thin lips and darting athletic eyes, she cornered Pasha to ask him a few questions. When he began to speak, she turned on the tape recorder. Nurzhan Bozhko overheard the answers Pasha gave and was stunned.

But I called the festival a stupendous success, said Pasha.

Yeah, said Nurzhan, and then proceeded to rant about the great majority of these so-called poets.

I don't rant, said Pasha.

That's true. You enlighten.

Bozhko, usually so miserly, bought Pasha a drink (Don't protest, you need it), because it was truly impressive his talent for shooting himself in the foot—under no circumstances did Pasha fail. Pasha laughed, and downed his drink, and felt like a hero, until they got back to the hotel and Sveta began doing something with her long fingers and an oppressive cloud settled over Pasha, like a fat lady plopping down in his lap, an obese lady with a vulgar smell and bubbling laughter that rolled over him in thick waves and made the room go black. He was asleep.

The next morning Pasha ate a bigger breakfast than usual, sucked a few extra sugar cubes with his tea, and took the luxury bus alone (the others, Sveta included, were determined to sleep in) to the campgrounds to catch the panel on trends of new sincerity in bourgeois cosmopolitan poetry, which from the very start suffered from low blood pressure and quickly devolved into mutterings, non sequiturs, and short-lived eruptions of disoriented tittering. And gossip. It was the beginning of a long day. Even the sun shone in a timid, noncommittal way, sensing that it would have to be putting in a sustained effort. Pasha stood outside the tent where a roundtable debate about theories of translation was in progress, and though he had a few things to say on the subject, he wandered off instead. Fifteen years ago his shoulders had been like balance scales with a small grapefruit on the left scale and a large blood orange on the right; now on the right scale was truth and on the left murder in cold blood. Every step Pasha took looked like an attempt to settle this imbalance once and for all, but every step only further deepened it. He walked. He realized that his face muscles ached from squinting so hard, yet he could hardly see a thing, and at the same moment he was gripped, very distinctly, by the wish to run into Brodsky, to just nonchalantly run into him and get to talking. No greeting or introduction, just business. This was late Brodsky, who never got to be old man Brodsky. Late Brodsky was the equivalent of present Pasha. An odd, moist paleness under Brodsky's eyes (that made his freckles look like bloated capsules of moldy water) would be the only sign he might not be feeling well. Otherwise, from his speech and manner, he might as well have been a man in his prime. They'd sit down in the shade somewhere, probably at a café where Brodsky could order a double espresso, though of course he shouldn't have been drinking a double espresso, and within seconds Pasha would be engulfed in the smoke from Brodsky's cigarette. The desire was so strong that Pasha even glanced up and searched for him in the crowds, which were growing, friends reuniting after their rest, after their nightmares. Pasha felt like a candidate for a heart attack. He went to get water and drank it down greedily, as if his thirst had been building for decades. As he drank, he was showing others, those standing around taking delicate sips from their tall glasses, just how superficial their thirst was. It had to be saved up, amassed. They shouldn't have been drinking at all.

But after sitting down at a secluded table in the shade, getting comfortable, what exactly would Brodsky have said? At first he would've made some jokes, been a tad too jovial, protecting himself, but what about after that energy was out of the way? Did Pasha just want Brodsky to repeat the wise, funny things he'd already heard Brodsky say in brief impromptu clips and live interviews from festivals such as this, or did he want Brodsky to impart his slight lisp to the more substantial written interviews, articles, and profiles that Pasha had already read, as he'd read them all, with the only difference being that they be personally addressed to him? Did he want others, passing poets, to see in whose company he truly was? Or was it enough to watch the soft contour of Brodsky's chin (he had no jaw, only chin) while seeing himself reflected in Brodsky's round, wire-rimmed spectacles? Of course not. It was Pasha who had something to tell Brodsky. Something urgent. He needed to unburden. No—he needed to plead his case.

Was there a way to do that in one broad stroke? And where

to begin? If for comprehensive purposes (and they were nothing if not comprehensive men) it was necessary to begin at the beginning, they'd be there for days or more likely weeks; he'd bore Brodsky to a second death. Pasha felt discouraged. He found a seat on a metal bleacher. A skinny woman with tense shoulders took a measured bite of her sandwich, the tinfoil like a cracked alien eggshell on her lap. He blocked the sun with his hand. In the distance the whitish shuttle bus was riding off and Sveta was entering the campgrounds. Not far behind, Bozhko was slinking along.

The fact of the matter, for one thing, was that the other night Pasha hadn't intended to shoot himself in the foot. No offense had been meant. He'd simply been stating the obvious. They were happy to be hosted by Georgia, to be treated like VIPs, and they were all enjoying themselves immensely—though perhaps he should speak for himself. He was happy, he was enjoying. And from the exponentially growing numbers of participants, it was clear that the festival mission was a stupendous success, as he'd said. Russian-language poets from across the globe were meeting and getting acquainted with one another's work, forging friendships and international partnerships, and so on. But did anybody really think it was possible that some hundred-plus Russian-language poets existed at any one time? A poet was born, not bred. The entire twentieth century had about a dozen (you among them, needless to say). And let's be honest: Since when did poetry benefit from a breakfast-is-included mentality? A luxury bus picked up the poets outside the hotel lobby at eight, and there was a shuttle every half hour afterward for those who didn't make it, transporting them with bathroom access to the campgrounds, where refreshments were served throughout the day. The poets had needed to know: Was the shuttle free of charge? Almost free, the Tbilisi representative had said, not quite. Be precise! There was a very minuscule fare, to be determined by each individual shuttle driver. This did not strike the poets as right. And eight A.M. was, by consensus, too early for the bus—how about nine-thirty? But events began at nine, and it was a half-hour drive on clear roads, which weren't at all guaranteed. Pity the poet whose reading was scheduled for nine! Though perhaps, if things really got rolling, many would be awake not already but still.

The bus schedule wasn't an issue for Pasha, who couldn't remember the last time he'd been able to sleep past dawn. The complimentary breakfast was a nuisance—he helplessly found himself filling a large plate, a small plate, and a bowl and then methodically emptying them into himself, adding layers of food onto the undigested layers from the previous night. But the campgrounds, littered with makeshift stages, sunburned faces, crammed tents, appealed to Pasha in that they resembled a flea market—everything drab, plentiful, on display yet camouflaged, visible and utterly overlookable. Pasha had patience, the key with both flea markets and poetry festivals (and baseball games, so he'd heard). Oftentimes the most awaited readings proved the dullest and the most captivating had an audience that could be counted on one hand, or so it was nice to think. But who was Pasha kidding? And if Brodsky wasn't around to listen as Pasha made fumbling attempts to explain himself— and by the looks of it he definitely wasn't—Pasha would proceed to do so to whoever was listening, because as he returned to roaming the labyrinthine campgrounds in what would appear to be avoidance of Sveta and Bozhko, he realized just how overdue such an explanation was.

He wasn't at the festival for what he could take away from the experience (a new poet to read, concept to mull, international collaboration to initiate), but for the experience itself— for the chance to roam patchy, bleached grasses in his Georgian vest, perhaps an occasional pipe between his hot, sandpapery lips, for good food and spontaneous conversation, often or always initiated by the other party. If he stood around for long enough, he was invariably approached by other poets, often female, who'd read his work and admired or even adored it, who weren't shy or reticent with their opinions and seemed to believe that just having them was a source of pride. They wanted to let Pasha know that they considered him a poet of genius not getting his due, no, it's true, he deserved far better treatment, a wider readership, international renown, and to be translated into every language imaginable, even Swahili. A scattered redhead claimed that his collection *Ancestral Belt* had been on her nightstand since 1995; a dark boy with emerald eyes, who might've been twelve, said that he'd been assigning Pasha's *Bestiary Cycle* in both his Mythology of Poetics and Poetics of Mythology courses for a decade; a woman in her fifties with one arm in a giant cast (or a giant arm in a fitted cast) said that she'd recently read his poem "Black Arch" in one of her classes and rather liked it, though she found the wordplay at the beginning rather tiring and it could've easily been half as long, but even so it was memorable, which was more than could be said for the other poems assigned in that class. Pasha relished these encounters more than he let on, his regular life in Odessa devoid of them, but he usually quickly lost the actual content of the compliment, retaining only warmth, like having been awoken from a pleasant dream. He carried around this wonderfully incommunicable warmth for as long as the heat held, potentially an entire afternoon providing he didn't happen to stumble into another encounter or a bit of news that froze him to the core, turning the saliva on his tongue to ice. But even when people weren't approaching Pasha to tell him of the influence his poetry had on them, that influence was alive in the air. It was real. No one had to be reading his poetry, and he didn't have to be writing it, and no mention of it had to be made, and still the influence was inarguably present, as present as the electromagnetic waves that miraculously allowed for cell-phone reception at the campgrounds in rural Georgia.

But currently there was a malfunction. Though people approached Pasha throughout the afternoon, not only did the heat not hold, it failed to appear. Real time had resumed—Sveta and Bozhko found Pasha, took him by the underarms, and led the way to the tent not where the conundrum of translation was once and for all being resolved but to the one with the red cross on the front, where a fat village beauty in a white uniform pinched his cheeks, called him Pumpkin Stew (for that was what he looked like), slammed a bag of ice on his forehead, and said heatstroke at least a dozen times, which was odd, as heat was the one sensation Pasha lacked. Equipped with a water bottle, a cap, and a few warnings, he was released. A few hours later, he read aloud to a packed auditorium; in terms of attendance, enemies were far more devoted than friends. The auditorium was large and had walls, and it couldn't have been on the campgrounds, but then where was it? This was bound to remain a mystery.

After the reading Pasha proceeded to let loose at the Mongolian barbecue and the ensuing festivities, staying late into the evening, refilling his glass with punch, letting himself be drawn into a conversation with three women and one homosexual ballad-composer that proved not entirely as frivolous as he would've imagined it had he excused himself instantly in his regular fashion, or maybe it was just as frivolous but livelier and more nuanced, occasioned with moments worth having if you were in it for the experience itself. Ten days out of the year, he could make such an allowance. Despite all the genuine fun and enjoyment, of which he would've told the reporter from *Znamya* if she hadn't lost her face, something was wrong. When the elevator took Pasha up to the forty-ninth floor, which he never realized was the top floor, thinking that there had to be another floor above, and after he managed to swipe the card so that the light turned green and let him into his room, where Sveta was already sleeping, the poor thing only able to take so much (though since when?), the oppressive mass again rolled over Pasha. First it crushed his toes, then it rolled off, and he thought with unspeakable relief that he'd been spared, but of course he was not.

He kept the lights off, and not for fear of waking Sveta. As a rule the first to fall asleep, Pasha didn't have this particular consideration installed in his brain. If a light had been needed, he wouldn't have hesitated to turn it on, provided he was able to locate the switch (not always so easy in these tricky hotel rooms). Pasha sat in the armchair by the wall. It began to feel like a wheelchair, so he went to stand by the window. Since he wasn't sleepy, he considered listening to music—nothing too serious, something modern and light, maybe Mingus. But he quickly stopped considering, knowing that he wasn't about to listen to any music.

The books that people mentioned when they approached him, Pasha realized, were old. The title he heard most often was *Ancestral Belt*, his first collection. *The Bestiary Cycle* was technically his third but truly his second (*Letter After the Quake*, dedicated to Renata Ostraya, didn't count). He'd written these so long ago they no longer felt written at all. Meanwhile his recent books, those of the past five years or so, were never mentioned. The explanation for this could be as simple as time—books required it. A collection needed to sit, some more than others. Not all response was instantaneous. And readers, merely human beings with their flaws, their daily worries, their limited attention spans, were uncomfortable with a writer's creative evolution. Biological evolution was swallowed like a bitter pill, or a pill that used to be bitter and now came in improved gel-capsule form, as if morphing from monkeys into us were the most basic concept to fathom, not murky or bizarre or frustrating in the least, certainly nothing worth questioning, in fact pity the fool who still did—but if a poet made his name with sestinas, God forbid he should torture the public with a villanelle; if he traded in binary structures for free verse, all the worse for him. And that's what Pasha had done, traded in something for something else, only it wasn't as concrete as binary structures or free verse, and he couldn't pinpoint precisely when the change had occurred. As a result he couldn't be entirely certain it had been voluntary.

Neither could he be sure the change had been his, considering he couldn't remember the last time he'd willfully changed anything other than wives. For as long as he could remember, he'd been consuming the same kasha for breakfast, quenching his thirst with the same mineral water from a spring somewhere not far from his current whereabouts, listening to the same cantatas on his Discman, exercising his heart on the same promenade in the center of Odessa, exercising his soul at Sunday services in the same cathedral, making the same rounds of cafés and restaurants, eating inordinate quantities of the same watermelon from Kherson, bathing in the same section of the Black Sea, composing poems at an unvarying rate with the same steadfast zeal at the same predawn hour. Yet. With each passing year, his surroundings became less recognizable, he felt more and more uprooted. Constancy of habit didn't buffer against a city, a nation, a society, perhaps a whole culture in decay. Though he could step outside and pass the places of his childhood, his schools, the hospital where his father had worked, the pediatric clinic where his mother had worked, it was as if the city had been moved to the moon—the structures were there, but the atmosphere had been sucked out. It was the irony of his life that he was more alienated and excluded in his native city than his family in their new land. He used to blame his mother, for not trying hard enough to stir him into action, for dying at the wrong time, in the wrong place, for everything not quite short of giving birth to him. Now he just missed her, Esther.

Sveta turned over, exposing a long white arm. For a moment it groped over his absence, then lay still. Pasha stumbled out of his pants and inserted himself under the arm, into the hotel-linen envelope, a welcome constraint. He couldn't move his toes and didn't want to. Getting a bit of rest wasn't a bad idea. In a day's time, they would be relocating to Tskaltubo, where the radon mineral springs were known to alleviate a variety of nervous ailments and circulatory conditions and the caves were touted as especially restorative for pulmonary diseases, which just might need relieving after the planned excursions to the famous dinosaur footprint and the private pool where Stalin had bathed. Pasha sighed. He was contented. And at the same time terrified, frightened, depressed. But that's enough about him. How about—

Frida couldn't make out the rest. The connection was wavering, Pasha fading out. Reception in rural Georgia wasn't so miraculous after all.

Me? she said. I'm fine. Actually, I've been doing some thinking. I'm probably going to stay awhile.

After a bout of static, Pasha screamed out, I said—how about my cats?

Your what? yelled Frida.

Cats, my cats! I trust you haven't forgotten about my cats.

She gulped. Of course not, she said. But I've got some news about your son. There's been a development in the drama. The wedding, it's back on. Talk about last-minute—and I thought *I* had trouble making up my mind! A conspiratorial tone had snuck into her voice. Aside from wanting to give Pasha the update and being glad to be the one to do it, as if her ability to provide information hot off the presses proved her worth and demonstrated how deep she'd wedged herself into their lives, she also hoped to bond with him over Sanya's fickle ways. Surely Pasha wouldn't approve of such volatile behavior.

That's Sanya for you, exclaimed Pasha.

It is, she said warily.

Pausing for a second, he said, Well then. I'll catch a plane out tonight.

A wave of panic shook her. Had a giant misunderstanding just occurred, and was she at the root of it? The wedding isn't until Sunday! she practically screamed. Sanya's not even in town! And don't forget, Sveta's family is occupying your bedroom.

Not a problem, said Pasha.

But—what about the festival?

The festival is fine, it's great, but I'm ready to pack it in, to be honest. I've been feeling under the weather, and besides, don't they say it's good to know how to make an exit?

Yelena Akhtiorskaya was born in Odessa in 1985 and raised in Brighton Beach, Brooklyn. She holds an MFA from Columbia University. She is the recipient of a Posen Fellowship in Fiction, and her writing has appeared in *n+1*, *The New Republic*, and elsewhere. She lives in New York City.